MIKI

BRATVA BLOOD BROTHERS #3

JAX KNIGHT

Miki
Bratva Blood Brothers #3
Copyright © 2024 Jax Knight
Published by Hudson Indie Ink
www.hudsonindieink.com

Miki/Jax Knight – 1st ed.
ISBN-13: 978-1-916562-97-4

PROLOGUE
MIKHAIL ROMINOV

LONDON - FRIDAY, MID-JULY - ANOTHER ENEMY DOWN

Slamming my fist into Siri's bloodied face for the last time, knowing the bastard was about to die, filled me with satisfaction. Blood coated my knuckles as I moved back to let my youngest brother, Marko, take another shot. Stepping aside, we allowed my friend and ally, Janusz Glowacki, to deliver his final blow.

As Glowacki pulled back, I nodded to my other brother, Ash. It was time. Ash stepped forward, smirked, and slit Siri's throat. Then we watched as Siri gurgled his last pitiful breath.

Glowacki's son, Dariusz, cut Siri's limp body down. My eyes narrowed as I stared at the man crumpled on the floor in a pool of crimson. I rarely felt satisfaction when I took part in a killing. None of us did, but this time I couldn't help myself, and I breathed a sigh of relief that another enemy was dead. Glowacki nodded to me in grim satisfaction, as glad as I was that the deed was done.

The Somali bastard, Siraaj Farah, also known as Siri, was the head of a gang called the Malia Boys. They had formed an alliance with another gang called the Broxley Estate Lads, known locally as the Broxys. They attacked our homes and family businesses and tried to break up our own alliance, so this outcome for Siri was inevitable.

In an unusual display of anger, my cousin Romi kicked the corpse.

"Fucking arsehole!" he cried, before turning and storming out of the room.

It wasn't often that Romi lost his cool over anything, but in this, I understood his anger. Siri had also kidnapped my sister, Romi's fiancé Sonia, and shot Romi. Romi was almost recovered now and thankfully, Sonia escaped virtually unharmed.

Unfortunately, we couldn't say the same about my other sister.

Two years ago, rogue members of the Polish Mafia, Lev Petrov, who had been Glowacki's second, and two of his soldiers, brothers Piotr and Szymon Nowack had killed my sister Krissa while they were conspiring to overthrow Glowacki's position as head of the Polish Mafia.

The night before they planned on murdering Glowacki and his family, they had gone out partying. Fuelled on drink and drugs, they had kidnapped a young woman off the street and raped and murdered her.

The three men had been so out of it they had left DNA evidence at the scene and were caught by the police. This had saved the lives of Glowacki and his family, but at a great loss to us.

At the time, we were led to believe that the men hadn't known who Krissa was when they attacked her. She was supposed to have been just a random woman to them.

However, we recently discovered that Petrov had recognised Krissa and contacted Siri who was apparently backing him in his plans, and Siri had told him to kill her.

Even if the bastard hadn't been a thorn in our sides for way too long, that fact alone would have been enough to sign his death warrant.

While I disliked torturing and killing anyone, as Pakhan of the Bratva in the UK, sometimes it was unavoidable. This was one of those times. We'd needed information from the guy, and he'd needed to suffer for what he'd done. The world was a better place without him.

My family didn't derive any joy from the suffering of others; but we didn't shy away from it either. We did what was necessary to protect ourselves and the rest of the Brotherhood. If there was an alternative way to handle our enemies, we utilised it. Otherwise, we brought them here, to the C, to die.

The C was short for the Smithson Crematorium, and it had been specially adapted so that we could deal with our enemies and dispose of their bodies easily and efficiently.

Dariusz and Ash started loading Siri's body into a body bag.

"We'll take the trash out," Ash said, grinning in a way that almost looked maniacal, as he zipped the bag up.

My heart clenched as I watched him. Ash was still coming to terms with Krissa's murder. He blamed himself for it.

Ash was supposed to pick Krissa up from a restaurant on the night it had happened, but he'd been running late and by the time he'd arrived, she was gone. The guilt had been eating away at him ever since.

Gracie, Ash's fiancé, had helped him deal with his anger issues over it and he was only now beginning to get over his guilt and grieve for Krissa properly. I just hoped that what we had learned from Siri tonight didn't set him back in his recovery.

Frustration filled me and I huffed as I walked out of the room behind Glowacki and Marko.

Siri had given the order to kill Krissa and had set up the recent alliance with the Broxys attempting to take us down. However, it would seem he had only been a pawn in the game. Someone else was pulling the strings. I bloody hated the idea of another enemy lurking in the shadows somewhere, just waiting to take another strike at me and mine.

Despite the torture he endured, Siri could not tell us who it was, since all his dealings had been via a go-between. We knew who that was, though. A lawyer named Nigel Simpson. One of our informants had already told us, but it was good that Siri confirmed it before he died.

As I showered and changed, I vowed I would find out who our secret enemy was. Nobody messed with my family or friends and got away with it.

CHAPTER 1
EILIDH CAMPBELL
GLASGOW – TWO WEEKS LATER –
DISILLUSIONED

t was early morning, and I was up and ready. It was my first day as a fully-fledged Detective Constable in the Criminal Investigation Department, for Police Scotland. I was seconded to the CID for a few months while I was in uniform, but this was me, now an actual detective.

For what seemed like the millionth time, I nervously checked myself in the mirror. Scrutinising my reflection, I gulped and nodded. With my hair tied neatly in a bun at the back of my head, a nicely fitted grey suit with a crisp white shirt, and black square-heeled ankle boots, I looked the part of a confident detective. Even if I didn't feel it.

Tears sprung to my eyes. Dad would have been so proud of me. I missed him so much. He was killed on duty almost three years ago, and the crime was still unsolved. There had been a major investigation at the time, but when no significant leads were found, it slowly dwindled off. Now it was just another cold case.

Still, I always kept hope that one day the breakthrough I had longed for, which would help bring my dad's killer to justice, would materialise. Yesterday, it finally did. Or so it seemed. I was still struggling to truly believe it.

Sniffing loudly, I swiped at my wet eyes with the backs of my hands. I would not cry. I needed to have my game face on this morning and act like I was happy to be going to work. Puffy red eyes were not part of my plan.

My mind flashed to the day before and the events that had changed everything for me.

When I returned from my usual morning run, I found a large brown envelope waiting for me on my doorstep.

There was no address or postage on the thickly stuffed envelope, only my name, Eilidh Campbell. Someone had obviously hand delivered it, but there was no sign of anyone in the quiet street.

Strange!

I took it into the house. Black and white pictures, which I immediately recognised were surveillance photographs, poured out as I emptied the contents onto my desk.

What the heck? Why would someone send me a load of photos?

As I looked through the first few images, I was filled with a growing sense of foreboding.

All of them showed my dad's partner, my new boss, and the man I called uncle, Detective Chief Inspector Roy Allen, in what appeared to be compromising situations. And he wasn't the only one. Several other members of the CID were in the photos, too.

What the hell are these?

Snatching up the rest, I shuffled through them, trying to make sense of what I was seeing.

Another man I recognised in the photographs was Aiden Mathieson, a well-known Glasgow defence lawyer. His clients were always the worst of the worst and included members of a notorious crime family.

One photo showed Uncle Roy and another of my colleagues taking a package from him, and another showed Uncle Roy handing Mathieson something. After closer inspection, I noticed yet another of the photos showed Aiden Mathieson giving a briefcase to Uncle Roy.

Each photo seemed more damning than the next, and I felt queasy.

I didn't want to believe what these photos were eluding to, but I couldn't stop my mind from going there. Were the photographs showing payoffs? I shook my head; surely not! But it certainly looked that way.

Bile rose in my throat, and I gulped it back. There had to be another explanation for what I was seeing. Maybe an undercover operation of some sort that I hadn't been aware of?

But if that was true, then why would someone take these photographs and then send them to me?

There was really only one explanation. Either my colleagues were corrupt, or someone wanted me to think they were.

But why?

As I reached the final three photographs, I froze in shocked disbelief.

"Oh, my god! No!"

A sob tore from my throat at the sight of my dad sitting in his unmarked police car on the night of his murder. He was reading something in a thin file.

With shaking hands, I moved the photo aside to look at the next one and immediately felt sick.

My dad lay on the ground, dead from a gunshot wound which had blown half his face off. A man stood over him, gun in hand. My vision blurred and my head swam. Bile rose in my throat, and I rushed into the bathroom, falling to my knees just in time as I vomited down the toilet.

My whole body shook with the horror of what I'd just seen. It wasn't as though I hadn't seen worse things. In the seven years that I had been in the Police, I most certainly had. But this was my dad, and that made it even more horrible.

I knew Dad was shot in the head, but thankfully I hadn't needed to identify the body. Uncle Roy had done that, and it was a closed coffin at the cremation. Despite being a police officer, I hadn't been allowed to see any of the crime scene photographs because I was family. So, witnessing my dad in that state for the first time was utterly shocking.

Lying on the bathroom floor, I took steadying breaths as I fought a battle against the vomit that kept threatening to rise again. Finally, my stomach settled, and I slowly climbed to my feet. My legs felt shaky, my body weak.

Clinging to the side of the sink for support, I rinsed my mouth. The water poured down my throat, cooling the burning sensation and helped wash away the rancid taste left behind by the bile. Then I splashed some water on my face and looked in the mirror. My shocked, pale visage stared back at me.

The images raced through my mind as I gazed at my reflection. I understood the message conveyed by the photographs, but I couldn't fully comprehend what I had witnessed. The distress of seeing my dad like that must have been messing with my head. Surely, it couldn't be true? I had to be mistaken.

Eventually, I recovered enough from the shock and nausea to return to the bedroom. Approaching the desk slowly, my dread built and sweat broke out all over my body as I slid into the chair and reached out a shaky hand. I didn't want to look at the photographs again, but I knew there was no choice.

My entire world shrunk down to the pile of images laid

before me. My eyes glued to my dad's prone form. The shallow breaths and small sounds in the back of my throat as I held on tightly to my emotions, the only other thing I was aware of as I studied the image, looking for clues.

There was little I could glean from the photograph that I hadn't seen already. I needed to know who the man with the gun was, but it was hard to identify him with his back toward the camera.

Closing my eyes, I turned the photo over. I'd tortured myself long enough. I would never look at that image again, but I vowed I would find the killer and make him pay, and anyone else involved.

Keeping my eyes closed, I took deep, steadying breaths as the vow took hold. As my resolve solidified, and my nerves calmed, I finally forced myself to pick up the rest of the photos and take another look.

As I got to the last image, one I'd not yet seen, I gasped. It revealed someone with the same build, hair, and clothing as the killer, handing over a file to Aiden Mathieson, who was standing next to Uncle Roy. The file looked just like the one my dad had been reading. I looked at the photograph again and stared at the face of my dad's killer. He was familiar. I'd seen him before. I couldn't remember where or who he was yet, but I would soon find out.

Why was he with Uncle Roy? There was only one conclusion I could draw. The one I'd tried to avoid. My Uncle Roy really was corrupt. That meant my colleagues could be too.

Not only that, but it appeared that they, or at least Roy, had something to do with my dad's murder.

Fuck!

As that thought took hold, I felt faint. How could he do that to my dad and me?

He was dad's best friend, his partner, the man who should have had his back.

Tears blurred my vision as I thought about how Roy had mentored me since Dad died. We were close. We always had been. And the other guys from my department, they'd been Dad's colleagues and friends too. These were all people I'd idolised. This couldn't be happening.

Had everything been a lie?

Wetness on my cheeks alerted me to the fact that I was crying. It felt like my world was falling apart; everything I thought I knew, the truths and people I'd held dear, looked up to even, were not real.

Anger infused me. I swept the photographs off the desk, screaming in frustration.

That's when I saw a small slip of paper I hadn't noticed before. It fluttered to the ground, landing on top of the mess I'd made. Picking it up, I saw the name John Aldridge, with a time and place for a meeting. Nothing else.

I'd cried myself to sleep after that, grieving the loss of my dad, the death of my illusions, and that nothing in my world would ever be the same again.

Shaking my head, I forced my mind back to the present.

Pushing aside the memories of yesterday, I stuffed the same slip of paper into my trouser pocket. That meeting was for later today, and I'd be there because whoever this John Aldridge was, he had answers I needed.

Throughout the night, I had looked through the photographs again—all but one of them—and now they were burnt into my mind. Technically, I should hand it all over to my boss and get him to re-open my dad's case, but since my boss appeared to be involved, that was not an option. Neither was going to anyone else at this time, because I did not know if any of my other colleagues were involved, and I didn't know how high up this corruption went.

It was actually frightening to think that I did not know who I could trust.

Opening the small safe I had in my wardrobe where I kept all my valuables, I stuck the envelope inside.

There was no other choice in the matter. I needed to investigate things myself, and I would start with meeting Mr Aldridge.

Closing my eyes, I took a deep breath, then headed for the door. It was time to go to work and face the men from the pictures.

How the heck I was going to deal with these men I'd called friends and colleagues without confronting them about my suspicions? I didn't know. My stomach churned with nerves as I drove, and even cranking up the volume on the radio couldn't distract my busy mind.

The closer I got to the police station, the more agitated I grew. Images of my dad's body, of his killer, then of my colleagues, flooded my mind, back and forth, until my breathing became shallow and my body trembled with a mix of anger, frustration, and hurt.

When I checked my reflection in the rearview mirror, I noted my pinched expression and narrowed angry eyes.

Not good.

If what I believed was true, my colleagues were not only corrupt, but they were also murderers, and I had to be very careful.

Pulling over, I parked, turned the radio off, and put the air con on full blast. Leaning back against the headrest, I shut my eyes and concentrated on steadying my breathing.

In, two, three.

Out, two, three.

I needed to be in control of myself if I was going to be successful in my task of uncovering the evidence of my colleagues' corruption, their link to my dad's murder, and bringing them to justice.

Eventually, I felt calm enough to continue my journey.

Revenge and avenging my father's death became my sole focus, and by the time I entered the police station and walked into the office; I had my poker face in place.

"Eilidh, welcome to the team," my new boss said, smiling brightly at me as I entered.

He walked over to me and put his arm around my shoulders. Forcing myself not to stiffen, I endured the overly familiar and very unprofessional greeting as he led me over to my new desk.

The rest of the team was there to greet me, grinning. Murmurs of *'Welcome to the team'*, *'Glad to have you onboard'* and similar greetings were banded about, but I barely heard them as I stared at the faces of my fallen idols.

Smiling broadly back, I kept my emotions tightly under wraps. I could do this. I'd make my dad proud and investigate this case like I would any other and bring down anyone involved. Starting with dear old Uncle Roy.

CHAPTER 2
MIKI

LONDON – SAME DAY – THE DOUBLE WEDDING

Sighing heavily, I shook my head and rubbed at the back of my neck as I read through the file of information Marko had compiled for me on the lawyer, Nigel Simpson. My shoulders ached, and I was tired, bone weary.

My eyes narrowed as I stared at the picture of the fucker on my screen with the young man, the very young man. Oh yes, Marko had come up with the goods and now we had what we needed to confront the bastard. Ash had wanted me to do it sooner, but I had waited. I'd made too many rash decisions recently, resulting in mistakes that had almost cost me my sister and cousin. So, I was determined to ensure I never made such a mistake again.

It seemed like I'd been knocking my enemies down like tenpins at a bowling alley lately. The problem was for every strike I got; more enemies racked up to take their place. Hopefully, Nigel Simpson and whoever his unknown boss was would be the last of them. At least for a while.

Pouring myself a shot of vodka, I downed it quickly, closing my eyes and enjoying the burn at the back of my throat. It had been a tiring few months, and I was extremely relieved that things had worked out.

After placing the photographs back in their envelope, I slid it in the file and locked it away in my safe. I'd soon be paying Nigel Simpson a visit and when I did, he would provide me with the information I needed to root out the last of our enemies. He just didn't know it yet. I'd tug the puppet's strings until he revealed the puppet master, and then I would eliminate them both.

However, that was something to be dealt with another day. Today was a day for celebration, a double wedding, and I planned on forgetting my problems and enjoying this special time with my family and our friends.

As if conjured by my thoughts, my uncle Maxim, Ash, Marko, and Romi entered the office, all suited and booted, looking their best, with huge smiles on their faces. I poured them all a shot and then another for myself.

"Nostrovia!" we cheered, before downing our drinks and heading out to the waiting cars.

A short while later, I watched my uncle walk my aunt Marta down the aisle towards Glowacki. Sonia and I followed behind them and as I walked her towards a thrilled-looking Romi, I couldn't help thinking about just how close I'd come to ruining everything.

Glowacki and my family had an alliance. Five years ago, we had united through grief and a common enemy during a war with the Albanians who had killed my parents and Glowacki's eldest son, Tomas. The alliance had continued to grow in strength over the years as Glowacki's family and mine came to know and respect each other. Even after the murder of my sister Krissa.

However, until now, we had kept the fact that we had a strong alliance quiet from our enemies, thinking that it gave us an edge. In hindsight, that had not been the best idea. Believing our association was on shaky ground had encouraged several enemies to unite against us, and we'd been forced to go to war with them.

When Glowacki initially proposed strengthening our alliance further with an arranged marriage between his son Dariusz and my sister Sonia, I had said no, not believing it was necessary. However, when the attacks had first begun, I thought perhaps the idea had merit after all, and agreed without considering the consequences.

Sonia was not happy about that at all. While Dariusz had not really wanted to get married either, he had agreed to it for his father's sake. However, my sister hated the idea and had been against it from the start. Initially, I had hoped she would come around, because Dariusz was a great guy, but she didn't.

When we discovered the relationship between her and Romi, my brothers and I reacted badly. Especially me.

Carrying on a relationship with each other had seemed wrong on so many levels at first, and I had been bloody furious.

Romi was our cousin through his mother's marriage to our late Uncle Petior. Technically, it wasn't an issue because there was no blood connection, but morally, it had felt wrong. Also, he was older than her by seven years, and it seemed like he had seduced her. I now know it was more likely the other way around. However, at the time, all I could see was my innocent little sister with an older, more experienced man.

Then there was the fact that Romi had sworn an oath as a *Bratva Blood Brother.* Years ago, when we were all young, a bunch of us took a blood oath to always protect each other and our families, especially our sisters. All of us Blood Brothers—me, Ash, Marko, Romi, my best friend Luca, and Ash's best friend Anton—all felt different levels of betrayal when we found out Romi was sleeping with Sonia. That was not the type of protection we had vowed.

Also, indulging in a relationship with Sonia while she was technically engaged to Glowacki's son was a massive issue for me as Pakhan. The problem was that such arrangements were unbreakable once shaken upon by two mafia leaders, unless a suitable alternative was found.

Breaking the agreement without an alternative arrangement would have been an insult. Glowacki would have had no choice but to retaliate or be seen as weak among the rest of his Brotherhood. That would definitely have threatened, if not completely shattered, our alliance.

Luckily, we had kept the arranged marriage agreement quiet because we had been busy dealing with the war with the Malia Boys and Broxys. So, when Glowacki and my aunt Marta became close as she helped nurse him back to health, he had agreed to amend the terms of the arranged marriage to them instead. It had been a godsend.

Especially after Sonia had been kidnapped, and Romi was shot while rescuing her. None of us could deny the depth of his feelings for her then, nor hers for him when she was inconsolable and refused to leave his side until he was over the worst. It was then we realised that nobody else could be better for her than Romi, our cousin, friend, and brother.

My folly could have ruined our family forever, something I didn't want to contemplate. I vowed never to make such a foolish, inconsiderate decision again, no matter how overwhelmed I sometimes felt as Pakhan.

The music ended, tearing my thoughts back to the present.

As Sonia took her place beside Romi, the joy on both of

their faces made my heart clench. I wished my parents were here to see this; they would have been overjoyed at seeing her wed.

Stepping back from the pair, I went to stand by Uncle Maxim, who smiled and placed a hand on my shoulder, squeezing it slightly. He was probably thinking about my parents, too, especially my dad.

Uncle Maxim was Dad's twin, just a few minutes older. They were identical, so spending time with him always gave me mixed feelings. I loved my dyadya and seeing his face was comforting, but it always made me sad, reminding me of happier times when my dad was alive.

Watching today's proceedings made me wonder what my dad would have thought of the double wedding.

Before we came to the UK and my father became Pakhan, the Polish and Russians had been rivals who barely tolerated each other. When Glowacki took over as head of the Polish Mafia, he was young and ambitious and tried to muscle in on our territory several times.

My father had subdued him quickly each time, and despite their rivalry, my dad had always treated Glowacki fairly. Eventually, they both came to a truce that grew into a grudging respect for each other, and the semblance of a friendship had begun just before my dad was murdered.

When I'd become Pakhan, I had felt way out of my depth, and often still did. However, Glowacki had offered me his hand in friendship, and I had taken it.

I was glad I had.

United in our grief, we formed an alliance, took on the Albanians, and thankfully won. Glowacki had been a good friend to me since and acted as a mentor. I respected him.

Dad had respected him too, but would he have agreed with the continued alliance and uniting our families?

"He'd be proud of you today and happy with how things have turned out," Uncle Maxim said, as if able to read my thoughts.

The registrar started the service, and Glowacki's smile widened as he gazed at my aunt. She beamed back at him, looking radiant as always. Aunt Marta was my dad and Uncle Max's younger half-sister and, at thirty-eight years old, was twelve years younger than Glowacki, but they were a good match. They had a lot in common.

My heart warmed as I nodded at Uncle Maxim. Yes, I'd made the right decision.

My gaze flicked to Sonia, who looked equally radiant, standing beside Romi, who was grinning like a buffoon. I'd never seen him look so happy.

Thank god, things had worked out.

As I observed the proceedings, I couldn't help sporting my own huge grin. Ash's fiancée, Gracie, was Sonia's bridesmaid and Glowacki's daughter, Magdalena, was Aunt Marta's. They all looked beautiful in their dresses.

Glowacki's son was his best man, and Ash was Romi's. Marko and Glowacki's other sons, Daniel and Sebastian, and our friends Luca and Anton, were the groomsmen, looking very distinguished in their finery. If I didn't know better, I'd even believe them to be the civilised beings they currently looked like. I smirked.

Outwardly we looked the part of polished businessmen, but underneath the veneer of civility lurked a darker place we often inhabited. The same place our enemies operated. That thought brought my light mood crashing down.

Scanning the grounds of my large estate, our home, I checked our security was in place, as expected. We'd gone a bit overboard for the wedding because even though we'd recently eliminated a huge chunk of those enemies, I refused to take any chances.

As the couples exchanged rings, I felt a pang of envy. I wanted someone who looked at me the way Aunt Marta looked at Glowacki and Sonia looked at Romi. Not that there was anyone in my life at the moment. In fact, there hadn't been for ages. It just never seemed to be the right time for me to pursue a relationship.

A little voice in my head said there never would be a right time, but I ignored it. There was no point thinking about love when there were far more important things to deal with, like having an enemy to track down.

On top of that, I wanted to concentrate on dispersing with some of our criminal activities over the next few years. Being born into the Bratva, my family and I had no option but to live a criminal life. But now I was Pakhan, there were things I could do to change that. Or at least minimise that part of our lives.

Uncle Maxim was based in St. Petersburg and he was the overall leader of the Rominov Bratva. His oldest son Viktor was in New York, and I oversaw the UK, but we both answered to Uncle Maxim. Thankfully, after everything that had happened to us in the last five years, Uncle Maxim understood why we didn't want to be a part of this life anymore and agreed we could leave so long as we found trustworthy allies to take our place.

Like myself, Uncle Maxim could be brutal when running the Brotherhood, but he was also a reasonable man who loved his family deeply and would do anything for them. Even if that meant letting them go.

So, my intention was to offload most of our criminal activities, a bit at a time, and concentrate on the more white-collar crime we had been specialising in of late.

The drugs smuggling route we managed for Uncle Maxim and our cousins in the States would be the first to go.

As we broke for photographs, I pondered my next moves.

Finding the right groups to take over the various parts of the route from us would not be easy, but I had some in mind. I needed to meet with them and make sure I chose wisely.

When you ran a criminal organisation, you couldn't just walk away. Not with all the enemies ready to seek revenge. It was necessary to set things up to ensure we remained surrounded by allies. Our future, and the future of my Bratva family in Russia and America, was at stake.

My father had always tried to keep a low profile here in the UK, which was helpful, and since taking over, I had done the same. I worked hard at maintaining the image of Russian Oligarchs and staying off the radar of the authorities, and I would continue to do so.

It was my dream for us all to be fully legitimate one day, but it was complicated and would take a lot of planning and I couldn't afford to make the wrong choices. Love would have to wait. I didn't have time for it.

As everyone gathered for a group photograph and I watched all the smiling faces, I breathed a sigh of relief.

Today, everyone was happy and safe. I hoped it stayed that way. Unfortunately, I didn't believe it would. I had a sense that things were far from over and I only hoped that whatever was coming next, we could all survive it.

But that was a concern for another time. For now, life was good, and it was time to celebrate.

Unwilling to let my thoughts disrupt my enjoyment of the rest of the day, I pushed them aside, plastered a smile on my face and headed off in search of a drink.

CHAPTER 3

EILIDH

GLASGOW – THAT NIGHT – THE MEETING

arrived at the address on the paper for my meeting with John Aldridge, with a few minutes to spare. It was a row of shops with offices above. I approached the door and confirmed it was the correct address. A small plaque above a buzzer stated, "Aldridge: Private Investigators."

Earlier in the day, I'd done a quick check of the address and so I wasn't surprised by this. Not surprised, but full of questions.

Who hired him? Why hadn't he come forward with these photographs sooner?

The door opened almost as soon as I pressed the button.

Feeling both excited and apprehensive, I climbed the stone steps to the upper floor. At the top, there were several small offices, all of which seemed locked up for the night except for one. A tall, thin man stood at the entrance.

"Miss Campbell, or should I say, Detective Constable Campbell, please come in," he said, beckoning me inside.

"I'm John Aldridge, and I am glad you came to meet me. May I say that I knew your dad, and I am sorry for your loss," he told me.

"Please, take a seat," he gestured to one of two chairs in front of a rather messy-looking desk with paperwork piled on top.

Several boxes were dotted about the room.

Was he moving in or moving out?

How did he know my dad? Where did he get the photographs? Why did he wait so long before sending them to me?

My head was buzzing with questions that I badly needed answers to, but I wanted him to tell me what he knew first. So, I did as he asked and sat down, keeping my mouth firmly shut.

As he took a seat on the other side of the desk, I watched him intently.

He took a deep breath before speaking.

"I was hired by your father to look into something for him not long before he was murdered. We met in the police force when I was a uniform sergeant before I was forced to leave to look after my sick wife. She had a brain tumour. I needed to care for her and our two children. After she died, I joined a retired police officer in his private investigator's business. I took it over myself when he passed away," he said.

He looked like he was waiting for me to ask something, but I still wasn't ready yet. I just continued to sit there quietly, observing him, and waited.

Once he realised I had no intention of speaking, he cleared his throat and continued.

"Anyway, your dad knew me and trusted me to look into things for him. He believed that some members of his department were taking bribes from criminals to ignore or lose evidence and even, sometimes, to plant evidence. He gave me a list of four names and told me his suspicions, but he didn't have any actual evidence and felt unable to make an internal complaint about his colleagues without it. So, he asked me to investigate on the quiet."

Nodding, I finally spoke.

"Go on."

"I spent a couple of days tailing the names on his list, two of whom I knew from my time in the force. The photographs I sent you, except for a few of them, were copies of the ones I took where anything suspicious occurred. I had already passed the originals, along with my report, to your father less than an hour before his murder. I met him where he was killed, and he had been reading it when I left him."

He looked away from me then and appeared lost in thought. I desperately wanted to ask my questions, but I bit my tongue to stop them from pouring from my mouth while I waited to hear the rest of what he had to say.

"The photographs showing his murder and the exchange with the man who was his killer were pushed under my door several days ago with a note advising me to ensure you received them and to tell you everything I knew."

That did it. I couldn't hold back any longer.

"Why didn't you before now? And why didn't you tell the detectives working on my dad's murder what you knew?" I asked, annoyance lacing my voice

Why had this man been sitting on evidence?

"I am truly sorry for what happened to your dad. He was a good man. However, after the evidence had gone missing from your dad's car when he was found dead, it didn't seem like a coincidence and I got scared."

He sniffed nervously.

"Thankfully, I didn't give him anything in the report or photographs that would have alerted anyone to my identity; otherwise, I may have been next. I didn't go to the police because I was unsure whom I could trust."

"You have to go to the police. We can go together. With these photographs and your testimony, they would need to reopen my dad's case and…"

"No," he shouted, cutting me off mid-sentence.

"I won't go to the police. That may seem cowardly to you, Miss Campbell, but I have two children who need me. They have already lost one parent, and I couldn't risk them losing another."

He paused, gulping, as I stared at him in anger.

"I had only been on the case for a couple of days, and the photographs were my initial findings along with this report," he said, handing me a thin file.

"It just states times, locations, and persons involved in the meetings shown on the photographs," he continued.

"As for the additional photographs, I do not know where they came from, who took them, or how they knew I had any involvement with your dad's investigation. That is all I know, and I have now passed it to you. You can do with it whatever you wish, but please leave me out of it. I have destroyed all other evidence of my involvement, and I will deny having anything to do with it if you try to involve me," he said, rising and coming around the desk.

"You need to testify, Mr Aldridge; I will get you protection!" I insisted, rising to face him.

"Your department is corrupt, Detective, and I don't know whom you can trust. Who knows how far up the corruption goes? I gave you the information I have to clear my conscience because whoever pushed those photos under my door obviously wanted me to. However, I have no intention of ever testifying," he said, opening the door.

"I was unaware that anyone knew I'd been helping your dad, but obviously, somebody did, and that concerns me. However, I am leaving town permanently. I wish you well, Miss

Campbell, and advise you to be very careful. I would hate for anything to happen to you, but I have given you all the help I can," he said, ushering me out and closing the door firmly in my face.

Shocked, I stared at it.

Did the guy seriously think I was going to let this go?

Furious, I tried to open it, but it was locked. I rattled the handle and pushed at it with my shoulder.

"Open the door, you arsehole!" I screamed as I banged on the thing.

"Leave, Detective. I've helped all I can!" he said through the door.

Frustrated, I leaned against the door frame.

"Please, Mr Aldridge!" I pleaded.

"No, I'm sorry, Miss Campbell, but I have children to protect. I won't get any more involved," he replied, and I could hear the conviction in his voice.

Fine, I would have to do this myself.

Clutching the file, I turned away from the closed door and walked back down the hall, letting everything I'd learned in our brief exchange finally sink in. It felt like my life really had been turned upside down.

It was all true. My dad was murdered while looking into corruption within the department that I now belonged to myself. I could no longer cling to the tiniest little hope I carried that somehow I had been wrong. There was no denying it anymore; my colleagues had to have been involved. Uncle Roy had to have been involved.

Memories of the times my dad and I had spent with Roy at his home, on holiday, laughing and joking together, and then me being hugged and comforted by Roy at my dad's funeral, assaulted me. Each memory felt like a punch to the gut, and by the time I reached the bottom of the stairs, I felt sick.

Shoving open the door, I ran out into the street, one hand holding the file, the other held desperately over my mouth in a vain effort to stop myself from throwing up. I just got to the end of the block of shops and turned into an alleyway before finally retching.

Bent over and using the edge of the building for support, I vomited on the ground as my stomach forcibly ejected the little food I'd eaten earlier.

Eventually, when there was nothing left, I took a deep breath and quickly wished I hadn't, because the smell made me dry heave. Backing away a few steps and keeping my breath shallow finally calmed the nausea, and I could stand up straight again. After wiping my mouth with the back of my hand, I staggered back to my car, thankful nobody was around to witness the evidence of my trauma.

Still feeling like shit, I climbed into the driver's seat and sat there clutching the steering wheel and breathing heavily as my anger built. All this time, Roy Allen had been lying to me, pretending to be grieving over my father's loss, when, in fact, it looked like he had been involved in his murder.

He won't get away with it! None of them will!

The vow I'd made that morning solidified in my mind. I was going to finish what my dad had started, expose the corruption in the department and bring his killer to justice. I would avenge my dad's death if it was the last thing I did.

CHAPTER 4
MIKI

LONDON – A WEEK LATER – THE BLACKMAIL

Standing outside the coffee shop, my eyes narrowed on the man as I took him in. He wasn't much to look at, pretty average; nothing about him stood out. He was small and lean, with a thin, pinched face, slightly receding hairline, and small wire-rimmed glasses. At first glance, you would likely dismiss him as no threat. I knew better.

Nigel Simpson was a prominent criminal defence lawyer here in London and while he might not outwardly exude power, as I had been told I did, he was definitely powerful and no doubt highly intelligent. He wouldn't be so successful if he wasn't.

So, while I knew I could bring him easily to his knees with the information I now held on him, I would still need to watch the slimy little weasel. He wasn't someone that could ever be trusted, even with the threat of blackmail hanging over his head.

The guy was as corrupt as they came. It was that corruption that had caused him to be a part of several conspiracies against me and mine. He was also a man who had a tendency to play hard and break the law, even as he upheld it, and those tendencies would be his downfall. Starting today.

Opening the door of the coffee shop, I made my way towards him, with Vlad, my friend and bodyguard, following closely behind.

Fisting my hands, I took a deep breath to help stay in control, as I slipped into the seat opposite him.

Finally, I was face to face with one of the men who had been orchestrating attacks on my family and the Polish Mafia for some time. They'd brought misery and upset to us and for that, they would pay. I tampered down the rage I felt at having to wait to take revenge on this little weasel. I couldn't give in to it, not yet. For now, I needed him.

Simpson looked up from reading his newspaper, and his breath hitched when he recognised me. Trying to pretend otherwise, he lifted his coffee towards his mouth, "Can I help you, Mr… eh?" he asked.

However, from the slight trembling of his hand as he drank from his cup, it was all too obvious that he knew exactly who I was… and was afraid. *Very good*, he should be afraid.

"I believe you know exactly who I am, Mr Simpson. Now, regarding how you can help me, I want the name of the person you work for. The one who has been behind the attacks on my family and business," I stated, my voice sounding pleasant, my expression anything but.

"I do not know what you are talking about!" he exclaimed before standing and picking up his briefcase, ready to leave.

"Sit!" I told him firmly, remaining in my seat.

Vlad moved to block his exit.

Tilting my head slightly, I silently watched Simpson look around the busy coffee shop, contemplating what he should do next. I smirked. The guy was trying hard to look like he was unaffected by my presence. However, the slight increase in his breathing and the acrid stench of sweat told the truth. The guy was nervous as fuck, and I couldn't be happier by that.

As seconds ticked by, I observed his inner turmoil, which was written all over his face. That was unexpected, disappointing, even. Considering his job, I had thought he'd be much calmer under pressure and certainly more able to hide his emotions. I had obviously caught him off guard. Well, if nothing else, being able to read him so openly would work in my favour. It would make bending him to my will that much easier.

Finally, obviously unwilling to make a scene, he sunk back into his seat, and I smiled evilly as I passed a large brown envelope across the table.

"Open it," I told him and leaned back in my chair, keeping my posture relaxed.

Simpson reached for it, and a second later, he blanched.

After several more seconds of absolute silence, as he stared at the contents, he looked into my eyes.

"What exactly do you want from me?" he asked, gulping.

Got you, arsehole!

The disgusting bastard was a married man who liked to mess about with young men, rent boys not much older than his fourteen-year-old twin sons, and he also had a penchant for snorting cocaine while enjoying their company. And we had the photographs to prove it.

So, now he would give me the information I needed, or I would leak the photographs to the newspapers.

As a criminal defence lawyer, Simpson had a lot to lose. Not only would he want to avoid the cost to his reputation, but being married to one of London's top divorce lawyers, I assumed he would do anything to avoid the considerable cost of divorce, too. He was well and truly screwed, and he knew it.

The guy was mine; I owned him now and he would soon learn exactly what that meant.

"We will start with your boss's name, and we can do it the

easy way or not; your choice," I smiled wider, not in the least bit friendly.

Simpson gulped loudly and looked down at the envelope again, contemplating his options. I gave him a minute to let the weight of his predicament sink in.

Finally, he put the contents back in the envelope and pushed it across the table towards me.

"Keep it; I have copies," I told him, and Simpson blanched again. So much so that I thought he was about to pass out on me. Geez, could this guy get any paler?

Letting out a long, ragged breath, he briefly closed his eyes. When he reopened them, he looked at me and I saw the internal debate going on inside him. I thought for a moment that he might have the balls to tell me to go screw myself, but then he looked away, and I knew he didn't.

Good. This man would tell me what I wanted to know, even if I had to take him somewhere more private and ensure that he did, but considering he was a prominent figure, I preferred to do it the easy way for now.

"Aidan Mathieson!" he finally said.

My eyes narrowed, and I frowned. The name was familiar, although I had never made his acquaintance.

"If I tell you what I know, will that be the end of it?" he asked.

When I said nothing, he continued talking, taking my silence for acquiescence, it seemed. Some of his colour returned, and he grew bolder, smirking as he spoke.

"I mean, a man like yourself knows all about the darker proclivities. Those of us with, shall we say, more specialised tendencies need to stick together. There's really no reason anyone else should find out about this. Am I right?" the little weasel said, licking his lips and darting his eyes around nervously.

My body tensed and my hands bunched into fists under the table as I held back the urge to smash the ugly fuck's face into a pulp. Instead, I forced myself to lean back and smirk.

Simpson returned it, obviously thinking I was agreeing with him. Stupid arsehole. Well, he would find out soon enough just how wrong he was, but in the meantime, it didn't hurt to let him think all he needed to do was co-operate and he wouldn't have to pay for his sins.

"Tell me everything, and hold nothing back," I said, my stare enough to imply the unspoken threats behind my words. It did the trick. The guy visibly paled again, gulping hard before finally regaining some of the composure he must have developed for the courtroom and nodding sharply in agreement.

———

As Vlad and I left the coffee shop a short time later, I couldn't stop my grin. I finally had the name of Nigel Simpson's boss. I was one step closer to making my family safer and eliminating the last of my enemies. Or so I hoped.

Trigger appeared beside us like a phantom, making Vlad grunt and take an unwitting step in front of me before he realised who it was. Thank god the guy was on our side because he could sneak up on a person faster than anyone could blink. Thankfully, he was one of my most trusted soldiers these days and was in charge of the guys assigned to trail Simpson.

"Watch him. We've got him by the balls, but I'm sure he'd do just about anything to weasel his way out of our hold," I told him.

"Will do, boss. Although I've got to say, I'm hoping he tries to do a runner. It's been a long time since I got to open up my baby and let rip. I'd love to give that bastard a run for his money," he replied, his entire face lighting up at the prospect.

"Well, if he does, be careful. No stupid antics and no fucking heroics," I warned, knowing it would fall on deaf ears.

"You bet, boss," he replied with a two-finger salute and a cheeky smile.

Chuckling, I shook my head as I watched him disappear down a side alley. Trigger had a way of making me smile despite myself. Even Vlad's lips twitched, his usual stoic expression dropping for a second. Since he'd been in my organisation, Trigger had embedded his way into my heart, and I considered him family. Just like I did Vlad.

Trigger had PTSD from his time as a sniper in the military. He'd been homeless and begging in the street outside our office building when Marko had met him five years ago, literally just after my parents were murdered. Marko had befriended him and persuaded me to give the guy a job with us. Despite being unsure of him, I reluctantly agreed because we had just started a war with the Albanians and needed more men.

However, Trigger had really proved his loyalty since then and, according to the therapist I made him go to, he was coping better with his symptoms. In fact, he was doing really well lately, and as a result, I had given him more responsibility. He seemed to actually be thriving on it. I was glad because I needed loyal guys, but I also needed them to be mentally stable. With hidden enemies all around, I couldn't afford for them to be anything else.

He was still a scruffy bastard that needed a bloody haircut, though. I smirked as I glanced down the alley and glimpsed long hair being shoved under a black motorbike helmet as he climbed onto the back of his 'baby'. That was another thing that had drawn Marko and Trigger together, their love of all things motorbikes.

While I could ride bikes, I preferred cars myself and owned several sports cars. It was just such a pity that these days I was far too busy to take any of my cars out for a run. I understood Trigger's remark all too well; I longed for a chance to take one of my babies out and let rip too.

There was nothing quite like the thrill of speeding along an open road in a sports car. Being a Pakhan really sucked sometimes. There was always so much to do and so little time for anything else.

Although now that we had fewer enemies to worry about, perhaps I could find a little more time for myself. Maybe I could even delegate more. Nodding to myself, I decided that as soon as I dealt with Simpson and Mathieson, that was exactly what I would do. I needed to make some time for pleasure. However, in the meantime, I had enemies to bring down.

"Where to?" Vlad asked.

"Home," I said with a heavy sigh as I climbed into the passenger seat and leaned my head back.

Reluctantly, I pushed thoughts of time for pleasure to the back of my mind and as Vlad drove us home, I thought over what I'd learned from the weasel.

Nigel Simpson was a successful lawyer and made decent enough money, but he had expensive habits. Habits that needed to be funded.

That's why the disgusting little shit had been happy to get paid to cause issues for mine and Glowacki's families by this Aiden Mathieson person. It made sense since Simpson was based here in London while Mathieson was based in Glasgow.

Checking my watch, I contemplated phoning Glowacki to update him. He'd want to know what I'd found out. However, he and my aunt Marta were on their honeymoon, so I decided against it. There was no reason it couldn't wait another few days until he returned home. After everything he'd been through, he deserved to enjoy this time with his new wife trouble free.

In the meantime, I sent Marko a quick text so he could get to work on digging up everything he could on Mathieson.

Simpson had been Mathieson's go-between with Siri and the Broxys; before that, he had been conspiring with Siri and members of the Polish Mafia against Glowacki.

And he'd given the order to kill my beautiful sister.

Fuck, maybe I should have just killed the little weasel after all.

Every part of me thrummed with the need to hit something, but I kept my rage in check.

No, he could still be useful! I reminded myself.

But when he wasn't, then I would gladly ring the fucker's neck, slowly, with my bare hands.

He'd pay just like the others had.

We'd ended the Nowack brothers when they were released on bail after their arrest. Petrov hadn't been bailed. He'd been remanded into custody and went to trial. He was given ten years. Not willing to allow anyone else to kill the fucker, I had ordered him to remain unharmed in prison as we waited for the day of his release.

However, that came sooner than expected when he cut himself a deal after agreeing to testify in a trial against his cellmate. We grabbed him before he could be taken into protective custody.

My mouth pulled up into an evil grin as I relished the fact that Petrov wouldn't be testifying in any trial ever again.

It was through torturing Petrov that we'd learned about Siri's involvement in our troubles and through Siri we'd found out about Nigel Simpson and now through Simpson, we'd discovered it was Aiden Mathieson who was behind it all and apparently ultimately to blame for everything that had happened to my family since the war with the Albanians.

This whole thing was getting more and more complicated

by the minute. My mind felt overwhelmed by it all. Just how many fucking enemies did we have?

This hidden enemy situation reminded me of a Russian Babushka doll, where each time you opened it up, there was another doll inside, until finally you got to the last one. I sure as hell hoped that Mathieson was the last of our enemies.

Anger filled every pore in my body, and I practically vibrated with restrained fury.

In the end, it didn't matter how many enemies we had or who had given the order to kill my sister, anyone who threatened the safety of my family would die.

Scraping my hand through my hair, my head ached with the depth of my responsibilities.

I needed a bloody drink!

As soon as I got home, I was going to pour myself a shot of my favourite vodka. Or maybe two!

Forcing myself to focus on the task at hand, I called Marko.

"How are things going?" I asked.

"It's done," he said.

Marko had been working on one of our cybercrime operations and had just confirmed we were now a couple of million pounds richer.

"Now I'm off out on my bike."

"Enjoy," I told him before hanging up.

He certainly deserved the break, and it was good for him to get out of his bloody office for a while. Even if I envied him his alone time.

God, what I wouldn't give to escape the confines of Pakhan and head out on my own once in a while.

I blew out a disgruntled breath. Maybe one day.

In the meantime, I consoled myself with the fact that at least the money Marko had syphoned out of an undeserving corporation's account would help finance the next stage of my plans.

Along with building up our legitimate businesses, we had been increasing our involvement in white collar crime, especially cybercrime. However, we only targeted the largest and most corrupt companies, and never individuals.

Fleecing an old person out of their life savings would not sit well with me; but fleecing millions from a dodgy corporation was entirely up my street, not to mention far more lucrative.

Not that I had a great understanding of that part of our business. That was Marko's domain. He was a fantastic hacker and ran a team of computer experts who worked on both our legitimate and not-so-legitimate operations. They were a great asset and one I would rely upon more in the future if my plans worked out as I hoped.

The first stage of my plans had been to cut down on the type of drugs we supplied and now we only dealt cocaine and Molly, or Mandy, as it was known here in the UK. The cocaine was brought in from South America via Europe, and we cut it in our lab before distributing it. We made our own Mandy from chemicals that we bought chemicals from China.

Soon I'd be handing that over to Glowacki. Once he'd rebuilt his Brotherhood and had enough men, that was. He'd lost quite a few during our recent attacks, so that had to be addressed first. Once he was back to full capacity, he'd take the drugs lab off our hands and take over our dealers and we'd be out of that side of things.

The next stage was to get rid of our responsibility for the drugs route, and I had begun negotiations about that already.

Those areas of my business were the ones that posed the biggest problem for my Brotherhood and family for two main reasons. First, they were the areas our enemies tried to muscle in on and had been the primary targets for the most recent attacks against us. Second, it was easier to get caught with those types of crimes. So, the sooner we got out of those areas, the better.

The issue was that if they fell into the wrong hands, it would be a disaster not only for my family here and our Russian and American counterparts, but it would also upset the balance of power and cause chaos in the UK. The consequences of any ensuing war would not only affect criminal organisations, but also innocent lives.

Therefore, it was absolutely vital that I chose the right organisations to take over from us. As Pakhan, it was my responsibility.

No bloody wonder I felt so overwhelmed at times. Not that I could show it. I always had to appear in control. Otherwise, I would appear weak, and that would make us an even bigger target than we already were.

My brother Ash was always going on about getting out of these areas sooner rather than later, but he didn't understand how complicated it was.

In our world, enemies held grudges for a long time and if I wasn't careful, I could make us vulnerable to revenge attacks. My whole brotherhood could end up wiped out if I made the wrong choices and aligned with the wrong people.

So, we needed people we could trust, who would work well with the other players in the game and also maintain a good relationship with my family and back us up should we need help against any future threats.

Sighing, I closed my eyes and leaned back against the headrest. Exhaustion settled into every part of my being, draining me of energy.

The last few years, especially since Krissa's murder, had taken their toll on me. Sometimes it felt like the weight of the world was on my shoulders. I longed for someone that I could share my life with; someone I could talk to, share my burdens with, and help me run things.

I huffed out a frustrated breath, annoyed at letting myself delve into those notions again. That was a pipe dream, and indulging in such dreams would only make me more depressed.

Instead, I shook off that line of thinking and opted for a nap. Turning my head slightly to get more comfortable, I let the world drift away, allowing myself a moment of escape from the ever-present heaviness of my responsibilities, for now.

CHAPTER 5

EILIDH

GLASGOW – THAT DAY – THE
INVESTIGATION

After my last night shift of the week, I left the office, throwing a quick "bye" over my shoulder as I headed for the door. It took all my effort to walk normally and not literally bolt from the station.

With a copy of my dad's unsolved case file hidden in my bag, I climbed into my car and sighed in relief.

God, it was getting harder to pretend that I was still clueless. How much longer could I keep my act up without cracking? I felt like a volcano, ready to explode any minute. I was so angry, but I knew I had to be very careful.

The week since my world had been turned upside down had been long and stressful. It absolutely galled me to know without a doubt that my colleagues were corrupt and responsible for my dad's death, and I was desperate to make the bastards pay. However, I needed proper evidence. I couldn't just go around accusing people without it.

Roy and the others must have been hiding their activities for years, so they would likely have an explanation lined up for what was in the photographs, I was sure. None showed any of my colleagues with dad's killer at the time the trigger was pulled, and they could easily plead ignorance on the matter. I didn't believe that for a second, but others might.

So, when I wasn't working, I spent my time following Aidan Mathieson around during the day, and looking for more information on the guy instead of sleeping.

I yawned, completely exhausted, then smirked. I was tired, but it was worth it. The bastards, Mathieson and my dad's murderer, had met up again.

Unfortunately, I hadn't been able to get close enough to find out what the meeting was about.

However, I followed the killer back to his flat. When he'd entered the building, I rushed over and took a quick photo of the names beside the buzzers. Suspecting the guy might have a record, I checked the names in the police database and got a hit. He was called Timmy Neilson, and he was one of Mathieson's former clients. That was no surprise, under the circumstances.

I'd made that discovery a couple of days ago. I didn't know of anyone in the police I could trust yet. So, I was still sitting on that information, along with the file and photos I had received from John Aldridge. My intention was to continue to gather evidence against anyone I thought was involved in my dad's murder and the corruption within the department. Then, when I had enough, I would figure out what to do with the evidence.

My eyelids drooped, but I shook myself awake. Lord, I was tired. I really needed to get some rest.

What had I been thinking about? Oh, yeah, I'd find someone to give the evidence to later.

The problem was, just a few hours ago, Timmy Neilson had turned up dead. Drowned in his bath. I didn't feel in the least sorry about that. Actually, I was glad the murdering bastard was dead. However, I couldn't help but wonder if it was a coincidence, or if someone had discovered that I was investigating. That was a distinct possibility because I didn't really believe in coincidences.

If anyone was on to me, I had to step things up and get the proof I needed as quickly as possible. I would have to be even more careful. Otherwise, I might find myself in real trouble or worse, dead. Just as John Aldridge had warned. A shiver of fear ran down my spine.

Blurry eyed, and distracted by thoughts of my next steps, I drove towards home practically on autopilot. I figured that in order to get evidence against both Mathieson and Roy, the best place to start would be their offices.

Roy was too smart to keep anything incriminating at the station, but he had a home office which I intended to check out. Our shift was off for the next seven days, and I knew the bastard was going out-of-town tomorrow on a golfing trip. Or so he claimed. Anyway, I planned on visiting my Aunt Maisie, his wife, when he was gone and checking his office out while I was there.

That was the plan for tomorrow. Tonight, I had another plan.

Yesterday, I had donned a dark wig and cap and taken in a bouquet to Mathieson's secretary, pretending it was a delivery from a nearby florist. That had allowed me to discover the exact location of his office while checking out the security.

My eyes drooped and my head slumped forward.

"Beeeeeeeep!"

The blast from a car horn jerked me awake.

I'd drifted over into the oncoming lane. A van zoomed towards me.

Shit!

Eyes wide with fear, I yanked the steering wheel to the left.

The van whizzed by me with a mere inches separating us.

The irate looking driver shouting something as he gave me the finger.

I did not know what he was saying, but I could imagine.

My body's fight-or-flight response sent me into a tailspin of horror at how close I'd come to being in a head-on collision with a van.

My heart pounded and my breaths came out in short, shallow puffs.

I sucked panicked air into my lungs.

Bloody idiot! Almost got yourself killed!

With my eyes glued to the road in front of me, and my hands holding the wheel in a death grip so it couldn't drift, I finally made it home in one piece.

Yawning wide, I parked outside my house and slumped back in the seat.

God, that was a close call. If I wasn't more careful, I wouldn't need to worry about anyone discovering my investigation and trying to kill me. I'd end up killing myself first.

I shook my head.

Stupid eejit!

Eventually, when I stopped chiding myself for my stupidity, I hurried inside the house, determined to get some sleep. I desperately needed to recharge my batteries, as I had important plans for this evening, and I couldn't mess them up by being too tired to think straight. Things were dangerous enough without me adding to it by not taking proper care of myself.

Until now, I had done nothing illegal in my investigations. Tonight, that would change.

As I readied for bed and brushed my teeth, I looked at my reflection in the mirror. The woman staring back at me wasn't the same one I was used to seeing. This woman had a hard glint in her eyes that I didn't recognise. She looked a little tougher than before, or maybe she was just a little less soft, a little less gullible, and a lot more jaded.

Sighing heavily, I had to acknowledge the fact that after the revelations of the past week; it was no wonder I'd changed.

Well, if the truth be known, until a week ago, I wouldn't have dreamed of breaking the law I had sworn to uphold to get evidence on a case. Of course, until then, I hadn't dreamed that I was working with corrupt police. In fact, I really never believed there were any at my station. Oh, I knew there had to be some in the force; I wasn't that naïve, just not in my station and not among those I knew.

Shaking my head, I couldn't believe the depths I was going to for the information I needed to end that corruption. If I was discovered, I could lose my career and end up in jail. Tears sprung to my eyes. I just hoped that wherever my dad was, if he was watching me, he understood what I was going to do.

"Sorry, Dad," I whispered, and hoped he would forgive me.

Breaking into Mathieson's office was definitely not how we had foreseen my career as a detective going.

CHAPTER 6
MIKI

GLASGOW – THAT AFTERNOON –
CLOSING IN

A few hours after returning home for our meeting with Simpson, Vlad and I were headed to Glasgow, with Marko in tow.

Sitting in the back of the SUV while Vlad drove as usual, Marko and I looked over the blueprints to the building which housed Mathieson's Law Office and discussed the plan for the night ahead.

As expected, the moment I provided Marko with Aiden Mathieson's name, he had got to work and within minutes we discovered Mathieson was an old-school friend of Simpson's wife. That was their connection, yet we still hadn't found the connection between Mathieson, Glowacki, and us. Marko had wanted a few more days to delve into Mathieson further and find out. However, I was sick of waiting.

It was strange because usually I took my time with everything. I liked to dot all the I's and cross all the t's and thoroughly plan for every eventuality before going ahead with anything. However, something compelled me to just go for it today. It felt like someone was tugging on an invisible rope wrapped around my mind, pulling all my thoughts towards Mathieson and that building.

The idea was ridiculous, yet I found myself unable to shake it off.

For years, this guy had been hiding behind the scenes, messing with us, no doubt laughing at us. The unknown puppet master pulling the strings of our enemies and playing us all for fools. But he wasn't unknown anymore, and I wouldn't allow his interference in my Brotherhood or Glowacki's any longer without consequence. We'd played by his rules long enough. It was time to change them.

Besides, we were due to meet with a contact in Glasgow in a couple of days anyway, so heading up a bit earlier felt like the right thing to do.

My fists clenched as I scowled at the picture of Mathieson that Marko had sent to my phone.

The smug expression on the guy's face made me seethe with fury.

On top of everything he had done, this fucking bastard had ordered my sister's death. I wanted to know why. What his problem was with us and if he was working with anyone else? And then he needed to pay. Him and that little weasel, Simpson.

Marko raised his eyebrows at me when I emitted a growl under my breath. I shook my head at his questioning gaze. He tilted his own head enough to see my screen and his wry smile told me he knew exactly what I was thinking. A pained look flashed across his face, and I knew he was picturing the last time we all saw our beautiful sister.

"We'll make him pay. We'll make them all pay," he reassured me, nodding.

Oh, they would definitely pay dearly for their sins. I still wasn't sure exactly how yet, but I longed to take at least one of them to the C, and Aiden Mathieson seemed the most likely candidate for a one-way ticket to the place.

When we were in the C, we were totally in control of everything.

Everyone entering was unconscious and properly restrained.

Clothes and personal items were removed, and forensic suits donned, before going into the kill room.

We never went in there alone but always with another person for safety.

After we were finished, we cleansed everything thoroughly and disposed of the bodies through cremation.

The C was our special place and the rules my dad had created, and we rigidly implemented, allowed us to literally get away with murder.

Dad was an amazing planner and strategist, and I tried to be like him as best I could.

That was why I didn't kill Simpson the minute I discovered his identity, even though I longed to rip out the bastard's throat. That was also why, although we were headed up to Scotland, I had no plans to confront Mathieson yet.

Not until I discovered everything I could about the guy and ensured there were no other unknown enemies lurking in the shadows. Sadly, the way things had been lately, I really couldn't discount that possibility. Time would tell.

"I'll give Jim MacArthur a call and see what he knows," I told Marko as he continued to dig into Mathieson's background.

"Miki. Good to hear from you," Jim answered in his gruff Scottish brogue.

Jim MacArthur was the head of the MacArthur gang from the south side of Glasgow, and one of the few people I was considering for offloading part of our drugs route to.

"Don't tell me you've called to rearrange our meeting?"

"Not at all. Actually, I was looking for a bit of information," I replied.

"Whatever you need," he said.

After filling him in on the situation, Jim confirmed Mathieson was the defence lawyer on the payroll of a rival gang. The Thomas gang were based in Glasgow's east end and were notorious throughout Scotland. They ruled their small territory through fear and violence and were, in the words of Jim, 'scummy bastards'. If Mathieson was involved with them, he was the lowest of the low.

However, that still didn't explain his obsession with hurting us or Glowacki. Neither of us had ever had any dealings with the Thomas gang. So, either Mathieson was working alone, and he was the one who had the issue with us, or there was indeed another player yet to be discovered.

Sighing heavily, I rubbed at the tension in my forehead, which was causing me a headache. It was frustrating that the answers still eluded us, but at least we were closing in on a key player.

Tonight, with the help of Marko, I would break into Mathieson's office and hopefully, that would provide me with many of the answers I so desperately needed.

Hiding behind the bins, out of sight of the security cameras, I waited.

The stink was disgusting. I guessed an office must have had a working lunch as leftover Indian takeaway and pizza boxes overflowed the bin, pushing the lid open enough to allow the stench of rotten food to permeate the air.

Taking quick, shallow breaths, I tried hard to avoid inhaling too deeply for fear that I might end up vomiting. I'd never live it down if Marko heard me spewing my guts up over a bit of leftover food.

Thankfully, I didn't have to wait for long and the lights in the building flickered off and then on again.

"Go!" his voice hissed through my earpiece. The alarm was off.

Relief flooded me as I escaped the offending smells and hurried over to the door, grabbed the handle, and pulled it open enough to slip inside.

Closing it over gently behind me, I smiled as I made my way in through the basement.

Marko had hacked the system and taken over the security feed a short while ago, recording footage that would now be shown on a loop by the cameras to hide my actions.

As the staff had already left for the night, there were no lights on the floors, but the stairs were lit enough light for me to see while I bolted up the five flights of stairs to take me to the fourth floor and Mathieson's Law Office.

Feeling exhilarated, and panting hard, I gasped out, "I'm here!" and a few seconds later, the office door unlocked. Fantastic!

My heart raced with the effort of the run and the thrill of the situation.

Slipping inside, I made my way over to Mathieson's private office and opened the door.

There were no lights on inside his office either, but I utilised the torch on my phone to help me see as I fired up his computer. Once it was on, I quickly linked it up to the gadget Marko had provided so he could hack into it and download the hard drive.

While that was happening, I hid several tiny cameras around the room. The feed from them would go directly to Marko's laptop and my phone. It didn't take long to do. This wasn't our first rodeo. We had done this sort of thing before.

Getting the hard drive information took the longest, and it was just completed when Marko hissed again, "Someone's coming!"

"The guard?" I asked.

"No, someone else appears to be breaking in!" he stated. "Hide!"

Shit! What? Who?

With just a few seconds to spare, I snatched Marko's gadget and shut down the computer.

After ducking into the small bathroom, I left the door just open enough so that whomever it was could see that it was a bathroom and hopefully ignore it while still leaving me hidden from view.

Tuning into the video feed from our cameras on my phone, I watched in silence, knowing the bit of light it produced could not be seen from within the office.

The office door opened, and I held my breath as I watched. A smallish figure dressed in black entered. Peering closer, I studied the approaching figure. It appeared to be female.

"Is that a woman?" Marko's question broke the silence, and I almost cursed, thinking I was about to be discovered before I remembered the earpiece lodged in my ear.

"Looks like it," I whispered.

A woman was breaking into Mathieson's office! Why?

CHAPTER 7
EILIDH

THAT NIGHT – THE BREAK-IN

As I hid in the shadows of the building across the street from Mathieson's office, I watched the goings on in the brightly lit foyer. The staff had left for the night and there was only one security guard left on duty. Perfect!

Once the guard left the front desk for his break, I crept around to the side entrance of the building, where I expected he would come out for a smoke. Just as he'd informed me he would when I spoke with him earlier this evening in the same spot after asking him for a light.

My nose scrunched in disgust at the thought. I hated cigarettes and didn't smoke, but had deliberately learned to do so while working undercover. It was an excellent way to strike up a conversation with strangers and get information, and it had worked perfectly yesterday.

Posing as a worker from the building I was now lurking beside, I casually remarked about looking forward to finishing work for the day. The guard told me he was working late into the night. After asking him if he found it boring working alone at night, he said he usually took a nap after his dinner, which helped pass the time.

Chuckling at the memory, I shook my head at how easily the idiot had given up vital information. Some security guard. Because of his penchant to say too much, I now knew he was working alone, would no doubt come out for a smoke on his dinner break, and would likely take a nap afterwards. I also knew where the smoking area was and the entrance he would use to get in and out.

While we'd chatted, I had also noticed that he had wedged a brick into the door, leaving it partially open, and I hoped he would do that again.

Movement caught my eye and my body tensed as I peered intently at the side door.

Yes! There he was. I was right. Stupid rent-a-cop was not the sharpest tool in the box!

Some security guys took their jobs seriously and were good at it. I respected that, but some were wannabe cops who couldn't make the grade and took a security job so they could pretend. Others were simply lazy time wasters who didn't really care. This guy fell into the latter category. Frowning at his approaching form, I muttered "useless" to myself before feeling guilty.

It was probably wrong of me to judge under the circumstances. Considering he was only watching over offices and not the crown jewels. Besides, for the measly amount of money he was probably getting paid, his lack of care was understandable, in a way. It also made things so much easier for me, so I guessed I should be glad of his lack of work ethic.

As soon as he exited the building and headed to the smoking shelter, I crossed the road and crept up behind him. When he had his back to me and his head down as he lit his cigarette, I slipped into the building, ran to the stairwell, and headed up the stairs to Aiden Mathieson's office.

Thank goodness I ran a lot because by the time I reached the fifth floor my heart was racing, and I my breathing was laboured. Who knew what state I'd be in if I wasn't fairly fit?

Before I left the stairway, I stopped to drag some much needed air into my burning lungs.

When my breathing had finally returned to normal, I entered the corridor and hurried towards Mathieson's office. Keeping my head down and my hood pulled forward to cover my face, I did my best to avoid the cameras in the hallway.

As I reached the office door, I took out the pass I stole from Mathieson's secretary as she left the building earlier. I scanned it, and it let me into the main office.

Yey! So far, so good. I worried that she might have already noticed it missing and notified security. Obviously not.

Using my flashlight to light my way, I hurried straight to Mathieson's own office and slipped inside. His computer was on, and as I pressed the keys, I saw it was just shutting down.

That seemed odd. I frowned. *Why would it still be on?*

Shaking my head, I ignored the question. I didn't have time to worry about it.

The top two drawers of his desk contained the usual sort of office junk. However, the bottom drawer was locked.

Taking out my special tools, I had the lock picked in no time. As I slid the drawer open, I smiled, happy that the skills I learned years ago were finally being put to good use.

Warmth spread through me, and a small smile tugged at the corners of my mouth as I thought about how I'd learned those skills.

My mum's cousin Joe had been a thief but, after a short stint in prison, he went straight. Luckily, he found a job with a security firm consulting on security measures. They found the knowledge he gained during his criminal activities exceptionally helpful, and although Joe always carried his set of tools with him, he never used them for illegal purposes again.

He just liked always having them nearby, like a security blanket, he once told me.

After Mum passed from cancer when I was a child, I found her jewellery box. It was one with a little lock, but there was no key. Unable to open it and not wanting to break it, I'd been distraught. Thankfully, Joe was there to save the day. He took out his special tools and showed me how to break into the box without causing any damage. I was only eight years old, so I thought it was great fun.

For years after that, whenever Joe was babysitting me or whenever I was upset and needed to be distracted, he would find me other locked things and let me play with his tools and break into them. He kept different things in his garage, including old safes, and spent hours trying to get into them. As I grew older, he let me help.

That had been a lot of fun.

Joe would also tell me stories about jobs he had done in his youth before he had been caught. I learned a lot from him about breaking into different places and the various security measures that exist in today's world, and I still had the small set of "Tools of the trade" he had given me for my thirteenth birthday.

He was long gone now, and I missed him as much as I did my parents. A wave of sadness hit me, and I squeezed my eyes shut and forced myself to get back to the task at hand.

So, because of Joe, I had skills. Maybe not the skills you would expect a police officer to have, but they came in handy whenever I had a robbery to investigate. They would certainly come in handy in helping me gain the evidence I needed to avenge my dad's murder.

Unfortunately, the drawer did not hold any hidden secrets. In fact, it was empty. In frustration, I reached inside and carefully examined the edges, but there was nothing I missed.

Quickly closing it up, I crept around, checking all the usual places people hide things, but again found nothing.

Pushing down feelings of disappointment, I took a step back and scanned the room. There had to be something. I was sure a man like Mathieson had lots of secrets, so where was he hiding them?

The computer was an obvious answer for some of them, but a lawyer like Mathieson would have hard copies of things as back up. I needed to find them. I glanced again at the computer and wished Joe had also taught me hacking skills. Unfortunately, that sort of thing was before his time and since I wasn't technically gifted, finding anything on the thing was a big fat no-no for me.

Narrowing my eyes, I zoned in on the picture on the wall behind his desk and smirked. Of course!

Moving it aside revealed the safe I'd suspected was there.

Really? Very cliched.

Chuckling, I shook my head. It seemed Aiden Mathieson was not too technical either. And not in the least original. However, that made it so much easier for me.

The safe was an old-fashioned dial type, too, which had obviously been there for some time.

Seriously, who still used this old shit?

"Hey, the old ones are the best!" I could practically hear Joe chiding me, and I smothered a chuckle behind my hand.

Checking my watch, I noticed there wasn't a lot of time left before the guard would be back.

Shit, I needed to hurry.

My skills were rusty, but excitement fizzled through me like a live wire at the thought of playing with my tools again.

Pulling my kit open, I selected the instruments which would do the job, put my ear to the door and in less than a minute, it was open. A sense of satisfaction flowed through me, and I grinned from ear to ear. That was fun! It was almost a pity it was over so soon.

Snapping a photo of the contents, I quickly riffled through them, taking pictures of everything before replacing the items back exactly where they had been. There was an enormous pile of cash and several passports with Mathieson's picture, but different names. It looked like this was where the shady lawyer kept his escape cache.

Stuffed at the back of the safe was a plastic bag with a gun inside. I froze and gulped, feeling sick as I wondered if it was the gun that killed my dad.

Closing my eyes briefly, I sucked in a deep breath, not wanting to even look at a weapon that might have ended my dad's life.

Come on, Eilidh, move, you haven't got time to freak out now. It might not even have anything to do with Dad!

Forcing myself to get moving, but unable to handle the bag with the gun, just in case, I used one of my tools to move it aside to ensure nothing else was hidden away. There wasn't, but that there was such a weapon in Mathieson's safe proved to me that the man was into some nasty shit.

This was the UK; we didn't carry guns here, and if it was evidence of a crime, it should be with the police and not a defence lawyer. There was no reason a lawyer would have a gun in a plastic bag in his safe unless he was keeping it as leverage for some reason.

Aidan Mathieson was either using it to blackmail someone, or to ensure his own safety. Whatever the reason, seeing it there made me nervous as fuck, and thinking it could be connected to my dad made me sick to my stomach.

It was too much. I needed to leave. I'd done enough snooping for one night. Besides, time was running out.

After shutting the safe and replacing the picture, I scanned the office to make sure nothing looked disturbed. Satisfied, I pulled up the hood of my jacket, ensuring it obscured my face as I slipped out of the office, closed the door, and with my head down, hurried back along the hall.

Intent on leaving as quickly as possible, I opened the door to the stairwell to head back downstairs. I had just started down the steps when my arm was grabbed and I was pushed up against the wall.

The breath whooshed out of me as a large body pressed tightly against me, and a hand covered my mouth.

The initial shock of being grabbed quickly wore off.

"What the fuck?" I mumbled behind his hand as I struggled frantically against a steel-like grip.

The guy was taller than me and built like a tank, and the way I was pressed tightly against the length of him left no room for me to manoeuvre. My pitiful attempts to break free of his hold were getting me nowhere. It was time to change tactics.

Just as I was about to go limp in his arms, so he was forced to change his grip on me, his body stiffened. He leaned in and hissed, "Quiet."

At that moment, I heard a door open below accompanied by whistling and the sound of footsteps. The guard was coming up the stairs. Shit!

Frozen in place, we held our breath and waited, listening to the steps getting closer.

Thankfully, the guard opened the door to the floor two floors below and headed inside. Geez, that was close. If I had barrelled down the stairs as planned, I would have run straight into him and been discovered.

That's when I realised that whoever had me pressed against the wall had just saved me from being caught. But who was he, and why?

CHAPTER 8
MIKI

THAT SAME NIGHT – THE MYSTERY WOMAN

As soon as the female exited Mathieson's office, I followed. Thank god she hadn't bothered to come into the tiny bathroom!

My mind was awhirl with questions. Who the hell was she? What had she been looking for?

"The guard is on his way up."

Marko's voice interrupted my thoughts.

"You need to get out!"

Shit! I cracked the door open and peeked out. The mystery woman was hurrying along the hallway. She seemed distracted and didn't notice me creeping up behind her.

"He's on level one and will head up, so wait until he goes onto level two or three, then slip past him and get out!" Marko stated.

Hell, the woman wasn't aware the guard was doing his rounds. If she kept running down the stairs, she'd be caught. I couldn't let that happen. If she got caught, the police would be called, and I'd be trapped here and likely caught, too. *Shit, shit, shit!*

There was nothing for it. I had to stop her.

Just as she opened the door and stepped into the stairwell, I grabbed her and pushed her up against the wall, holding her tightly against me with a hand over her mouth. She attempted to struggle and speak.

"Quiet," I whispered. She froze, and we heard whistling and footsteps as the guard entered the stairwell below.

She gasped and looked up at me, her eyes widening as she realised just how close she'd come to being discovered. With our bodies pressed tightly together, faces inches apart, we could do nothing but stare at each other.

The most gorgeous amber eyes I had ever seen held mine prisoner as the world around me lost focus. A sense of peace filled me, unlike anything I'd ever known.

Whoever this woman was, I knew in that second that she was going to have an impact on my life beyond this brief encounter, and I smiled as I checked out the rest of her.

Pressed up against her as tightly as I was, I couldn't help but notice her curves. *Nice! Real nice!*

Several strands of dark red hair peeked out from her hood, which had fallen back just enough to reveal pale, flawless skin, and full pink lips. She was stunning. Completely breathtaking.

After what felt like ages, the guard opened the door two floors below and headed inside. I breathed a sigh of relief and slowly removed my hand from her mouth.

"Who are you, and what are you doing here?" she asked.

Her voice sent a shiver of pleasure down my spine as I caught a trace of a sexy Scottish accent. She was a local.

"I could ask you the same thing?"

She never answered. Instead, she appeared to be checking me out the way I had her.

"I guess who we are doesn't matter, and as for what I am doing? No doubt something similar to you!" she stated with a slight frown that made her nose scrunch up.

God, that was so cute!

She took a deep breath and leaned in closer.

Did she just sniff me?

Yes, I was sure she just sniffed me, and I liked it. Grinning, I sniffed her in return, and wow, she smelt so good. Something citrusy with a hint of cinnamon and maybe chocolate. It made me want to lick her. My cock jerked its approval. *Oh hell!*

My mouth was suddenly dry, and I licked my lips. Her eyes tracked the movement, and as if pulled by an invisible force, I dipped my head. Her own tilted up at the same time, and I took it as an invitation. Before I could think better of it, I brushed my lips against hers. Their welcoming softness made me groan, and she shuddered in response, opening her mouth to let my tongue delve inside.

Fuck, she tasted as good as she smelt. Better even. All the blood rushed to my cock, and I felt it hardening between us.

Shit, what was going on with me? I was reacting to her like some horny teenager.

Seriously? I chided myself. This was hardly the time or place for me to be getting turned on, but I couldn't seem to control my body's response. She was making sexy little mewling sounds, which made it hard for me to even think straight, never mind try to stop. I deepened the kiss, loving her responsiveness.

A voice penetrated my haze of lust, and I realised it was Marko.

"Where the fuck are you? And what are you groaning for? Miki, what the hell is that noise?" Marko asked as the door below us opened again.

That brought me back to my senses like a bucket of water thrown over me. I pulled away from the siren, and we both stood staring at each other in shock while trying to quieten our panting breaths.

Expecting the guard to hear our breathing, we peered over the railing, but luckily he was whistling away to music he was listening to through earbuds. He pulled open the door of the floor directly below us and disappeared inside.

God, that was close.

"We'd better get out of here before the guard comes back," she whispered, pushing past me and heading quickly downstairs.

Unable to do anything else but follow, I checked out her bottom as she descended the stairs.

When she stopped just before the door the guard had disappeared into, she caught me looking. Smirking, she raised her eyebrows at me in question. Shrugging, I returned her smirk without remorse.

Well, I was a hot-blooded guy who hadn't been laid in a while and we'd just enjoyed a searing kiss that had made my toes curl after all.

Smiling at the memory, I waited, watching her as she sneaked a look through the small glass window in the door before nodding at me, sprinting past and continuing down the stairs. I kept pace until we got to the ground floor. She headed for the side entrance, but I pulled her back.

"This way, Little Miss Red!" I said, gesturing towards the emergency exit in the basement.

At first I thought she was going to protest, but thankfully she didn't and instead let me lead the way. Once in position, I let Marko know to unlock the door again. Almost immediately, the lights flickered. I grabbed her hand, and then we were outside and running.

Once we got a block away, I kept hold of her hand as we slowed down to catch our breath. I told myself I needed to find out who she was and what information she had on Mathieson, but in truth, I was reluctant to let her go. However, I could see the wheels turning in her mind now that we were no longer in danger of being caught and realised she was about to bolt.

Uh uh, baby! I pulled her back as she tried to run.

Turning her around, I pushed her into a nearby doorway, pressing her up against it. Just like before. Only this time, instead of putting my hand over her mouth, I grabbed her face, tilting her chin, and captured her mouth in another searing kiss.

Expecting her to fight this time, I was relieved, and a little surprised when she didn't. Instead, she clutched my jacket and returned the kiss with an enthusiasm which excited me.

Lifting her up high, I literally plastered myself against her, desperate to be closer to her. She must have had the same thought as she wrapped her legs tightly around me, grinding against my hard on.

God, I want her!

"What the fuck?" Marko's voice hissed in my ear.

"Are you kissing that woman?"

Shit! I had forgotten he was listening.

Ignoring him, I reached into my pocket, pulled out a card, and removed a tiny object. Forcing myself to break off the kiss, I rested my forehead against hers and slipped my hand behind her neck and stuck it to the label of her hoodie.

After gently setting her down on the ground, I took a couple of steps back to stop myself from grabbing her and kissing her again.

"What's your name?" I asked.

"Tell me your name," I demanded when she hesitated.

She opened her mouth to speak, then clamped it shut, shaking her head.

"I need to go!" she cried, then turned and bolted off down the road. My body wanted to give chase, but there was no need.

"Marko, open your system and trace the tracker I just put on the woman," I said.

"Got her!" he confirmed within a few seconds, and I grinned.

Little Miss Red might think she could escape me, but she would soon discover that she could only get away from me if I allowed it. Even if I didn't want to know what she was doing at Mathieson's and what information she had, I wanted more of those kisses, and that alone ensured we would see each other again. Soon, very soon!

When the SUV pulled up, I was still grinning at the thought. Vlad was driving, as always. Marko was in the backseat with his laptop open, so I climbed into the passenger seat, hoping to avoid too much scrutiny from him.

Noting my expression, Vlad simply raised his eyebrows and smirked, but said nothing about the incident I knew he would have overheard too. Good man. He could always be relied on to be discreet.

Turning away again, he simply asked, "Where to, boss?"

"Take us back to the hotel," I replied.

"Want to tell me what the hell you were doing back there?" Marko asked.

Settling into the seat, I ripped my balaclava off, scratching at my beard, and ignored him.

The bloody thing always made me itch. I hated wearing it, but it hid my identity and so it was a necessary evil sometimes.

"You were kissing her!" Marko cried incredulously when I continued to ignore him.

"Don't know what you are talking about," I told him.

"I heard you. We both did," he stated.

"There must have been something wrong with the earpiece," I said, smirking.

"No chance!" he exclaimed.

"She must really be something if you jumped on her within seconds of seeing her," Vlad said quietly.

"She is," I said, grinning like a fool.

"Now shut up and drive," I told him, before leaning my head back against the headrest and closing my eyes.

"Fuck," Marko mumbled under his breath, obviously thinking I'd lost my mind. Maybe I had. For a petite, red-haired, Scottish lass with amber eyes I could drown in and a mouth that made me want to come from the slightest taste. Yes, maybe I had.

"Send me the app for her tracker," I said as an afterthought.

I'd be keeping a close eye on my Little Miss Red until I saw her again. My cock hardened at the thought. It was going to be difficult waiting for that moment. We'd only been apart for a few minutes, and it was already too long.

When we reached our suite at the hotel, I went straight to my room and headed for the shower, where I spent an enjoyable few minutes reliving those kisses while relieving my aching cock.

CHAPTER 9

EILIDH

THE FOLLOWING DAY – THE FOUR SUSPECTS

Despite sleeping well, I woke up early the following morning feeling restless. My mind kept drifting back to the mysterious man, our kisses, and his sexy as hell voice.

Chuckling, I couldn't believe I kissed him like that. I didn't even get to see his face, but I didn't need to. Just from the beautiful silver-grey eyes and his smile, I knew he was handsome. And that accent of his, which I was sure was Russian, my god; it made me want to come on the spot.

Nevertheless, what I had done had been reckless and entirely out of character. I should be concerned about that, but I wasn't. It didn't matter that we had met in such odd and frankly dangerous circumstances; I had been immediately drawn to him. I couldn't explain it, so I decided not to try. With all the upset I had been through recently, my entire world turning upside down, it was no wonder I had taken solace in a few minutes of pleasure.

And he had smelt so good! A mix of spice and ginger with an undertone that was all male. Yum! Warmth flooded my face as I remembered blatantly smelling him.

Oh my god, did I really do that? *Yip!* my inner voice chipped in, making me groan and facepalm in embarrassment.

Yet even my embarrassment didn't stop the rush of liquid to my core just thinking of how he had smelt.

God, I cringed when I thought of how wantonly I'd acted. Although, who could blame me, really?

The pull of attraction I had felt the moment he had pressed his large body with all those hard muscles against me was unlike anything I'd felt before.

Between his gorgeous eyes, his smell, his luscious sexy lips, his panty-melting kisses, that voice, and the hard length of him against my body, it was no wonder I hadn't been able to resist. He was the full package and then some!

My body shivered with lust. I was only human, after all, so I refused to be ashamed of practically throwing myself at the man. Even if I did!

Well, actually, he lifted me up, and I just wrapped my legs around him the second time we kissed. So technically, I didn't actually jump on him, but it wasn't far off. And deep down, I knew that I really wouldn't mind doing it again.

Sighing, I pushed that thought aside.

Under any other circumstances, I would be thrilled to see the man again. Unfortunately, that wasn't something that could happen. The thought filled me with sadness, as if my body mourned his loss. But it would have to mourn. That brief but exciting encounter we had yesterday was all it was going to get.

After all, the guy was breaking into a building. If that hadn't been enough to tell me he was obviously a criminal of some sort, then the dangerous vibe he exuded certainly was. It didn't matter that I was hugely attracted to him. Steering clear of him was definitely for the best.

But his kisses! And those lips! That little voice said again.

Seriously! I admonished myself.

No more throwing myself at random strangers, no more kissing them, and definitely no more thinking about their lips!

My body slumped, and I suddenly felt depressed by the thought.

What was going on with me? This was all out of character. It definitely had to be a reaction to all the stress I was under. I was simply going to put the incident with Mr Sexy Lips down to a moment of temporary insanity and forget all about it. And him. Especially him.

Curiosity tugged at me, though.

My police senses were tingling. I really wanted to know why he was breaking into that building. He was obviously a thief up to no good.

Like you? My inner voice questioned.

Shit, my inner voice was pissing me off today. I might have acted like a criminal by breaking into Mathieson's office, but I was not a criminal, I told it fiercely.

But you stole the secretary's pass too, the annoying little voice sneered.

Huffing heavily, I ignored it.

Everything I had done was necessary, but it didn't make me a criminal. I was a police officer; I upheld the law. It just so happened that I needed to break it on this occasion to bring my dad's killers to justice and expose the corruption that got him killed.

It was hard not to see the irony in that. However, I consoled myself that the end justified the means under the circumstances.

The thought that until a week ago I wouldn't have dreamed of doing such a thing entered my mind again and I pushed it quickly aside, not wanting to admit that my world was no longer as black and white as I'd believed.

Regardless of my current actions, I was a police officer and so I couldn't go around associating with criminals. Even sexy ones!

Besides, I was on a mission and didn't need the distraction.

Although, to be honest, I was lucky that Mr Sexy Lips had been there last night. If he hadn't been, I would probably have been caught in the stairwell by the security guard. If he had detained me and called the police, how the hell would I have explained things? I had to be more careful.

That was the second time I put myself in danger yesterday.

My heart pounded and my stomach churned at the thought of how close I'd come to nearly losing everything. It made me wonder if doing all of this on my own was the right thing to do. Perhaps I should look for some help. But who? There was really no one I could trust.

Tears sprung to my eyes as I realised that there was nobody in my life who had my back. Nobody who truly loved me. Nobody who was there when I needed them.

God, what I wouldn't give to have someone to share things with. A man who loved me and who would help me navigate life's traumas. Someone I could love in return.

But there wasn't anyone, and dreaming of such things was stupidity.

What about Mr Sexy Lips? That annoying little voice piped up again.

No, not him. Definitely not!

Shaking my head, I swiped angrily at the tears that were running unbidden down my face.

I would just have to do this on my own and make sure I didn't kill myself or get arrested in the process. Losing my life or my job would not bring my dad's killers to justice. No matter what, that had to be my priority, and I had to ensure I didn't mess things up. It was time to toughen the hell up!

Thinking back over yesterday, I noted my errors. The first

was not allowing myself proper rest, and the second was not controlling my emotions. I was putting my stupidity in nearly running straight into the guard down to my upset over seeing what I believed to be the gun that killed my dad.

However, that was no excuse; I was trained to work better under pressure and in stressful situations. From now on, I needed to stay clear-headed and focused. I had to keep a grip on my emotions, and I had to stop getting distracted, and that included by gorgeous men.

Images of the mystery man and our antics flashed through my mind, making a mockery of my vow to forget about him. I huffed, annoyed with myself. The man was way too distracting.

No matter how I tried, I couldn't focus on anything but the feel of his lips.

They really were sexy lips.

Aargh!

Damn that man. I needed to get out, go for a run, and clear my head.

Grabbing my running clothes and trainers, I pulled them on in annoyance, huffing and mumbling about purging the annoying male from my mind.

It was a chilly morning. The crisp air assaulted my lungs as I ran. However, every breath felt like a cleansing of my mind and body, so I pushed myself hard, concentrating solely on my breathing until all other thoughts disappeared.

———

Eventually, with a clearer mind and feeling more in control of myself, I returned home.

After a long shower, I felt refreshed, more focused, stronger and ready to take on the world. Or at least my colleagues. Alone or not, I could do this!

Opening my phone, I downloaded the photos I took in Mathieson's office onto my computer to look through them. It definitely was some sort of escape cache that confirmed, without a doubt, that the asshole was corrupt.

However, there was nothing there I could use against him or Roy. I had stopped calling him Uncle Roy. He wasn't my uncle, and he no longer deserved the privilege of being an honorary one. The thought of calling him uncle ever again made me want to puke. The fucker!

Thinking about him reminded me it was time to call Aunt Maisie. After a brief chat, she invited me over for dinner later in the evening, just as I had hoped.

Afterwards, I settled at my desk with my notebook and started making notes.

I had four prime suspects regarding the corruption in my department. All of whom were on my shift, and most of whom were long-serving prominent members of the CID Roy, Sergeant John McBride, and two Detective Constables, Steven Ridley, and my partner, Martin Johnson.

It was time to gather my thoughts and get properly organised.

Starting a file on each of the officers, I wrote out everything I knew about them, no matter how insignificant. I spent the rest of the morning thinking about the various incidents I had witnessed at work that were in any way odd, jotting down everything I could remember as I tried to figure out exactly what these officers were involved in.

There was one incident a few months ago involving Sergeant McBride while I had been on secondment. We had been driving around and the Sarge had told me he needed to talk with some of his informants about a case he was working on.

Naturally, I thought nothing of that. Using informants was a big part of a detective's life, and many informants would only speak to a particular officer. So, when I was told to wait inside the car as he went around various pubs and clubs chatting with people, it didn't ring any alarm bells. It was boring but not unusual.

However, as the night wore on, I thought his behaviour seemed a bit off. It had been almost as if he was on edge, and I got the impression the Sarge was nervous about my presence. Especially when he talked with the bouncer at the last club we visited. He kept glancing towards me as he spoke. I pretended I wasn't watching and saw him slip something to the guy, who then gave him something in return.

It had seemed a little shady, but I had scoffed at myself for thinking that and ignored my concerns. I'd simply thought that the Sarge was paying an unofficial informant for the information he was getting instead of going down the normal route.

Usually, criminal informants—also known as Covert Human Intelligence Sources—were properly sanctioned and paid for out of police funds. However, not everyone who gives out information to the police regularly wants to be an official informant. I'd just thought the Sarge was acting a bit off the books, but thoughts of him actually being corrupt hadn't entered my mind.

In hindsight, I now knew it likely was something nefarious after all.

To make matters worse, that was just one of several similar incidents I'd witnessed involving the Sarge and my partner Martin during my secondment.

Shaking my head in disgust with myself, I wondered how the heck I hadn't questioned things sooner.

Shame filled me as I realised just how naïve I'd been. I'd trusted my colleagues and as a result, I'd missed so much.

Well, the blinkers were off. My eyes were well and truly

opened now, and in some ways, I wished I could go back to that time of blissful ignorance, but unfortunately, there was no going back. All I could do now was to bring these officers to justice and redeem myself for my stupidity and blind faith in men that didn't deserve it.

The alarm on my phone went off, telling me it was time to put yet another part of my plan into action.

Grabbing a backpack, I packed my gloves, tools, and some lunch and headed to Martin's house. If he wasn't home, I planned on breaking in and looking around. If he was, I would just observe for a while and see if anything came of that.

———

A short while later, I pulled into Martin's street and parked near enough to his house to watch any comings and goings.

Within minutes, he appeared with a gym bag, jumped into his car, and drove off in the opposite direction.

Yes! I grinned as he passed my hire car, oblivious to my presence. My luck was in.

My foot tapped impatiently, and I fidgeted with the strap of my bag, desperate to get on with my mission, but I forced myself to wait.

Finally, when I was sure he would not return, I left the car and slowly approached his home.

After checking nobody was watching, I slipped around the back.

Having been to his house a few times before, I knew he didn't have an alarm or any dogs. I also knew that the back door was old and had an old mortice lock, and my handy little toolkit held a skeleton key that would open it easily.

After a bit of jiggling, the door opened, and I beamed. Cousin Joe would be so proud!

Unsure of how much time I had, I went straight to Martin's home office. Unfortunately, the time wasted searching through it proved pointless when I found nothing of interest. In fact, it looked like it was rarely used.

Disappointed, I moved on to his bedroom. Inside his wardrobe, he had a small safe. It had a keypad, and I took out a small container of powder used for lifting prints at crime scenes and brushed the contents over the pad.

Fingerprints could be seen on four keys. It only took me a moment to realise that the numbers matched the date he'd been made detective.

Ha, easy!

A rush of excitement filled me as I grinned and keyed the date in, and the door popped open.

Just like at Mathieson's, Martin had another passport with his photo, but a different name and an enormous pile of cash. Wow! It seemed being a corrupt officer was very lucrative. The most interesting thing, however, was a notebook which had been hidden underneath some other paperwork.

Just like before, I snapped a photo of the contents before looking through them.

The notebook held names, dates, times, and amounts. Some small amounts and some much larger amounts. I wasn't sure what it was, but my gut told me it referred to something illegal. Otherwise, why would it be locked in here with everything else?

The notebook was obviously important, and I needed to figure out what all the entries related to, but that would take time. So, against my better judgement, I took it and slipped it into my backpack.

After closing the safe, I wiped the powder from the keypad, then made my way out of the house, ensuring the back door was locked before I left.

Back in the safety of my rental car, which I'd hired for my snooping, I laughed. That was easy! For a police officer, Martin's security was appalling. However, it made it quicker for me to get in and out, so I wasn't complaining.

Before heading home to change for dinner with Aunt Maisie, I drove to the nearest off-licence to grab a bottle of gin and some wine.

I'd always loved Aunt Maisie and got along well with her, even though she was a bit of a lush and loved a good drink. Tonight, I intended to use that to my advantage. The plan was to ply her with drink and, when she was passed out drunk, I'd check the house.

CHAPTER 10
MIKI

After leaving Marko at the hotel to continue collating information on Mathieson, Vlad and I headed off to our meeting with Jim MacArthur.

Since Vlad drove, I sat back and shut my eyes, intending to go over the proposition I was about to discuss with Jim in my head. Instead, the minute I closed my eyes, all I could think about was her; the hot little Scottish lass I was longing to see again.

She'd haunted my dreams all night and as soon as I woke up this morning, I checked in with Marko, desperate for any information he had on her. Thankfully, he'd been hard at it, and now I had not only an address for Little Miss Red, but a name too.

Smiling, I turned her name over in my head; Eilidh Campbell. Very Scottish. I liked it. It fit her well.

While I knew I couldn't get involved in anything long term with the little siren, another brief encounter wouldn't hurt. My cock leapt, making its agreement of that idea known. Eilidh Campbell had information I wanted and when I saw her again, I planned on getting it, but I also planned on taking full advantage of the opportunity and stealing more kisses.

Hell yeah! My libido practically screamed at me as my cock hardened at the thought. I definitely wanted to get another chance to explore Little Miss Red's lips again, along with anywhere else she might let me explore. I had thoroughly enjoyed our brief encounter, and I was sure that the little taste I had of her could be the start of something amazing if we had the chance.

Unfortunately, if anything happened, it could only be a temporary liaison. She was obviously a local while I lived in London. I was a Bratva Pakhan with a lot to deal with and she was, well, I did not know what she was, but unfortunately, it didn't really matter. I had already established that I didn't have time for a relationship, and if I ever found the time, I would have to be careful who I built one with.

Being the head of a Mafia organisation meant that whomever I became involved with would need to be someone I could not only be happy with, but someone I could trust implicitly. My life, my family's life and the rest of the Brotherhood would depend upon it.

It was just such a pity that my Little Miss Red, the only woman ever to have stirred my emotions and set my libido on fire, wasn't someone I could pursue. Disappointment flooded me. That was fucking depressing.

But that didn't mean we couldn't have a brief fling. That thought sent my spirits soaring. My cock jerked in approval, liking the idea as much as me.

"Almost there," Vlad said, breaking into my daydreams.

As we pulled up to the small country pub where our meeting was taking place, I pushed all thought of Little Miss Red and our next encounter aside. I'd let myself think more about the sexy lass later; in the meantime, I had an important meeting with Jim MacArthur to get through, and I needed to concentrate.

A couple of Jim's men greeted us at the entrance to the pub and frisked us.

We might be considered friends, but that didn't mean security would be lax. The MacArthur gang hadn't got as far as they had and been around as long as they had without being both well-organised and careful. That was the main reason we liked working with them, so I could hardly take exception when they continued to display the level of caution I expected from them.

Once the preliminaries were out of the way, we were escorted inside. The pub was empty except for a man behind the bar, Jim MacArthur, and his two sons, who were sitting at a table in the middle of the room, each with a glass of whiskey in front of them.

Vlad and I shook hands with the men before sitting down.

"Bring us another bottle of the good stuff!" Jim shouted to the barman, and he came over with a bottle of Macallan and poured us each a dram. Vlad shook his head.

"Not for me. I'm driving," he said.

"What can I get you?" the barman asked.

"Water's fine," Vlad replied.

When we all had drinks in front of us, Jim lifted his.

"To friends," he said, and clanked his glass with mine as we downed the amber coloured nectar inside.

God, that was good! I wasn't a big whiskey fan, preferring my native vodka, but I did like Macallan with its smooth, sweet taste.

"How are Lisa and the grandkids?" I asked.

Jim's daughter Lisa had just had twin girls, and he was over the moon about it. They were his first grandkids, and he had a tendency to brag about them whenever we talked. So, I knew that chatting about them would relax him and his boys, and make them even more receptive to our negotiations.

"Bloody beautiful! All three are doing well. I'll show you their pictures," Jim said, beaming as he pulled his phone out of his pocket.

"Now you've done it," Jamie, Jim's eldest lad said, smirking.

"Yeah, once you get him started on those babies, you'll never get him to stop," Drew, his youngest, said, groaning.

"They're all we ever hear about these days," Jamie agreed.

"You'd think he had nothing else to talk about," Drew stated, smirking.

"Shut it!" Jim said, elbowing him.

"Ouch! That hurt!" Drew said, grabbing his stomach in mock pain.

"See, now that he has other babies to coo over, he couldn't care less about us!" Jamie said in an exaggerated sorrowful tone, his eyes full of mirth.

"You're thirty! You haven't been a baby in a long time," Jim laughed and shook his head.

Their good-natured ribbing brought a smile to my face. They were a close family, just like mine, and that was one reason I felt an affinity with this gang.

"Besides, if you want me to coo over you, get the hell on with finding a wife and making me some more grand weans, and I will be more than happy to coo over them, and you!" he said to Jamie, giving Vlad and I a wink.

"Nae chance!" Jamie huffed, looking almost horrified at the thought.

Drew sniggered at his brother.

"You, too!" Jim said, sounding more serious this time.

That shut the pair up, and I bit back a laugh.

"Anyway, I was about to show you the grand weans," Jim said, ignoring his boys and opening his phone.

Vlad and I spent the next ten minutes smiling and nodding as he showed us every photograph he had of the 'weans'.

Apparently, they were two of the most beautiful babies there ever was. They just looked like any other babies to me, but I took his word for it.

Despite their words to the contrary, it was easy to see both of his sons were just as enamoured by the newest members of their family, if their own cooing over the twins was anything to go by.

When the photographs finally dried up, our talk turned to business and the reason for the meeting.

"What did you think of the proposals?" I asked as Jim poured us another whiskey.

We'd worked with the MacArthur gang for years and they'd proved trustworthy. In fact, Jim had run the Scottish side of our drugs route since before my folks died, but his involvement stopped just at the border with England, where my guys took over.

I was hoping to persuade him to expand into the English side as far as Manchester, where another of our allies could assume control. Hence the reason for our visit.

I'd already sent my proposals to him overnight to look at, so I didn't need to go over everything today. This was more a time of questioning and deliberation to determine if expansion was possible for him.

Jim nodded slowly and his eyes turned shrew before he answered.

"It seems like a good proposition, but we'd need to discuss the logistics more, and the other players, both in situ and the ones you hope to bring into play," he said, sipping his drink.

Gone was the doting grandad of earlier, and he was all business now.

Negotiations got underway in earnest after that and about an hour later, Jim and his lads excused themselves to go talk in the backroom. It was a big proposition, but one I felt they were ready for, otherwise I wouldn't have offered them the opportunity.

"Do you think they'll accept?" Vlad asked.

"I think they'd be fools not to, given that Jim's sons are both old enough now to take on more responsibility and they already run this side of things. They certainly have enough men to control the route and with their knowledge of everything, it's less of a learning curve for them than it would be for another player," I replied.

"Besides, if we offload the English side of things from Manchester upward to anyone else, they need to work with the new people too, and that is a hit and miss. No, I believe Jim will do his utmost to secure this expansion for himself."

Vlad nodded his agreement and sipped his water. Pouring myself another shot of whiskey, I thought things through once more. My proposal was a good one and Jim would accept it. I was confident about that.

Of course, it wasn't without problems, but the MacArthur gang was already well versed in dealing with those, anyway. Expanding their operation with our help really shouldn't cause them anymore issues.

Bringing drugs into the UK was a dangerous business, so we utilised several methods of transport, changing them regularly to avoid detection. We also had various points of entry, all of which were scattered around the south of England. However, once they entered the UK, they were moved through London, then on to Manchester and distributed to the rest of the UK from there.

My Brotherhood ran all the operations until the Scottish border, where Jim took over, the Welsh border where another gang took control, and Liverpool, where the Irish Mafia then transported them over to Northern Ireland and then into Eire.

That meant I needed to dispose of everything until those points. I hoped that today would see the start of that.

Jim and the lads returned wearing grins.

"We'll see how it goes with the first three shipments and if there are no issues, you've got yourself a deal, Miki, lad," Jim said, shaking my hand.

My stomach churned with excitement, and I grinned widely, relishing the thought that my dreams were finally underway.

To seal the deal and celebrate our closer union, Jim ordered some vodka, and we downed a shot together. Its taste exploded in my mouth, and my mind immediately flashed to the memory of a kiss which had done the same thing.

Suddenly, I had an overwhelming desire to share my news with my Little Miss Red. Dismissing the idea as foolishness, I told myself to get a grip and turned my attention back to the MacArthurs.

With the business out of the way, we discussed Mathieson a bit more.

"He's as corrupt as they come, and bloody smart with it. The polis cannae pin anything on the slimy wee git," Jim told me, his accent becoming thicker the more he drank.

"That's because he's got so many of them in his pocket!" Jamie said.

"Yeah, rumour has it that the DCI himself is one of Mathieson's men," Drew added.

Interesting!

"Who's that?" I asked.

"Detective Chief Constable Roy Allen. If the rumours are true, he's been working with Mathieson and the Thomas gang for years. Since so much of the evidence against them is lost or destroyed. I'd say that was likely true," Drew further clarified.

"He's not averse to planting evidence for Mathieson, either. That's how several of our men are rotting in jail right now," Jamie told me.

We continued to talk about Mathieson and his pet police officer a bit more before it was finally time to leave, and we said our goodbyes.

———

Back at the hotel, I called Ash to check on things in London and quickly updated him on my productive meeting with Jim. Ash had everything under control. Simpson was under twenty-four-hour surveillance, and Marko's guys had hacked his phone and email to ensure he didn't double-cross us and warn Mathieson that we were on to him.

The rest of the afternoon I worked on my laptop answering emails and looking over reports, but I couldn't stop my thoughts from drifting to Little Miss Red and wondering what her reaction would be when I sneaked into her house tonight.

Hopefully, despite the unorthodox entrance I had planned, she'd be amenable to providing me with whatever information she had on the guy.

We'd played back the video from the break in and saw exactly what she'd done. Breaking into Mathieson's safe was impressive. Little Miss Red had skills.

She certainly does! The little voice in my head agreed, making me smirk.

My mind took me back to the encounter we had, and I licked my lips in anticipation of spending more time with the hot little Scottish lass I was longing to taste again.

My daydream was just getting to a good bit when Marko mumbled, "Shit!"

"What is it?" I asked as his curse pulled me from my thoughts.

"Your Little Miss Red is a cop!" he stated, sounding shocked.

"What?" I asked, looking at him sharply. He was kidding, right?

"Yep, a cop, one of Police Scotland's finest," he said, a grin spreading across his face.

Shit! A cop? Surely not?

"You were kissing a cop!" he teased, waggling his eyebrows at me.

"No, I wasn't," I said, glaring at him. Not believing him. He had to be teasing me.

He laughed.

"Oh yes, you were. And loved every second. We heard you, remember?" he teased me again, grinning and making stupid kissing sounds which reminded me of Sonia.

I sighed, trying to stop my lips from twitching at his stupid antics. Sometimes I wondered if I was the only grownup in my family.

"What's going on?" Vlad asked, emerging from his bedroom where he'd gone for a nap.

"That woman Miki was kissing is a cop," Marko said.

"He's kidding," I told Vlad, desperate for it to be true.

"Nope," Marko replied, shaking his head, and his wide grin showed just how much he was enjoying this. Little shit!

"Meet the newly promoted Detective Constable Eilidh Campbell," he said, as he turned his laptop to face us with a flourish.

"Shit!" Vlad said, voicing my thoughts.

Aw hell. It was true. There on the screen was my Little Miss Red, wearing a police uniform!

That sexy little kisser was a cop?

I couldn't believe it.

No other woman made my body react the way she did. I bit back the bitter sting of utter disappointment. Getting involved with a cop was not on my to-do list, not now, not ever. In my line of business, it was a dangerous move. Cops were the enemy. Okay, some, the bent ones, were useful obviously and you might do business with them, but you didn't fuck them.

Any idea I had of fooling around with Little Miss Red while I was here in Glasgow was out of the question now. Damn it.

Fuck my life!

"So, what do you think a detective constable was doing breaking into Aiden Mathieson's office?" Marko asked.

"No idea. I guess that is another question for Little Miss Red to answer when I visit her tonight," I stated in response.

"You're still going?" he asked incredulously.

"Hell yeah," I replied.

"Are you sure that's a good idea?" Vlad questioned me, the look on his face showing he thought I was making a big mistake.

"She still has information which could be of use to us. We don't know why she was there, but her actions were not normal for a detective. So, either she was looking into Mathieson unofficially, or she's a bent cop. Whichever it is, the little siren was there illegally, just like us. It can't hurt to ask what she knows. She doesn't know who I am, and I'll keep my balaclava on to ensure it remains that way," I replied.

"She's police. It's too big a risk," Marko argued.

"What's she going to do, arrest me and risk me telling her secret? No, it won't be an issue. Getting her to share any information might be, however, but it's worth a shot," I told him, making it clear I'd made up my mind.

"If you say so," Marko mumbled unhappily.

Anger filled me, and narrowing my eyes, I shot him one of my death stares. He was becoming as annoying as Ash.

It was rare for me to have to justify myself as Pakhan. My argument was the truth. I wanted to know what she had on Mathieson and if it was of any use to us.

And you need to see her again! A little voice in my head said, but I refused to acknowledge its presence. No good would come of thinking such thoughts. My visit was business. Purely business!

CHAPTER 11
EILIDH
THAT NIGHT – GETTING MORE EVIDENCE

When I arrived at Roy's house, I handed Aunt Maisie the bottle of gin. It was only 8 p.m. but I could smell from her breath that she had already started drinking. There wasn't much left in the wine bottle sitting on the kitchen worktop, it looked like she'd had at least three glasses before I'd arrived.

Good. The sooner she got drunk, the sooner I could have a good look around.

"Thanks, honey," she said, smiling at me when I topped up her glass.

She quickly grabbed it and took several large gulps, and I realised her drinking had got worse lately.

Aunt Maisie was usually a happy drunk, but as I watched her dish out our dinner, I couldn't help noticing that she seemed more subdued than normal. Observing her closely, I wondered if she knew about Roy or suspected his criminal activities. Could that be the cause of her drinking? It was certainly a possibility.

Roy had never been short of money over the years, but Maisie had received a large inheritance from her dad when he passed away. Any large purchases were always explained away as coming from that source. However, what if that was not the case? Then Maisie would surely have at least wondered where Roy got the money. Right?

Was she suspicious? Or totally oblivious? Or worse, was she, in fact, aware and complicit in his actions?

Staring intensely at her, I twisted my lips as I pondered the situation.

She noticed.

"Everything all right?" she asked.

"Yes. I was just wondering how you made your lasagne, and if you'd teach me sometime?" I said quickly to cover my real thoughts.

"Sure, I will, sweetie. Next time you come over, come early, and we'll make it together," she replied, beaming at me.

"Great," I said, avoiding her eyes as a sense of shame washed over me.

Maisie might have her flaws, but she was kind and always happy to help. She'd been good to me and my dad over the years. Despite her heavy drinking, she was a good person. Too good to have been complicit in Roy's actions. She couldn't know.

Another pang of guilt assaulted me, making me feel nauseous as it finally dawned on me that my investigations were going to have a severe impact on Maisie and the rest of her family.

How would she feel when she found out that Roy was corrupt and that he had killed my dad? It could break her. Their sons were successful businessmen now, too. I'd no idea what a scandal involving their dad would do to them.

Damn, Roy! How could he do this to us all? Anger replaced my guilt as I thought of the man we'd all loved and how he'd betrayed us. It was his fault, and he needed to pay for everything he'd done. Bringing Roy to justice was the right thing to do and I would do it, no matter the consequences. I couldn't let any feelings of remorse get in the way.

Pushing aside the lingering guilt, I forced myself to focus on the task at hand. Getting the evidence that I was here for was crucial to my plans and so I refilled Maisie's glass and forced myself to make small talk with her as we ate dinner.

Even when she was under the influence of alcohol, Maisie was a superb cook. Dad and I used to love coming over for dinner when I was growing up. However, on this occasion, every bite of food I took tasted like ash in my mouth. But I shovelled it in, chewed and swallowed regardless as we talked.

When her wine was finished, I plied her with gin and tonic while I pretended to sip my glass of wine. She never noticed that I hugged the same glass throughout the meal, never topping it up.

As we filled the dishwasher, she put on some music, and we laughed and danced. She was back to her usual self again, and it was nice to see, but my heart clenched when I considered the possibility that this might be the last time I spent in her company like this.

When everything was finally revealed and Roy went to prison as I intended he would, things would be different between us. I just hoped that when I turned her life upside down, she could forgive me.

My guilt was back, and as the evening wore on, my nerves felt frayed. Eventually, having finally had enough and barely able to stand, she retired for the night.

"Night, sweetie," she slurred as I helped her remove her shoes and climb into bed.

Maisie assumed I was staying over in the guest room, like I often did when I came to visit. However, I had no intention of sleeping in Roy's house ever again. The mere thought of it made my stomach churn. Nevertheless, I didn't tell her that.

––––––––

A short while later, when Maisie's light snores told me she was fast asleep, I snuck into Roy's office.

After a quick look through his desk, where I found nothing, I moved to his safe. I knew he had one as I'd seen it before, and thanks to Joe, I knew exactly what I needed to break into it. Opening my backpack, I took out the little electronic device and got to work. It unlocked with a click, and I grinned.

Who knew illegal stuff could be so much fun? *Well, I guess the criminals did!* I chuckled at my thoughts, then quickly sobered up when I saw what was inside. *Not a game, Eilidh!* I reminded myself sternly.

The safe wasn't any larger than the one Mathieson had in his office, but I couldn't believe how full it was. It was literally crammed with big brown envelopes, a notebook, a smaller lock box, and a small black holdall full of cash. Shit!

As usual, I took some photos on my phone and then started removing the items. This was going to take a while. Thank God that Maisie was asleep, and Roy was out of town.

Each envelope had a name on the front. Inside were details of the person named and a lot of photographs, showing the person in compromising situations. It seemed like Roy was using the contents of the envelopes to blackmail these people. I went through all the names, which I noted were in alphabetical order. Geez, he was an organised blackmailer.

There were several names I recognised, including two judges, some lawyers, a few businessmen and a reporter. There were also files on the other three officers from my shift. Why would he be blackmailing them? Or maybe he wasn't. Yet.

Maybe some of them were being kept just in case he needed to use them in the future? It was hard to say.

Shaking my head in disgust, I wondered just how long Roy had been collecting all of this stuff. His entire career, by the look of things. He was due to retire soon. I guessed this was his nest egg.

My stomach churned and my dinner threatened to make a comeback as I took in the evidence of his corruption. I'd convinced myself that Roy was simply a bent cop being paid to do someone else's dirty work. A small fish in a big pond.

However, as I looked at the contents of his safe, I knew without a doubt that I'd been wrong. Roy was no small fish; he was a shark!

There was no way I was going to have time to take photos of everything. So, I decided to just snap photos of the envelopes and some of their contents inside and leave the rest. That would surely be enough.

When the safe was empty, I settled on the floor beside my haul and hesitated, staring at the envelopes.

Did I really want to see all the shit these people got up to? Did I really want to learn their secrets? Because once I knew them, it wasn't like I could forget them.

Fortifying my resolve, I opened the first envelope.

There was no choice. No matter what dirty little secrets were revealed, I had to know. This was evidence, and I was a detective.

All of this would be found during the official investigation at some point, anyway. As soon as I could find someone to trust enough with this information. After that, the secrets would be out in the open and it would be up to the police officers involved to deal with them.

Almost an hour later, I cracked my neck to release the tension and rubbed at the bridge of my nose. A headache was coming on. I needed to finish up soon and get out of here. There was just one more envelope, Aiden Mathieson's, which I'd saved for last.

Opening it up, I poured everything out onto the floor. The first photograph that fell out showed Aiden Mathieson kissing my dad's murderer.

I froze and stared at it.

Timmy Neilson was obviously not just a hired killer, as I had first assumed. He was Mathieson's lover!

Revulsion coursed through my veins as I went through the rest of the photos, which showed the pair snorting coke, drinking, and having sex together or indulging in orgies. They were all pretty graphic, but that wasn't the issue for me. What sickened me was that these were the men responsible for my dad's murder. I hated they were out partying and having fun after what they had done. It wasn't right.

Bile rose in my throat, and I gulped it back, grimacing, as I looked at the last couple of pictures. Dear god. Mathieson had killed his lover. Why?

And how did Roy get these photographs?

I shook my head. It didn't matter. Roy was hiding evidence linked to an ongoing murder enquiry. Mathieson was walking around a free man because of him. Roy really was a bastard.

After stuffing the photographs back into the envelope, I returned it to the safe, just as I'd done with all the others when I'd finished with them.

Stretching my body was a relief. Between the sitting and the tension in my bones, I was bloody stiff. I was nearly finished, though. Only the lockbox needed to be checked.

Inside, just like with Mathieson and Martin, there were several passports with false names. I noted there was none for Aunt Maisie, but there was one for a woman I hadn't seen before. A young woman about my age who looked a hell of a lot like me, in fact. Chills went down my spine as I stared at her image.

Poor Aunt Maisie, it looked like the bastard was cheating on her. The similarity to me, though, was uncanny and made me uneasy. Why did she look so like me?

It didn't matter, I'd had enough. It was time to go.

Pleased with my findings, I closed the box, put it back in the safe and then checked the picture I'd taken at the beginning to ensure everything was back in its proper order. With how organised it had been, it was likely Roy would notice if the slightest thing was out of place.

Satisfied that everything looked as it should, I closed it up and headed for the door.

Peeking into Aunt Maisie's room again, I checked she was still sleeping peacefully and left a note to say I'd got up early as I had to meet a friend. That way, she wouldn't be concerned when I wasn't there in the morning. Setting it on the table next to her bed, I slipped silently out of the house.

It was the early hours of the morning and tiredness seeped into my bones as I climbed into my car. The tension of the evening and the revelations uncovered in those envelopes had me exhausted.

As I pulled out of Roy's street, the hairs on the back of my neck stood up and goosebumps broke out on my skin. It felt like I was being watched. Checking my rear-view mirror, I sighed in relief. I was just being stupid. The roads were empty. It was just my imagination working overtime. There was nobody there.

Dismissing my concerns as paranoia, I turned my attention to who the heck I could trust with all the information I had gathered.

Roy's boss, Detective Chief Superintendent Mathews, came to mind. He was the overall boss of the department, but I didn't know how high the corruption went. Surely not that high?

But what if I was wrong?

It might be better going to COPFS instead. COPFS, formally known as the Crown Office and Procurator Fiscal Service, was the body that investigated allegations of corruption in Police Scotland. They'd be the best people to take my evidence to. However, after seeing so many files on people from that department, I'd need to ensure it didn't go to one of them.

First thing in the morning, I'd start looking into the members of that department for someone that could be trusted.

With that decision made, I pulled into my driveway and parked.

As I climbed out, the overwhelming sensation of being watched returned. My skin prickled, and I shivered.

Spinning around, I froze and held my breath as I scanned the street, looking for the source of my unease.

Nothing moved. Utter silence filled the air, but I remained stock still, waiting just in case. Seconds stretched out and when there was still no sound or movement, I let out a slow breath and shook my head. I was definitely becoming paranoid.

This investigation was taking its toll on me. The quicker I found someone to get my evidence to, the better. It was time to get some sleep. I obviously needed it. My nerves were frayed.

CHAPTER 12
MIKI

THAT SAME NIGHT – EXCHANGING MORE THAN INFO

It was getting late when I finally approached Little Miss Red's house, doing my best to ignore the way my heartbeat increased and my stomach churned with excitement the closer I got to her home. It was simply the thought of discovering what she knew, I told myself, and nothing at all to do with seeing the sexy little siren again. Nope, nothing at all!

There were no lights on, and her car wasn't in the driveway, so I figured she was out. I'd no idea where she might be at this time, but it didn't matter. I planned on waiting for her, anyway.

Breaking into her home was easy with the help of Marko's hacking skills. Her alarm was disabled in no time and taking a leaf from her book, Marko had provided me with a skeleton key to her door, which worked perfectly.

Since she wasn't home, I took the opportunity to look around. There were some photographs of Eilidh with an older man, who, from the family resemblance, I presumed was her dad. There was an old one of him in a police uniform.

That fit with what Marko had found out about her. He'd said her dad had been a police officer but was killed on duty and the person responsible hadn't been found.

Careful not to disturb anything, I planted a bug in her home phone and cameras around the house. Once I had them in place, I settled down in the leather armchair in her living room, and checked the feed to make sure I'd set them up correctly, as I waited.

The minutes stretched on as I sat there in the dark with only the ticking of the clock on the wall breaking the silence. With nothing else to occupy me, my mind bombarded me with thoughts of her and no matter how I tried, I couldn't shut them down. Every second of our encounter replayed in my mind, and with each memory, my cock grew harder.

Fuck, I wanted that woman!

Groaning, I tried to shut down my thoughts; nothing could happen between us, I reminded myself, just as the front door opened and in walked the source of my fantasies.

Excitement filled me. My woman was home.

Damn it! She's not mine! I scolded myself.

Eilidh wasn't my anything. She couldn't be. I tried to convince myself of that, but it was no good. It didn't seem to matter that she was supposed to be my enemy; the woman had got under my skin and there was no denying it.

My eyes feasted on the sight of her, taking her in fully for the first time as she turned on the hall light and removed her jacket.

She was wearing a silky-looking t-shirt which matched her amber eyes, a sexy short brown mini skirt which revealed smooth bare thighs and brown knee-high boots. The effect had me almost salivating.

She was even more beautiful than I'd realised and that mass of long red hair which was no longer hidden away was magnificent. Truly magnificent, and I ached to run my fingers through it.

She didn't see me sitting in the dark and as she turned to head upstairs; I called out.

"Evening, Little Miss Red."

She gasped, twisting to look in my direction, squinting into the darkness.

As I stood and moved towards the light, her eyes widened. It was obvious she recognised my outfit from the evening before because, thankfully; she didn't scream or run. But I could tell she was thinking about it, as her eyes flicked to the front door and back again.

"Don't be afraid, sweetheart," I told her.

"I just came to talk."

"What the fuck? How did you get in here? And how did you find me?" she asked in a rush of questions.

I chuckled.

"No plans on fucking you tonight. Through the front door, and I have my ways," I answered as I walked towards her.

"Don't come any closer," she said, backing up a step.

Doing as she asked, I stopped a few feet away from her, far enough for her to feel safe but close enough to catch her if she ran.

"Who are you?" she asked, a small hitch in her voice betraying her nerves.

"A friend," I replied in a steady voice, careful not to make any sudden moves.

"Why are you here? What do you want?" she asked, looking worried.

She was skittish. It was understandable. I'd broken into her home, and I was wearing a balaclava and gloves. Of course, she would be scared.

"I'm just here to talk," I told her again, though by her frown and the way she chewed on her bottom lip, I didn't think she believed me.

The moment she decided to run, I saw it on her face. My predator instinct kicked in and I was on her before she could get far.

In a move that was fast becoming a habit, I grabbed her, swung her around, and pressed her against the wall. My heart pounded with exhilaration and my dick hardened at her closeness. I hadn't felt this excited in years. It was thrilling!

Before I could think better of it, I lifted her up, forcing her to wrap her legs around me.

"Hi, beautiful," I said, smiling as I looked into her gorgeous amber eyes.

"Put me down!" she cried, wiggling around, pushing uselessly at my chest. Her weak attempts at breaking out of my arms only added to my excitement.

My cock thickened between us, making her breath hitch. It wasn't like she could miss it with our bodies pressed so closely together.

"Relax, sweetheart, you're safe," I said, leaning down to nuzzle her ear.

"You shouldn't be here," she said, her voice a mix of annoyance and breathy desire.

"Probably not, but here I am. My intention was to simply talk. However, you have a way of distracting me with thoughts of more pleasurable pursuits," I murmured, nipping at her earlobe.

"It's not my fault. You're the one who keeps pressing your big body against mine," she chuckled.

Grinning, I looked at her. So much for this visit being purely business. What a lie that had been!

"You're the one with the hot little body, gorgeous eyes, flaming hair, and lips that I've imagined wrapped around my cock since the last time we kissed. So, I'd definitely say it was your fault," I smirked, watching her eyes widen and her cheeks pinken with every word.

"You're blaming me for your X-rated fantasies?" she laughed incredulously.

"Hell yeah!" I laughed back, enjoying the unexpected flirtation.

"You've been thinking about our kisses too, haven't you?" I asked, trying not to sound desperate to hear her confirm I wasn't the only one who couldn't get those kisses out of my head.

"Maybe," she murmured, clearing her throat and avoiding my eyes.

"Liar." I smirked.

"Fine. Yes," she said, tilting her chin in defiance.

Yes! I felt like I'd won a gold medal with just that one little admission.

"I haven't been able to get you out of my head," I said, my voice low and filled with lust as I looked deeply into her eyes.

God, I could get lost in them. When I looked at her like this, the entire world faded away until she was all I could see. I liked that.

Her breath hitched, and she licked her lips, drawing my attention to her mouth, the wetness beckoning me to taste her again.

Don't do it! The annoying voice in my head said. But I ignored it.

There was a sense of inevitability as I leaned down and captured her lips. She returned my kiss with as much passion as she had last time, pressing closer to me and rubbing her core against my hard on.

Adrenaline flowed through my body, and it felt as if every nerve ending had woken up. It was as if I'd been asleep before her and now I was alive, born from her kiss.

"You taste as good as I remembered," I murmured, brushing my lips against her cheek before I returned to devour her lips again.

My cock jerked, and I really wanted to continue what we were doing, but I knew I couldn't. No matter how wonderful she tasted or how great she made me feel, or how well she responded to me, I needed to stop. I'd already taken things too far. They couldn't go any further. She was a police officer. An enemy to the Bratva and I needed to remember that.

Sighing, I reluctantly set her back on her feet, but held her close and kissed the top of her head. Not quite willing to let her go just yet.

"We need to talk," I mumbled into her hair.

She stiffened.

"Eh, not sure that we do," she stated.

"Yes, Eilidh, we do," I said firmly.

"You've been looking into Aiden Mathieson, and I want to know why and what you have found out."

"Uh uh," she said, shaking her head.

"I don't even know who you are or what you look like, and I won't be telling you anything unless you plan on divulging why *you* are digging into Mathieson. If you want information from me, you'll need to trade me for it," she stated, lifting her chin and glaring at me in defiance.

My Little Miss Red was fiery, just like her hair. Her defiance was as much of a turn on as her responsiveness and I didn't know whether I should kiss her or spank her.

However, I'd expected she'd want something in return, and I was prepared to give her some information.

"Okay."

"You will?" she asked. She obviously hadn't expected me to agree.

I nodded, then unable to help myself, I picked her up again and strode into the living room.

Turning on the small lamp beside the sofa, I sat down with her on my lap.

Of course, Eilidh didn't need to sit on my lap to discuss our information, but I wanted her there and so I indulged myself. Soon our time together would be over, and we'd never see one another again, but for now I wanted her close.

"Let me go!" she said, squirming to get off.

"Not going to happen." I shook my head, wondering what the hell I was thinking, keeping her there as she wiggled her sexy little bum on my crotch.

My cock was as hard as a rock, throbbing angrily with need and all her wriggling was only adding to the torture. Yet, I loved every second. So, she was staying right where she was. Who knew I was a masochist?

"Sit still, and we will talk about Mathieson, or keep squirming and I will take it as an invitation to take our kiss further and ravish you," I told her.

She froze, and I suddenly realised what the heck I'd just said. Damn it! This needed to stop.

She's the enemy! I reminded myself.

It didn't matter. Neither my cock nor my heart were convinced.

"You are bloody annoying," she said, huffing out a breath in frustration, but she settled against my chest and my heart clenched at how good it felt to have her in my arms. I closed my eyes for a brief second to savour the forbidden sensation.

My body was hyper aware of hers. Every rise and fall of her chest, every beat of her heart, the warmth of her bottom against my groin, her smell, the tickle of her hair against my chin, all of it felt like heaven. God, how I wished we could have more than just these few moments.

"Okay, talk," she said, her voice pulling me from my thoughts.

She was right. It was time to get back to the reason I was here.

Sitting up a little straighter, she looked at me. I was about to speak, but she licked her lips, distracting me. I stared, mesmerised and unable to form a coherent sentence. Hell, I wanted those lips on me again, everywhere, on my mouth, on my body, wrapped around my cock.

My mind assaulted me with images of her on her knees sucking me off. I groaned at the thought, my cock jerking at the image and leaking a little pre cum. Oh hell!

"Well?" she demanded, and I blinked suddenly back in the room again.

Geez, I had to get a grip on my unruly thoughts. It dawned on me that perhaps I should let her move off my lap after all, but I dismissed the thought as soon as I had it. No, it might be torture having her sit on me, but it was the most exquisite torture I'd ever endured, and I was quickly becoming addicted to it. So, I kept her there.

However, I needed to conduct an exchange of information and so I had to stop being distracted. Taking a deep breath, I focused on what I had to say.

"I am a businessman. Aiden Mathieson has been behind several attacks on my businesses and my family, but I don't know why. I was at his office the other night to find out."

I had told her the truth, but kept things as vague as possible.

"And did you?" she asked.

"Not yet. That's why I'm here. To learn what you know," I replied.

"What sort of attacks?"

"Ones that cost my family and that of a close friends family dearly," I told her.

She looked at me and pursed her lips, well aware that I was holding back and not willing to divulge any more.

It wasn't possible. Not when she was a police officer. Revealing too much could be the biggest mistake of my life. She might be a sexy little thing, but that didn't mean I could trust her. In fact, it probably meant I should definitely not. If I wasn't careful, I'd lose myself in her and end up disclosing information that could get me jailed, or worse, dead.

Changing tactics, she asked, "What's your name?"

"You can call me Miki," I said.

Divulging the nickname I went by wasn't an issue. Lots of people were called Miki. She didn't know my full name and hadn't seen my face, so it was doubtful she would find out who I was. Or at least that's what I told myself, but deep down, I knew that I simply wanted to hear her say my name. Just once.

"Well, it's nice to meet you, Miki," she said with a smirk.

"It's nice to meet you, Eilidh," I replied, and I swear my heart leapt in my chest at the sound of my name from her lips.

God, I had it bad. This was so not good. I needed to move things on and leave before I did something stupid.

"Now you," I stated with a nod of encouragement.

Eilidh stared at me, her eyes narrowing as she looked deep into mine. I could see her police brain working. She was sizing me up. Little Miss Red knew I was dangerous and likely a criminal, despite my businessman façade. After all, what sort of businessman breaks into office buildings? *Shady ones*: I had no doubt she was thinking.

However, she had done the same. Why? There was a story behind that, and I wanted to know what it was. I wanted to know everything about her.

My body leaned towards hers of its own accord as I silently watched her debate what information she would divulge and what she would hold back. I understood. After all, I had done exactly the same.

Her frown was the cutest thing, and her pursed lips called to me to kiss them.

God, she was distracting. I gave myself a mental shake.

Get your head in the game, man! I chided myself.

"Talk," I said, then pressed my lips firmly together, so they didn't pucker up and plant themselves on hers again as they really wanted to do.

"My father was a police officer, and he was killed on duty almost three years ago. I think Aiden Mathieson had him killed," she stated.

Well, shit! I hadn't expected that. I'd already learned about her dad's murder and that nobody had been arrested for it. However, I hadn't connected it with her being at Mathieson's office.

"Why do you think that?"

Eilidh bit her bottom lip and squirmed in my lap again, obviously unsure if she should tell me.

As she unconsciously squirmed, her bottom rubbed across my hard as fuck cock. She needed to stop doing that; it was becoming too difficult to ignore. If she continued, I was going to end up throwing caution to the wind and take her right here on the sofa. My control was about done.

"I saw some photographs of a man I believe killed my dad. I think he was in some kind of sexual relationship with Mathieson, and I think Mathieson paid him to kill my dad," she said finally.

"Who is he?"

"Was," she said, "His name was Timmy Neilson, but he is dead. He was found drowned in his bath. I think Mathieson did it. I was in his office looking for evidence, but there was nothing there to link him to either murder," she stated matter-of-factly.

"What else can you tell me about him? What did you find in the safe?" I asked.

"Nothing. I can't tell you anything more," she said, sounding annoyed.

Then she pushed up and off my lap, stepping out of my reach.

"Time for you to go!" she said.

I didn't move, shocked by the sudden change in her demeanour. One minute she was talking and the next she'd clammed up. I didn't like it. Little Miss Red knew far more than she was telling me, and I wanted to know exactly what it was.

"Why don't we work together?" I said before I could think better of it.

"Sorry, not happening!" she said, heading to the door.

"Why not?" I asked her. Not because I didn't understand her reasons. They were likely similar to my own. But because no matter how much I knew she was right and I should leave, I couldn't bring myself to let this be the end of us.

"Well, the first reason is obvious. I'm a police officer and you are likely a criminal and anyway, you don't have any information for me and I'm certainly not providing you with information which is needed for a police investigation. So, we are done here. Goodbye, Miki," she said, unlocking the door.

"But you weren't there officially, were you, Eilidh?" I asked.

"Breaking into offices is illegal and certainly not part of any official operation," I said, crowding her.

The look of fear that flickered over her face made me take a step back. I raised my hands in supplication.

"You're safe with me, Eilidh. You've nothing to worry about," I reassured her.

She shook her head.

"You need to leave," she said, opening the door.

No! my mind screamed.

My body refused to move.

Eilidh was right. I really should leave. She had decided not to divulge anything else, and she was correct; I didn't actually have anything useful to trade her with. Yet despite everything, I simply didn't want to.

"I could help you," I said, not really sure why or what I meant by that except that I really didn't want this to be the end of things between us. Not yet.

"I don't need any help," she said, indicating to the door with a sweeping gesture.

Yeah, I got the message.

Feeling defeated, I sighed heavily, forcing myself to move. As I stepped forward to go past her, and our bodies brushed together. Her breath hitched. Mine did too, and we stared at each other. Suddenly, there was no way I could leave. The connection between us was too strong, as if an invisible force tied us together and wouldn't let us part.

"All right, if that is the end of our business, let's get personal."

Without thinking, I pulled her into my arms, grabbed her head, and kissed her like my life depended on it. She gasped in surprise, and I took advantage, thrusting my tongue inside her mouth.

Little Miss Red froze, and my heart stuttered, sure she was going to resist, and I'd have to leave after all. However, a second later, she was moaning into my mouth and kissing me back with the same amount of passion.

Fuck!

What the hell are you doing? This is so not a good idea! My rational side shouted at me, but I ignored the party pooper, lifted Eilidh up and quickly carried her upstairs.

When I reached the top, I kicked open a door, happy to see it was a bedroom. Walking to the bed, our tongues still entangled, I lowered her onto it without breaking the kiss.

My trainers were toed off and my hand was up her skirt in seconds. She was wet; I smiled in satisfaction. My fingers stroked lightly over the fabric that was in the way of my prize, and her hips bucked.

My cock throbbed, straining against my pants. Eilidh was so fucking responsive.

Straddling her hips, I moved my hand up to her top and pulled it up over her head and then quickly removed her bra, letting her breasts fall free.

God, they were beautiful. I loved them.

Eilidh's nipples hardened under my gaze, and I took one into my mouth and sucked before moving on to the other. She moaned and squirmed beneath me as I took my time, lavishing attention on each of her luscious tits.

Mewling sounds of pleasure escaped her, and she reached between her legs and rubbed her wet pussy, but I grabbed her hand and pushed it away.

"Uh, uh, that's my job, baby," I murmured against her ear as I shifted position.

Shoving my hand into her knickers, she shivered as I lightly stroked the hair over her mound before I pushed a finger into her slit. It slid in with ease and I added another, thrusting deep. Her breaths came in quick succession, her chest rising and falling rapidly as her desire grew.

The slickness of her channel made thrusting my fingers in and out easy. Pressing my thumb against her clit, I circled it with every inward movement, changing the pressure with each inward and outward stroke.

Eilidh squirmed against my hand, and I groaned. My cock badly wanted to replace my fingers, but it was too soon. It throbbed angrily, not liking that, but it would need to wait. There was no way I was going to let this finish too soon. I was going to savour every second and enjoy her with every part of my body. My cock would just have to deal with that and wait its turn.

I continued to play with her pussy while I nibbled and sucked on her nipples. She hummed in pleasure and the sound was almost my undoing. My cock leaked pre cum inside my trousers. It badly wanted to explode.

Not yet! I willed the bastard to behave, refusing to be rushed.

It was time to truly savour the delicacy before me, but I had to continue to maintain my anonymity, and I knew just how to ensure that.

The headboard was one of those metal ones with an intricate design which was just perfect for what I had in mind.

My Little Miss Red was about to fulfil one of my favourite fantasies I'd had about her since we'd met. She moaned in protest as I moved my hand away from her pussy, but I captured her lips again and gave her boobs a squeeze to appease her.

Pulling her hands over her head while still kissing her, I held them together with one hand and quickly undid my belt with the other. Her eyes were heavy with lust, and she didn't seem to notice as I wrapped my belt around her wrists, then looped it around one of the metal pieces and fastened it.

When I pulled away, my breath caught as I took in the beautiful sight she made. Eilidh was the sexiest woman I had ever seen. My eyes scanned her body, devouring every inch of her as I licked my lips and imagined everything I was going to do to her.

She blinked, suddenly realising she was lying there topless

and tied to the bed with me looming over her, fully dressed. Her eyes became panicked, and she struggled against the belt.

"What the fuck are you doing?" she cried.

"Relax, baby; you're safe. I won't hurt you, but I am going to fuck you," I said, while removing my clothes.

She relaxed and smirked as her eyes watched my unwitting strip tease.

"I thought you weren't planning to?" she said, smiling coyly.

"Plans change. I'm going to make you come so hard you see stars," I told her, standing there wearing only my balaclava.

She surprised me again by chuckling and said, "I hope that isn't just an idle boast."

"No, baby, that is a promise," I vowed, crawling over her again.

"You aren't even going to let me see your face?" she asked with another chuckle.

"Not this time," I said, grinning.

Shit, I made that sound like there would be another time, and there couldn't be. Damn it!

Well, at least I could enjoy this time, I consoled myself as I kissed my way down her body, removing the rest of her clothes as I went, until she was left in only her knee-high boots.

God, I was so looking forward to having them wrapped around me when I thrust into her.

My cock jerked painfully again, making its annoyance at having to wait known. *Patience! You'll get your time soon! But first, I need to make Little Miss Red come.*

Delving between her thighs, I lifted her legs over my shoulders and licked at her wet pussy. Little Miss Red was soaked, and I loved it. She tasted great, and I lapped her up as she moaned and pushed herself upwards, trying to get closer.

Her need spurred me on, and I licked and sucked her as she panted and moaned beneath me.

My excitement increased with hers until I felt lightheaded with desire.

As I continued to lick her clit, I thrust a finger into her tight core. She bucked her hips, and I added another finger, then another, making her cry out in pleasure as she bucked harder.

All my focus was on the woman that had me burning with desire for her. As I licked and sucked on her most intimate parts, I looked up into her eyes. The heavy-lidded look of lust she gave me filled me with longing. I wanted to see that look on her face always.

There was no time to process that thought as she came with a cry and all thought flew from my mind. All I could do was watch in awe as she thrashed mindlessly beneath me, her tight sheath rippling around my fingers.

Determined to milk every drop of her orgasm, I kept thrusting until finally her cries died down. But she wasn't done.

"More, I need more. I want you inside me," she panted, wriggling against me.

I was surprised she wasn't exhausted by how hard she had just come. It flattered my ego that she was so desperate for my cock.

"Greedy girl," I smirked, feeling like a fucking sex god.

"Please, Miki, I need you inside me," she begged.

My heart clenched. I loved hearing her say my name while she begged me to fuck her.

"Whatever you need, sweetheart," I said as I positioned my cock at her entrance and wondered how the hell I was going to find the strength to walk away from her.

CHAPTER 13
EILIDH

STILL THE SAME NIGHT – FINDING MR
SEXY LIPS

What the hell was this guy doing to me? I'd just had the best orgasm of my life and yet I wanted more. No, not wanted. I bloody needed it, as if my life depended on it.

"Please, Miki, I need you inside me," I begged.

"Whatever you need, sweetheart," he smirked at me.

Gulping, I licked my lips as he positioned his cock at my entrance. My pussy still tingled with the remnants of my orgasm, but it wasn't enough. He needed to be inside me.

I wrapped my legs around him, crossing my feet to hold him close, as he rammed into me with one swift thrust. A grunt tore from my throat at the intrusion, which stretched me to the point of pain.

"God, you're tight, baby. Did I hurt you?" he asked through clenched teeth, his muscles straining with effort as he held himself poised over me, his eyes searching my face.

My heart felt ready to burst with love at the sight of him holding himself back in case he'd hurt me.

Wait, what? Love?! What the hell was I thinking?

This was sex, one-off, mind-blowing sex and nothing more!

Miki kissed my forehead, pulling me out of my worrisome thoughts.

"You okay?" he asked again, his eyes full of concern.

"Yes, I'm fine. You're just big, that's all. You're stretching me, but it's good. Keep going, Miki, please," I replied, leaning up and kissing him.

Wanting to encourage him, I tightened my legs more and lifted my hips.

Miki thrust again, grunting loudly as he buried himself deeper this time. The sensation of fullness was exquisite and made me moan and whimper as he continued to move in and out, over and over, twisting his hips slightly whenever he was buried up to the hilt, hitting me in just the right spot.

I badly wanted to kiss him. Leaning towards him, he took the hint and brushed his lips against mine. The minute he had, it was as if he could no longer hold back. He pushed me back against the bed and proceeded to ravish me as he'd threatened to do earlier. There was no other word for it. He pounded into me like a wild thing and kissed me as if he had been lost in the desert for days and my mouth was the only source of moisture to keep him from dying.

Our chests rubbed together as he pounded into me. The friction sending electric jolts from my hardened nipples straight to my pussy.

"I'm going to come!" I screamed out as I felt myself balancing on the precipice, ready to fall into what I knew would be the best orgasm of my life. Even better than the one I'd just had.

Oh, my goodness, the guy was a sex god. He had to be. No real man could feel this good. Or certainly no man I'd ever met before had ever made me feel like this. Not that I'd had sex with that many, but I'd had a few relationships and compared to those guys, Miki was definitely in a class of his own.

My hips rose to meet his thrusts, matching his rhythm as we created our own minor symphony of pleasurable sounds.

Miki's groans and pants and my cries and whimpers were music to my ears. He was the conductor of my desire, and he certainly knew how to play the best tunes.

My body shook as another orgasm burst from me, pulling his own with it.

"Fuck!" he grunted as he ground his hips one last time, his hot cum shooting inside me.

He held still, his face buried in my neck as the last drops of his seed filled me.

After a few minutes, he gently pulled out and moved to lie beside me, cuddling close to my body. We lay there panting hard in the aftermath of our incredible orgasms.

"Wow!" he said with a chuckle as our breathing finally returned to normal.

"That was amazing," I agreed.

"Shit! We didn't use a condom!" I cried when I felt his sticky cum dripping down my thigh.

He shot to his elbows and looked at me as if the reality of the situation had just dawned on him, too.

"I'm clean," he told me in a rush.

"Me too, and I'm on the pill, so we should be fine," I confirmed and breathed a sigh of relief; thank fuck. What the hell had I been thinking?

Mr Sexy Lips nodded, but for a second I thought I caught a brief flash of disappointment in his eyes. Nah, don't be dumb, I told myself as I dismissed the idea as nonsense.

"Want to untie me now?" I wriggled, pulling at my hands.

"But I like you all tied up and at my mercy," he teased, running his hands down my body.

The look in his eyes told me he was up for round two and while I would love to indulge in another tussle with him, it was dangerous. The man was getting under my skin, and I had enough problems to deal with, without adding man trouble to the mix. I was reluctant to end this, but we had to, before things went too far.

If they hadn't already!

"Uh, huh! Untie me!" I said, my lips twitching in amusement.

Miki did what I asked. Then I watched him as he turned to pick up his trousers and I got a glimpse of his muscular back and tight ass.

God, he was so sexy! It was like a reverse strip tease. I'd thoroughly enjoyed watching him remove his closed earlier, but I was having just as much fun as I watched him put them back on. More so even because now he was taking his time, and I could get to really look at his hot body.

My Mr Sexy Lips was tall, broad shouldered and muscular. Big everywhere, in fact, and yes, that included down there. Wow, no wonder I was stretched so full!

He must work out a lot to keep that physique, I thought as I admired him from head to toe. Oh my, he really was a feast for the eyes. I wasn't sure if I was reading too much into his actions, but he seemed as reluctant to end things as I felt.

Sadness filled me as I resigned myself to the fact that our time together was over.

Why did he have to be a criminal? Why couldn't he be someone I could be with?

Does he really have to go? Maybe we could fit in another round, or two, after all? Let's pull him back to bed, the naughty little voice in my head said.

Hell, I wanted to do just that. My palms itched to grab him to me, but I restrained myself, turned away from his gorgeousness and forced my hands to put on my hello kitty pyjamas instead. They weren't sexy, but at least they were cute, and I would not go searching around my drawers for something more flattering when he was about to leave.

My heart sunk as we finally faced each other again, fully clothed. This was it, the end of whatever was going on between us. Sorrow threatened to overwhelm me at the thought of never seeing him again. Geez, I had it bad. I really didn't want him to leave, which was utterly crazy.

When Miki first appeared in my house, I hadn't wanted him in my space, but it wasn't because I thought he would hurt me. Not knowing him, I should have been more concerned about that, yet I hadn't really felt danger from him. Oh, he was dangerous, that I knew without a doubt, but I hadn't believed he was a danger to me. However, the real reason I hadn't wanted him in my home was because I was insanely attracted to him, and that was not good.

There was more to this man than he let on and I had to admit I was intrigued by him, but with everything else going on in my life, I didn't want to know more. It wouldn't do me any good to get any more involved with him anyway because we were worlds apart and there was no changing that.

Police officers and criminals didn't mix. Well, not unless the police officer was corrupt and while I might break the law to bring killers to justice, I wasn't now and never would be a corrupt police officer.

Despite saying he was a businessman; I knew Miki had to be some sort of criminal. I believed what he told me about Mathieson and his reason for breaking into the office was true; it was all the parts he missed out that put my police senses on full alert.

A normal businessman would go to the police with their problems or, at the very least, hire a private investigator, but he wouldn't be running around illegally breaking into offices by himself. And he definitely wouldn't be so adept at doing it.

My Mr Sexy Lips was not the innocent businessman he pretended to be. Just exactly what he was involved in, however, I didn't know. And that was the reason we couldn't work together even though I could use the help.

We stared at each other for what seemed like ages, neither of us saying anything and neither making a move. Tension crackled between us. It seemed we were both reluctant to end this. Shit, this was hard.

Eventually, he broke the silence.

"Cute," he said as he scanned me up and down.

Laughing to lighten the mood further, I gave him a quick twirl.

A slow, sexy smile spread over his face, and he chuckled as I finished the twirl with a flourish.

Fuck, I could lose myself in that smile and those gorgeous grey eyes. Damn, I really had it bad. This was why I hadn't wanted him in my house.

I'd fallen hard in lust before, but after a quick fuck, it would normally be over with. These things always fizzled out fast. What we just did should have been enough to get him out of my system. That was the only reason I allowed it to happen. We'd wanted each other, and we'd scratched an itch, but that really should have been the end.

So, why wasn't it?

Because this is way more than lust!

Shit, I knew I should have made him leave.

Too late now! That bloody little voice said, sounding way too gleeful.

That's when I realised it wasn't over. It didn't matter that we shouldn't see one another again; it was inevitable. This was not the last time we would get down and dirty.

However, I needed to be cautious; I didn't know whom I was dealing with, and I may be enamoured by him, but I couldn't afford to let that influence me. The man was hiding something, and until I knew what it was, he couldn't be fully trusted.

So, I needed to learn who he was, after all.

As Miki sauntered towards me, I made a show of fishing around inside my bag before pulling out a lip balm and applying it.

"What do you plan on doing about Mathieson now, Eilidh?" he asked me.

"Get the evidence I need and bring him to justice!" I stated as I walked purposefully towards him, rubbing my lips together, successfully getting his attention where I wanted it.

"Well, be careful," he said, his eyes riveted to my mouth.

When I reached him, he took me in his arms and kissed me briefly on the lips. Before he could let go, I grabbed him around the waist and gave him a quick hug.

The minute I let go, he turned and, without looking back, rushed out of the bedroom door. A few seconds later, the front door closed. He was gone.

Bye Mr Sexy Lips. See you soon.

Smirking, I went to the bathroom to clean myself up.

Seeing Mr Sexy Lips tonight wasn't entirely a surprise. I had found the little tracker he placed on my hoodie and knew he had traced me home despite my best efforts. Therefore, I had thought I might see him again. I just hadn't known when.

After finding the tracker, I'd replayed our encounter and realised that he must have been in the office when I was searching through it. He had likely been doing the same thing before I'd disturbed him, and he'd been forced to hide. Obviously in the little bathroom. That's why Mathieson's computer had still been powering down when I entered.

When the mysterious Russian had revealed himself and saved me from being caught by the security guard, I'd been curious about why he'd been there and knew he had to have been curious about me, too.

However, him breaking into my home tonight had been unexpected, as I had an excellent security system. That he had bypassed it meant that he had someone very talented working with him. Although, to be honest, I knew that already when they hacked into the security system of Mathieson's building. So, I guess it really shouldn't have surprised me.

When Miki asked to work with me, my first instinct was to decline. After all, he had divulged nothing during our so-called exchange of information. That had been disappointing, and I'd been determined to make him leave before I ended up spilling any more of my own discoveries. However, he'd stayed and now things had changed. My feelings in particular.

My mystery Russian had tracked me down, and now I was going to turn the tables on him. Then I'd figure out my next move and perhaps, just perhaps, I'd agree to work with him after all. At present, it wasn't in my best interest, but life had a way of throwing you a curve ball when you least expected it and so that could change at any time.

If it did, the more I knew about him and where to find him, the better. So, I'd placed the tracker on the inside of his belt.

Mr Sexy Lips thought he was smart, tracking me down, keeping his cards close to his chest and his identity hidden. But he forgot something vital. I was a detective, and investigating was my thing. By wearing his balaclava, he expected to remain anonymous. He really underestimated me if he thought that would stop me from finding out who he was.

Besides, if he was using technology and a hacker, I thought he might have placed cameras in Mathieson's office. If that was true, he could end up with information that could be vital to my case. That in itself was a good reason to see the guy again, and if we had another intimate encounter, I would not complain.

Settling back onto the crumpled bed where we'd just been playing, I opened my phone and logged into the tracker app, readying myself to play a different type of game. He might think he was the one in control of this little chess match he had going on with me, but I would soon show Mr Sexy Lips the error of his ways.

Smiling, I watched the little dot move away from the area.

Game on!

After making sure the tracker was doing its job, I climbed into bed, intent on getting some much needed rest. The exhaustion I'd felt earlier had returned, and I badly needed to sleep.

As I snuggled under the covers, I sniffed hard.

My sheets smelt of sex and hot Russian male. With a huge grin on my face, I replayed what we'd done. What a night!

Settling into a comfortable position, I relaxed and hugged the pillow where Miki had briefly lain and closed my eyes, expecting to fall asleep right away. However, my brain wasn't ready to rest despite my exhaustion and no matter how hard I tried to fall asleep, the bloody thing eluded me.

But I kept trying anyway, tossing and turning for hours, until I couldn't take it anymore.

Fuck it!

Annoyed and frustrated, I threw the covers aside and got up.

Too many questions about Mr Sexy Lips were on my mind and there was no escaping them. So, I opened the tracking app again and checked its position. Smiling, I noticed that the little dot had remained in the same place... the Hilton Hotel... for quite some time.

Bingo!

Next, I looked up Russian names to see what Miki might stand for. Mikhail seemed the most appropriate choice.

With a name and location, I was one step closer to solving the puzzle of my mystery man.

Something Miki forgot about when trying to hide his identity was his tattoo, which was beautiful and completely unique. It was on his upper left arm and was the face of a grey wolf with piercing silver-grey eyes, just like Miki's.

The first time I'd noticed it, something about it niggled at me. However, I'd naturally been far too distracted at the time to think too much about it. Now I was sure I had seen it before.

Frowning, I pursed my lips and tutted when I couldn't think where.

Since the sexy Russian was likely a criminal, the obvious answer would be to check the police database when I got back to work in case he was on file. Yet I doubted that. While I believed the guy was indeed a villain, and he was obviously good at breaking into places, he didn't seem like your usual run-of-the-mill thief. Or the type to get caught.

Besides, I really didn't think him being a criminal was how I recognised his tattoo. There was some other reason for that.

My head ached trying to remember.

The sense of power and danger Miki exuded and his comments about being a businessman made me think he was used to being in charge. It was likely this man was very successful and probably hid his criminal activities behind a legitimate businessman's façade.

Closing my eyes, I focused on the image of the wolf in my head. Around its neck was a collar with a tag that depicted an eight-point star with the letter R inside it. The star resembled the one used by the Russian Mafia.

Could Mr Sexy Lips be connected to the Bratva?

Chewing on my bottom lip, I pondered that.

There was no Bratva operating in Glasgow, or Scotland, as far as I knew, but we had them here in the UK. So, it wasn't outside the realm of possibility. The Russian accent and my view that his criminality was hidden behind the businessman's façade certainly aligned with that theory.

As I waited to feel guilt over the fact that I might not just have slept with a thief, I might have slept with a Mafia man. I was shocked when it didn't come.

Shit!

My black and white world had truly become skewed if that idea didn't bother me. A few weeks ago, I was sure it would have horrified me. Of course, a few weeks ago, I viewed the world in a way I now knew was completely naïve.

Taking a deep breath, I came to terms with the idea.

What was done was done. I couldn't change it and, if truth be known, I didn't want to. The guy had rocked my world and whether or not he was Bratva, nothing would change that. And nothing would stop this obsessive attraction I had for him, either. We had chemistry, and that was that.

God, those kisses! That sex!

My pussy throbbed as my mind went down that rabbit hole again. I clamped my lips tightly down on the giggle that threatened as images flashed in my brain like a private porn show.

God, I wished my friend Lisa was around so I could tell her all about Mr Sexy Lips.

As my best friend, she'd love to hear all about my exploits with the hot Russian. We'd met on our first day at university before I joined the Police. She'd been studying journalism, and I'd studied English. We'd hit it off immediately and had remained besties ever since.

Unfortunately, she was currently travelling abroad with her boyfriend, Danny. She was a successful travel vlogger, and he was a photographer. They made a great team, and I expected to hear news of an engagement soon. I'd helped Danny pick out a ring for her before they left last month for their new adventure, but I knew he was waiting to find the right moment to propose.

The pair had been in a relationship since our university days, too. Lisa and Danny were made for each other. Personally, I envied them because I hadn't been so lucky in love. Oh, I attracted enough men, but just never the rights ones. After a string of unsatisfying relationships, I'd become jaded with dating and until my sexy Russian, I had been celibate for some time.

Lisa was always telling me I was a born-again virgin, so she would be really pleased to hear my dry spell was finally over. She'd love to hear all the gory details.

Although, to be honest, even if she had been here to gossip with, I wouldn't have been able to tell her any of this because she'd likely want to help with my investigation and put herself in danger. There was no way I'd ever allow that, so it was just as well she was far away from all of this.

That didn't stop me from missing her like crazy, though.

To compensate, I pulled up her vlog. Her beaming face filled the screen, and I laughed and smiled as I replayed her latest videos.

She showed off a henna design a Malaysian woman had just painted on her hand and that's when I had my light bulb moment.

I gasped, excited.

Flicking through Lisa's old vlogs, I grinned when I found what I was looking for.

Yes!

This vlog was from when she attended the opening of a new London club called Glitz. I remembered the vlog because the club looked amazing. It was owned by a Russian family called Rominov.

The image of the wolf's collar sprung to mind. R for Rominov?

Checking her linked blog, I discovered the parents were dead, and the business was run by the siblings and a cousin. They were said to be quite private and shied away from media coverage, but there was a rare photograph of the family in front of another of their businesses with their names underneath; Mikhail, Sashenka, Marko, Sonia, and Romivick.

As I looked at the face of Mikhail Rominov, butterflies erupted in my stomach. It was hard to tell the colour of his eyes from the picture, but he was tall and muscular, with a handsome face, dark hair, a beard, and very familiar.

Underneath, Lisa had added some other rare photographs that were obviously taken by paparazzi. One of them showed Mikhail on a yacht wearing only swim shorts, and his glorious chest was on display, and there on his upper left arm was the tattoo.

Mikhail Rominov was my mystery Russian, Mr Sexy Lips himself.

Gotcha babe!

Smirking at having already discovered who he was and where I could find him, I printed out his photographs and the other ones of his family and then snuggled back down in bed to study them.

They were a good-looking family, but Miki was the sexiest, with his dark hair and beard. Call me a cliché, but I had a thing for guys that were not only tall, dark and handsome but had beards and tattoos.

I'd been drawn to the man from the moment I had sniffed his scent in the stairwell of Mathieson's building. However, after our amazing sex, and now studying his gorgeous features, well, I had to say; I was well and truly infatuated with the guy.

It had happened so fast, and might not be love exactly, but it was definitely more than mere lust. I wasn't a great believer in love at first sight, or in this case, first sniff. That sort of thing was only for books.

However, I couldn't get him out of my head, and it definitely bordered on obsession. I had the distinct feeling that meeting Mr Sexy Lips was going to have a profound effect on my future, and I wasn't sure I liked that.

Staring at his image again, I had to admit; he was gorgeous and obviously rich. I doubted I could do better. The only problem I could see with this infatuation was the fact that we so obviously came from different worlds. Miles apart in so many ways. Could this thing between us really bridge that gap?

Who knew?

With everything else I had to deal with, I didn't want to think about it anymore. A sense of inevitability washed over me again and I sighed. Whatever was going to happen between Miki and me, fate could decide.

CHAPTER 14
MIKI

A FEW DAYS LATER – THE REASON FOR
THE VENDETTA

Marko had come up with more information on Mathieson and we'd been monitoring the bugger since. I now knew exactly who he was and his link to my family.

The reason behind his vendetta with my family was simple; my father had been the one behind his father's downfall.

Why he had also targeted Glowacki, we still hadn't found out. It might simply have been because of our alliance, but no doubt all would be revealed, eventually.

When we'd moved to the UK, and my dad tried to establish himself as pakhan here, he had trouble with a local gang funded by a corrupt banker. As the banker was so prominent, instead of having him killed, my dad anonymously ensured that the local police discovered evidence of his corporate corruption. He'd later been jailed for fraud and embezzlement around twenty years ago and had committed suicide in jail.

Aiden Mathieson, also known as Simon Aiden Hughes, was the banker's son.

After the scandal of his father's incarceration, Simon, his

mother, and sixteen-year-old sister had left London and changed their names to Mathieson to escape the paparazzi.

They had gone from being a wealthy family to barely getting by. His mother suffered from depression after that and eventually she took her own life too, leaving Mathieson to look after his sister while working and studying law. At some point, he had obviously found out about my dad's involvement and held a grudge.

In other circumstances, I would probably have felt sorry for Mathieson. He and his family were collateral damage in a war neither of us was a part of.

However, my father was dead now and instead of Mathieson's grudge dying with him, he'd transferred it to the rest of my family. And for that, there was no excuse.

The worst thing was, he had given the go-ahead to kill my beautiful sister. A woman innocent of any wrongdoing and undeserving of his ire or the suffering he inadvertently caused.

Of course, the arseholes who murdered her might have done so anyway, but Mathieson ensured it. Any possibility of sympathy died with that thought.

The fucker should have let bygones be bygones and left us the hell alone. My hands itched to do the guy some damage, and I growled in frustration.

It pissed me off I had to wait, but, like his father before him, he was too prominent a figure to just kill. And like my father before me, I needed to come up with a plan for his demise that didn't come back to haunt me.

There was no way I would risk his death causing any more suffering for me or mine.

So, I'd wait, and I'd plan. Then when the time came to deal with him, I'd make sure he suffered dearly for every one of his crimes against us, but especially for Krissa's death.

Of course, in order to do that, I needed to formulate my

plan. I was usually good at that, but I was currently finding it difficult, as I kept getting distracted by one sexy little police detective. Little Miss Red was proving to be more than a passing fancy.

It had been a few days since we'd been together, but she was never far from my mind. Like a phantom, she haunted my dreams, and every waking moment was filled with thoughts of her. No matter how I tried, I could not get her out of my head.

Every time she entered my mind, my body reacted with lust. It was driving me mad. My bloody cock had remained at half mast as if in mourning of her pussy since I'd left her bedroom and no matter how I tried, no amount of DIY could fix the problem.

There was no denying it. I had to see her again.

It didn't matter that she was a police officer and an enemy. My heart wanted her, my cock wanted her, and my whole bloody being screamed for her.

I wanted her more than I'd ever wanted anything in my life. I had to have her!

My mind was consumed with thoughts about how to make her my own, so much so, I could think of nothing else.

Making her mine was the only way I would remain sane and the only way I could stop being so bloody distracted by her. If she belonged to me, and I belonged to her, then I knew I'd be finally able to focus again.

That would be a hard thing to achieve. But I had to believe it wasn't impossible.

Marko had done a lot of digging, and we found out that her boss, Detective Chief Constable Roy Allen, had been Eilidh's dad's best friend and partner at the time of his death.

Jim MacArthur had already informed us the guy was corrupt, but Marko had also found out about a few others in her department. They'd all been taking bribes from Mathieson for years. That was obviously how he'd kept most of the Thomas gang and many others out of jail.

Naturally, I knew all about corrupt police, as we had several on our payroll, but I hated them even though they were vital to keeping my family and business safe. Anyone who would sell out their family, friends, and morals for money was the lowest of the low, in my opinion. So, I naturally hated Roy Allen and his team of corrupt officers.

The fact they were Eilidh's colleagues made me hate them more.

Not only were they on the take, but apparently they were blackmailing several prestigious people. That was a very dangerous game to play and one I was well versed in myself. However, when I played that game, it was in order to protect my family from harm and not simply for personal gain.

Yes, I was a bad man who did bad things, but I did them with a moral code of ethics that guys like these didn't have.

My Little Miss Red was working with these men, and that worried the hell out of me. Even worse, if Mathieson had killed Eilidh's dad as she suspected, then they might have been involved. If any of them discovered she was investigating Mathieson, who knew what they would do?

My heart pounded, and my stomach churned at the thought of Eilidh coming to harm.

It didn't help that our surveillance of her uncovered the fact that she was not just investigating Mathieson as she had told me, but was also looking into her colleagues.

She'd been following them whenever she could and had watched as they met with several unsavoury characters from the Thomas gang, among others.

I was so terrified she would get caught; my body literally broke out in a cold sweat every time I thought about it.

My sexy detective was good at what she did, but she was

alone, and these men were not stupid. It was only a matter of time before her activities were discovered. She needed to be kept safe.

That was why I had brought up a couple of our men from London and had them, or Vlad, following her.

My plan wasn't developed, but my mind was made up. I'd deal with these men for her and bring them to justice for what they had done to her dad. I wasn't sure how to do that yet and still get Mathieson for myself, but I would figure something out.

Then, when all of this was over, I'd contact her and attempt to woo her away from the police and into my life.

Again, I didn't know how I was going to do that or if my attempts would be in any way successful, but my feelings for her ran too deep not to try. In the meantime, she would be looked after by my men.

Despite my worries for Eilidh, as the morning wore on, I attempted to focus on my discussions with Jim MacArthur and various phone calls to my Uncle Maxim and Cousin Viktor as we sorted out the re-routing of our drug trafficking route. It took a lot of planning and was a logistical nightmare to set up initially, but now we had things figured out to everyone's satisfaction. I was happy about that, but completely worn out.

Giving in to my exhaustion, I told the guys I was going for a nap to get some peace. When I was alone in my room, I pulled up the footage of Eilidh's house. All was quiet there, but I had expected that as she had returned to work today. Marko had checked her shift pattern, so I knew she was on day shift and wasn't due to finish work for another hour at least.

However, I liked to monitor things in Eilidh's absence. She had an excellent security system, but it wasn't good enough. If I could break in, someone else could. Okay, it had taken the help of Marko to do it, but I wasn't the only one with a hacker at my disposal and with all the danger she had put herself in with this investigation of hers, I wasn't taking any chances.

Marko was monitoring all communications in and out of the station to ensure that we knew where she was at all times, and Vlad was on her tail today, so I knew she would be fine. If anything concerning happened, they'd soon let me know.

Having put my mind at ease that she was still safe, I settled on the bed for a badly needed rest and closed my eyes. With a smile on my face, I drifted off to sleep quickly, dreaming about long curly red hair fisted in my hands as I thrust into a sexy little police detective.

CHAPTER 15
EILIDH
THAT DAY – NEEDING AN ALLY

t had been a few days since I had discovered the identity of Mr Sexy Lips, and I was doing my level best not to obsess over him and failing dramatically.

However, despite my constant distraction, I'd spent my free time spying on the corrupt members of my team and slowly gathering more information against them.

Although I only harboured suspicions about Roy having an affair with a young woman, I'd discovered for a fact that my married sergeant was doing the dirty deed with his neighbour who was half his age.

Dirty prick! I felt sorry for his wife.

What was bloody frustrating, however, was that while I had observed more dodgy behaviour by my colleagues, I had discovered nothing I could use to link their corruption to Mathieson, or my dad's murder, beyond the photographs I got from John Aldridge. And they would be too easy to explain away, without more evidence to back them up.

The information I had found during my illegal activities wouldn't be enough because it was inadmissible in court. I'd simply needed to know what I was dealing with and get an idea of what I should look for, so that I could find something that could prompt the police to investigate further.

Sending anonymous photos of the contents of the safes I'd broken into would get me nowhere. No procurator fiscal would touch them and no judge would grant a warrant to search premises based on them because again, they could be easily explained away or be deemed a set up.

After days of snooping around and doing everything I could think of to find out what I needed, I had nothing, and I'd run out of ideas.

Rubbing at the tension in my forehead, I puffed out an exasperated breath.

Of course, there could be something worthwhile on Mathieson's computer. Perhaps it was time to pay a visit to Mr Sexy Lips.

Sighing heavily, I pulled my hair back and tied it up.

I'd need to think about that later, as I was back at work today.

Dread filled me as I finished getting dressed. It had been hard enough working with these guys before, but after investigating them, the very thought of them sickened me.

The drive to the station only made me feel sicker the closer I got.

My feet dragged as I walked through the doors of the police station and my legs felt like lead as I climbed the stairs to the CID office.

Pull yourself together, Eilidh!

It was time to get my game face on again, otherwise I would set off their alarm bells, and that was definitely not something I wanted to do.

———

Being back on duty with Martin was a nightmare, and I didn't know how long I could keep acting as if nothing was wrong. Thankfully, we were kept busy with various appointments, but every second with him dragged out, making it feel like one heck of a long day.

Especially since Martin kept making jokes about us getting together outside of work in his usual flirty way. He was a handsome guy, but he knew it. A real ladies' man who liked to have a new woman on his arm every time he went out. That kind of man wasn't my type. So, even before I'd become obsessed with my silver eyed Russian, I'd never have gone out with Martin, but I had found his flirting flattering and a bit of fun. Now it just made my skin crawl, and I didn't want to be anywhere near him.

However, something I discovered early on about my partner was that he liked the sound of his own voice. Once Martin started talking, he could keep doing so for a long time, with little input from anyone else. I quickly surmised he preferred it that way.

So, in between appointments, and desperately fighting back my revulsion, I kept him talking with a few strategically placed questions.

Normally, he wasn't concerned by my lack of response. His oversized ego meant that typically he assumed everyone was hanging off his every word. Truth be known, often they were. Martin was a charmer, and with his good looks, he was usually the centre of attention. He was the sort of man that many men wanted to be, and many women wanted to have.

Usually, I only had to smile, nod, chuckle occasionally, or make some non-committal noises during one of his long monologues to keep him happy. So, I hadn't expected him to notice when I zoned out, thinking of how to deal with Miki and my rising feelings for him.

"You seem really distracted today, Eilidh. Is something wrong?" His voice broke through my thoughts.

Turning towards him, I couldn't suppress my shiver as his eyes drilled into me while he waited for my answer.

Oh, no!

Unease crept along my spine, and my gut churned.

Was he suspicious of me? Did he suspect what I was up to? Or worse, did he know?

There was no way to be sure. It could just be that for once he'd noticed my distraction, but my gut told me there was more to his question than that.

My heart pounded in my chest, and I gulped nervously as sweat broke out all over my body.

Calm, Eilidh, stay calm! I pleaded with myself.

"Nothing's wrong, it's just hormones making me feel unwell," I told him, shaking my head and offering a weak smile. I prayed he'd take my response for embarrassment at admitting my female hormones were interfering with my mood rather than nerves.

Crossing my fingers, I hoped the excuse would be enough for him.

Heat crept up my neck as he assessed me, but thankfully, my pinkened cheeks appeared to do the trick and he nodded.

"Okay, sweetie, no need to be embarrassed. Do you want me to stop and get you some chocolate or something?"

Martin smiled at me sympathetically.

"No, I just need to get home. I can't wait for the shift to be over," I said truthfully.

"Well, we are done here for the day, so we'll head back to the station, and I'll arrange for the statements to be typed up, and you can disappear off home a bit early then," he replied.

"Great, thanks," I said, relief washing over me.

As soon as we returned to the station, I made my excuses and got the hell out of there.

My concern that my colleagues might be on to me meant I needed to step up my plans.

As soon as I got home, I pulled on some dark clothing, I grabbed a sandwich and some water, stuffed it into the bag I used when out on surveillance, and within less than half an hour, I was in my car and headed back to the station.

Parking at a good vantage point, I waited.

Not long after, I saw Martin's car leaving the car park. I followed behind, keeping a suitable distance between us since I no longer had my rental car.

The way he'd looked at me today had me on edge. Although I knew I should probably steer clear of him and focus on one of my other colleagues tonight, for some reason, I felt compelled to get back out and follow Martin instead.

We sped along the motorway for a while, and I expected him to take the next cut-off and head home, but he didn't. He continued on before taking the exit that I knew led to a small hotel instead.

As he pulled into the carpark, I slowed to a stop and waited until he got out and headed inside carrying a holdall.

Once he'd disappeared through the door, I parked my car around the corner where he wouldn't see it. Jumping out, I ran to the entrance and peeked inside just in time to see him go through a set of double doors towards the Spa and gym.

Hurrying back to my car, I pulled out my backpack and headed back inside. I had a friend who worked in the Spa here as a beautician, and I knew my way around and had used the gym several times before as a guest, so it was easy to look like I belonged there.

After removing my jacket, I left it in the changing room.

Thankful that I had a sports top, leggings, and trainers on, so I looked the part.

Stepping into the gym, I ducked behind some equipment, trying to avoid being noticed as I checked around the room, but Martin wasn't there. In fact, for the early evening, it was very quiet. There was only an older couple working out together by the weights and a young man running on the treadmill. Shit!

Maybe he was still in the changing room?

Heading back into the corridor, I stopped outside the men's changing room and listened at the door. It was useless. I couldn't hear anything, so I quietly opened the door a crack and peered in.

Nobody was in the immediate area, but I could hear voices from somewhere inside. Praying I wasn't about to come upon some unsuspecting guy in his birthday suit, I ducked inside and crept towards the voices.

They were hushed, but I recognised Martin's voice as one of them.

"I need you to watch, and if I am right, then we have a problem that will need to be sorted," he said.

"Just how *sorted* are we talking?" the other voice asked, emphasising the word sorted.

"Depends on just how much of a problem we have. Find that out first, then get back to me, and I'll deal with it myself," Martin said.

The other voice responded, but I couldn't make out what he said. Hearing footsteps coming my way, I ran to a toilet cubicle and hid behind its door, holding my breath.

The changing room door opened and closed, but I remained where I was, straining to hear anything else.

Within seconds, another person exited, then there was silence. I waited a little longer, then crept out of the cubicle and rushed for the door.

Damn it. I must have missed most of their conversation.

What the hell was that about? Was it about me? If it was, I could be in big trouble.

Peeking into the gym, I saw Martin running on the treadmill. There was no sign of anyone else with him.

As soon as I got back into the women's changing room, I grabbed my bag and left.

Thank god there were no speed cameras in the vicinity and no police cars on patrol as I sped along the road like a formula one driver on speed.

All the way I kept checking over my shoulder as if a car was suddenly going to be following me.

The rational part of my brain told me I was being dumb. Nobody was following me. After all, neither Martin nor his associate had known I was there, but my churning gut, shaking hands and overall sick feeling said I didn't believe it.

Regardless of whether I was being followed, I had to assume that the conversation I'd overheard was about me. After the way Martin had acted today, taking more notice of my demeanour than usual, which was out of character for him, I was convinced of it.

Of course, there was the slightest chance I was wrong. I might just be being paranoid, but I didn't believe so. My gut said they suspected me, and I needed to listen to it.

Suddenly, I felt very alone and very frightened.

The words John Aldridge said to me kept playing over and over in my mind. What if he was right, and I ended up with a bullet in my head like my dad? Just another unsolved cold case. Bile rose in my throat as I realised how screwed I could be.

Shit! I couldn't do this alone.

My mind whirled, and I felt dizzy.

I'd been a bloody fool. Anything could happen to me, and then my dad would have really died for nothing, the corruption would go on, and those involved would get away with everything. That couldn't be allowed to happen.

I needed an ally, and there was only one person it could be. It was time to go see Miki and take him up on his offer to work together and trade information. It looked like fate had decided, after all.

Turning my car around, I headed to the Hilton.

CHAPTER 16
MIKI

Pounding at my door alerted me to a problem, and I awoke with a start.

Cursing loudly, I jumped out of bed naked and opened the door. Marko was there, looking worried.

"What is it?" I demanded in annoyance.

"Vlad just called; your detective is on her way up here."

"Shit!"

She found me?

I hurriedly pulled on some trousers and a shirt and rushed out into the other room just as there was a knock at the suite door.

What was she doing here, and how the hell did she find me?

And thank god she had.

I'd been climbing the walls all day, desperate with the need to see her, and now she had come to me.

Excitement at seeing my Little Miss Red made my heart pound and adrenaline rush through my veins.

But she shouldn't be here!

Closing my eyes, I took a deep breath and tried to get a grip on my emotions, which were all over the place.

"Open it," I told Marko as I stood off to the side, still trying to bloody compose myself. If I didn't, I would likely grab her and kiss her immediately she walked through the door.

"Hi, I'm here to see Miki," Eilidh said.

"Who should I tell him is calling?" Marko asked.

"I believe you know," she replied with a chuckle.

Taking another deep breath, I stepped around Marko and gulped as her beautiful face grinned up at me.

"Nice to see you again, Little Miss Red," I drawled, trying to appear cool while my heart hammered like a jack rabbit against my chest.

I saw the way her eyes widened at my nickname for her. She liked it. Of course, it wasn't the first time she'd heard it, but I could tell by the secret little smile tugging at her lips that she enjoyed hearing it.

"Hi, Miki," she said with a look of triumph.

A slow smile spread over my face as I stood there staring at her.

Eilidh was pleased to see me, but why? Had she been pining for me as much as I had for her, or was there another reason for her visit?

My emotions warred with each other as I watched her face, waiting to see if she said anything else.

I wanted her here, but I wasn't ready for her.

This was not part of my plan.

Well, to be honest, I didn't have one yet. My mind was set on pursuing her and, if possible, winning her for my own. But for that to even be an option, I knew I would have to gain her trust and then somehow her loyalty and love so that she would want me, despite my criminal background.

That would take some convincing, but considering that her colleagues were corrupt and might have had something to do with her dad's murder, I guessed her faith in law enforcement might have been shaken.

Eilidh was twenty-eight and had been a police officer for seven years. She'd followed in her father's footsteps and was now a detective like he had been. However, any pride she'd felt in that must have been severely affected by everything she'd discovered.

It was sad, and although my heart went out to her, I had to admit that it gave me hope. After all, she would need to give up her job for me, but if she was less than enamoured with it after discovering all of this, that would certainly benefit me.

Maybe once I helped her deal with those officers and Mathieson, she would be glad to leave the police. I mentally crossed my fingers and hoped that would be the case.

We could be great together. She was supposed to be with me; I knew it with all my heart. But she could not remain a police officer and be with me. That was impossible. Being a Bratva pakhan wasn't conducive to having a relationship with a police officer. My brotherhood would not condone that.

"Are you going to invite me in?" she asked, sounding calm, but I caught a flash of worry in her eyes.

Did she think I wouldn't? I might not have expected to see her yet, but I would work with it. Starting right now, I'd begin trying to win her to my side.

Grinning, and licking my lips, I let my heated gaze drift over her, ensuring she was in no doubt that I was glad she'd come.

She gulped and her face flushed slightly, making it obvious her calm façade was just that. My Little Miss Red was as affected by me as I was by her.

My heart soared.

"Come in, beautiful," I said, deliberately thickening my accent as I opened the door wider and gestured for her to enter.

I had noticed the effect my voice had on her before and was going to use it to my full advantage. Of course, my voice wasn't the only thing that thickened.

Throwing caution to the wind, and uncaring about Marko standing a few feet away, I pulled her into my arms and kissed her.

She gasped in shock, obviously not expecting that reaction, but she quickly got over it and kissed me back. As it always did when we kissed, the world fell away until only the two of us were left.

Marko cleared his throat, and I heard him sniggering as my tongue delved inside her delicious mouth. Ignoring him, I continued to kiss her. However, his chuckle broke the moment for her, and she pushed away from me, redness crawling up her face.

God, she was cute when she was embarrassed. I'd have to make that happen more often.

Russians weren't known for public displays of affection, but we were half Italian, so it wasn't unusual for us. And I was more than happy to show my growing affection for my Little Miss Red in front of Marko, or anyone else for that matter. In fact, I'd be proud to do it. The world needed to know she was mine, and I was hers. A sense of rightness settled over me at that thought.

After glancing between Marko and myself, Eilidh cleared her throat and spoke, "I think we should work together after all."

"I agree!" I stated and noted Marko's look of surprise.

He recovered quickly, throwing me a questioning look from behind her back, which I ignored.

"This is my brother Marko," I told her, gesturing towards him as he came to stand beside us.

"Hi," she said, smiling.

"Hi, Little Miss Red, I have heard a lot about you," he stated, taking her hand and kissing it, as he gave me a mischievous look.

Annoyed, I pushed him away from her.

"Keep your kisses to yourself," I said, my jealousy clear.

Eilidh raised her eyebrows and smirked as Marko sniggered.

Damn it!

I'd wanted to play things cool and seduce her slowly but surely, earning her trust. Yet, I'd already kissed her and showed my possessiveness, and she had only been in the room a few minutes.

Oh well, I didn't really like games anyway, so it was best that she knew how deeply she affected me and that what had happened between us was more than just sex.

However, her mere presence interfered with my equilibrium, and I needed to regain some control. Otherwise, I'd be divulging all my secrets before I was ready.

"It would appear I underestimated you. I didn't think you'd find me, Detective. Although I am very pleased you have," I said, emphasising the word detective.

I wondered how the hell she did, but at the same time, I was thoroughly impressed.

"Well, you tracked me down. It seemed only fair I returned the favour. So, I did my homework," she replied with a smirk.

"When did you find out who I was?" she asked, narrowing her eyes.

"The day after we met," I told her truthfully.

"Like you, I do my homework," I said in a playful tone with a wink.

She nodded, looking at Marko with suspicion. Her lips pursed and I could almost hear her brain working as she put two and two together, beginning to understand that Marko was the person relaying information to me during our time at Mathieson's office.

"Tell me what you have discovered about Mathieson," she demanded with a tone of authority that brooked no argument. Little Miss Red had put her police hat on.

"I'm happy to share," I said with a smile.

Marko's mouth twisted with uncertainty. My Little Miss Red shot me a triumphant grin.

"Let's share what we know and work together. If you think you can," I said, opting for a more formal tone like her and trying my best not to sound too eager. I wasn't sure what had brought her here or why she'd changed her mind about working together, but I didn't want to scare her off after her reluctance the other night.

"Fine!" she said, holding out her hand for me to shake.

She was definitely being all business now, and I'd play along, if that made her more comfortable, but only for a while.

"Come sit down and we'll talk."

Placing my hand lightly on her waist, I drew her over to the sofa. Unlike the other night, I didn't pull her on to my lap, but god how I wanted to. My cock gave a jerk in agreement.

"I was just about to order something to eat from room service. Can I get you guys anything?" Marko asked.

"A steak with all the trimmings," I said, suddenly realising how starved I was.

"Have you eaten?" I asked.

"Well, no, but I'm not very hungry," she replied.

"She'll have the same," I said to Marko.

"You need to eat," I told her firmly.

"Unless you don't like meat?" I asked, raising my eyebrows in question.

"Yes, I do," she nodded and sighed in submission, obviously seeing my determination.

"Then a steak it is," I repeated to Marko, who was already phoning the reception with our order.

Since I was the type of guy who always needed a plan, I formulated a quick plan of seduction in my head as we waited for Marko to finish giving our order.

Step 1 – make her comfortable with me.

Step 2 – gain her trust.

Step 3 – make her crave me.

Step 4 – win her love.

Step 5 – gain her loyalty.

Step 6 – claim her as mine.

It seemed simple enough. Now all I had to do was implement it, starting with Step 1.

"Why don't you tell me how you found me?" I asked, deciding that letting her impress me with her skills would be the best way to get her to relax and open up.

"The same way you found me."

She smirked, and I grinned back.

"Yes, I know about the tracker you put on my hoodie."

"Did you keep it? Where is it? Can I have it back? It's a prototype," Marko said, butting into the conversation.

"Yes, I kept it. It's at my house. And yes, you can have it back, Marko," she said with a laugh.

"So, how did you track me?"

Eilidh might have found my tracker, but I hadn't found hers. She looked at me, leaned over and put her hands around my waist, and touched my belt. Suddenly I was transported back to when she hugged me before I left her house the other day and had an *ah ha* moment.

My sexy police detective smirked as she held her hand up and showed me a tiny device not much bigger than a pinhead. She waggled her eyes at me, and I chuckled, impressed by her ingenuity.

Reaching for it, I looked it over. We used similar devices all the time, but Marko was always inventing his own.

"Can I see?" Marko asked, and I passed it to him.

"Nice!" he said, sounding impressed, before passing it back to her.

It was very high tech and very expensive. I didn't think Police Scotland would have the budget for that. When I said as much to her, she laughed again.

"Definitely not. It's my own. I got it from a source of mine and, like my breaking into Mathieson's office, it is not part of a legal investigation. As you had already surmised, I am investigating Mathieson alone in my own time," she told me, confirming my original belief.

Marko settled on the sofa opposite, and I glared at him.

"Don't you have stuff to do?" I asked, gesturing with my head that he needed to leave.

He chuckled and stood.

"Yes, boss," he replied with a two-finger salute. I rolled my eyes. Cheeky bugger! If he wasn't channelling his inner Sonia, or Ash, it was Trigger.

"Don't do anything I wouldn't do," he said, winking.

Eilidh chuckled, and I shook my head.

"Get out of here," I said, my lips twitching as he headed off to his room, making loud smooching noises like the fool he was.

As Eilidh stuck the tracker into her backpack, I was glad she'd only found that one and not the one in her car or the cameras I'd place around her house. I doubted she would be in quite such a good mood if she had.

"How did you break into his office, anyway?" I asked and was amazed by her answer and especially how she came about her very specialised skills.

If I hadn't been there, she might have been caught, but

otherwise she had done a good job of scouting the place out, gathering the intelligence needed, getting into the building, and searching the office. And, of course, breaking into his safe was a truly impressive feat.

My sexy detective was obviously good at planning things out, and she'd thought of everything. Her only problem had been doing it all alone. With no proper backup, she'd been vulnerable.

It struck me just how alike we were. Both of us liked to plan things out and each of us was doing illegal things behind a legal façade, and both doing them to avenge our family. Not only that, but we had a common goal: to make Mathieson pay for his crimes.

Of course, our idea of how to do that might not be the same. I intended to kill the bastard when, no doubt, she intended for him to go to jail. That didn't matter, Aiden Mathieson would be mine in the end, no matter what.

For now, I would concentrate on taking him down, along with her colleagues. Those guys could go to jail if that was what she wanted, but Mathieson would go to the C.

"Your cousin Joe certainly taught you some useful skills," I said, observing her reaction.

This Joe character had been a criminal who'd gone straight, and Eilidh obviously overlooked his past and loved him despite it. I was a criminal who wanted to go straight. Did that mean she could love me, too? My heart gave a leap at the thought.

"He sure did. Although I never expected to put them to use in real life," she said ruefully.

"I guess not," I replied, pursing my lips.

Despite being enamoured with Eilidh and determined to make her mine, I knew I had to tread carefully. She was still a police officer after all, and until I had her loyalty, I would need to ensure I didn't divulge all of my family business or all of my plans to her.

I'd fallen hard for this woman, but no matter my feelings, I couldn't jeopardise my family's safety. Before I told her everything, I needed to be sure she wouldn't betray me. Gaining her trust and loyalty was therefore vital.

At some point, I would need to tell her precisely who and what I was, but I wasn't ready to do that yet, and I doubted she was ready to hear it.

Dinner arrived, and we settled down to eat.

As I poured a glass of wine for myself and some water for her, I mulled over how best to start building her trust. Being as truthful as possible was the best way, I decided as I chewed a piece of steak and thought of how to begin my story.

In the end, I told her everything I'd learned about Aiden Mathieson and his vendetta against my family, his involvement in Krissa's death and the recent attacks against our businesses.

Eilidh must have seen just how hard it was for me to talk about Krissa, because she reached over and took my hand.

"I'm so very sorry about Krissa, Miki. That must have been very hard for you," she said, squeezing my fingers.

My heart clenched as I looked at the sympathy on her face. It felt good to have someone acknowledge my feelings. Usually, I hid them behind a mask of authority, unable to appear vulnerable in my position, but with Eilidh, it didn't seem necessary. Opening up and being vulnerable with her felt right.

Finishing my story, I glossed over my father's part in Ewan Hughes's arrest, pretending my dad was just a businessman who'd come across some information about a corrupt banker and anonymously passed that information along to the authorities, only to have his involvement discovered later by Mathieson.

It was all true. I just omitted any mention of my family's involvement in the Bratva or our illegal activities.

My sexy detective would still be suspicious about my criminal side, but she was smart enough to know I wasn't going to just pour all my secrets out to a stranger. For despite our attraction and the wonderful sex we'd had, that was what we were. Strangers. At least for now.

With dinner finished, we moved to the sofa again, and I listened intently as Eilidh reciprocated with her own information. I nodded now and then in encouragement while she told me everything she'd learned about her dad's murder and the corruption in her department, which confirmed she'd been investigating her colleagues along with Mathieson.

As Little Miss Red talked, I didn't let on that I knew about any of it, as I wanted to be sure she wasn't holding anything back. She wouldn't tell me everything unless she trusted me enough, so I was over the moon when she did. Obviously, allowing her to see my upset over Krissa had been the right move. I mentally high-fived myself. It looked like I had step 2 – gain her trust, well underway.

However, the thought made me feel guilty about holding a huge part of my life back from her, but it was too soon. I'd let Eilidh know everything about me when the time was right. Hopefully that wouldn't be too far in the future, because I longed to come clean and have her accept me for who I was.

Patience! I reminded myself. My family's safety had to come before my own needs. I was pretty sure she had a good idea who I was anyhow, but I wouldn't confirm it. Not yet.

Finally, after we had discussed everything, she stood to leave.

"I'll send copies of all of my files to you when I get home so you and Marko can look at them," she said.

We arranged to meet again tomorrow when she'd finished

work to discuss our next move. Then it was time to say goodbye.

"Are you sure you wouldn't rather stay?" I asked, pulling her into my arms and nuzzling her neck.

"No. I'd better get home," she sighed, the reluctance in her voice clear.

"I have an early start and need to copy those files before I grab some sleep. It's difficult enough to get through a shift with those men as it is, without adding exhaustion into the mix."

The thought of her anywhere near them made my stomach clench with worry and I tightened my grip on her, not wanting to let her go. However, I had to.

"Alright, but be careful and if you need me, call me," I said.

I had already given her my phone number, just in case.

She nodded, and I brushed her lips lightly with mine. She gave me a tight squeeze around the waist again and I pulled my head back, laughing.

"Tracking me again?" I asked with a chuckle.

She chuckled back and shook her head.

"Nope, you're safe. It's in my bag," she grinned.

"Good. You don't need to track me, Little Miss Red, because I assure you I'm not going anywhere," I said but held back from stating, "because you're mine now." I had a feeling it was just too soon for that. My plan of seduction was going well. I didn't want to spoil things now.

Finally, we pulled apart, and I walked her to the lift. As the door closed, she blew me a kiss, and I grinned. As soon as she was gone, I rang Vlad so he would follow her home and ensure she got there safely.

Back in my suite, I sat on the sofa and went over the evening in my mind.

Little Miss Red impressed me more each time we met. Every little thing I found out about her made me even more enamoured and yet there was still so much to learn. I looked forward to becoming more acquainted with every part of her, physically and mentally. Especially physically. I smirked as the semi hard cock I'd had all night jerked in agreement as it always did when I had such thoughts. Tomorrow couldn't come soon enough.

Holding back from ravishing her the way I'd longed to do had been a bloody arduous task, but Eilidh's actions showed me it was worth it. I was sure Little Miss Red craved me as much as I did her. Step 3 was in the bag!

Of course, I might think I was halfway through the steps in my plan of seduction already, but that didn't mean I didn't still need to work to secure each step. It was time to up my game.

Smiling, I rang the reception and ordered flowers.

CHAPTER 17
EILIDH
STILL THAT NIGHT – ALONE AND SCARED

As the lift closed, I gave Miki a little wave and blew him a kiss. God, the man was gorgeous and just one glance from him had my pussy clenching in anticipation.

It was ridiculous how my body craved him. And not just my body, my mind, too. He really was the sexiest man I'd ever encountered, and my fingers had itched to touch him all night. How the heck I'd kept my hands to myself I'd never know. It was definitely a testament to a strength of will I hadn't realised I had.

When he'd asked me to stay the night, I'd almost agreed, but it was late. Jumping his bones would have been fantastic, but I forced myself to behave and leave. It was one of the hardest things I'd ever done and that was annoying as hell and bloody ridiculous.

The man had me in the palm of his hand, and I wasn't sure how I felt about that. Despite all he told me, he was holding some very important information back. And that was the real problem. Until I knew everything about him, he couldn't be truly trusted.

Not only that, but when I found out the gory details of his life, some of which I already suspected, I didn't know how I would deal with it. As a police officer, if I learned about his criminal activities, I was duty bound to investigate them and bring him to justice. Or at the very least, report him to someone else. And yet, every bone in my body screamed against that. The very idea of asking Miki for help and then betraying him made me sick to the stomach.

As I walked to my car, I felt like I could cry.

Geez, get a grip, girl! I chided myself, feeling like a bloody fool.

Mr Sexy Lips was trouble; I needed to be careful about how far I took things and just how much of a hold he had on me. If I didn't watch out, he could very well break my heart.

Although, the way he'd looked at me tonight, I could tell he was struggling to keep his hands to himself as well. Perhaps he was having the same concerns as I was.

We came from two opposite worlds and although we might bridge the gap for a while; it wasn't something we could do permanently. Not unless one of us changed.

I'd tried to be businesslike tonight for that very reason, but my attempts at maintaining a distance between us weren't very successful.

Shit, I really shouldn't have let him kiss me and I definitely shouldn't have kissed him back, or flirted, or blew him a kiss, or any of that.

This was a dangerous game I was playing, but I needed help with my mission. Nevertheless, my heart or my career, or both, were at stake. It was a leap of faith to believe Miki was someone I could trust with the information I'd supplied tonight and the information I would send when I got home. My heart told me I was right to believe in him, but my head recommended caution.

One thing this evening had taught me was that keeping a professional distance from my Mr Sexy Lips was impossible. So, when we succumbed to our mutual attraction again, and I knew for a fact we would soon, and probably often, I would simply have to ensure that my heart remembered that it was only sex.

There couldn't be anything else.

A lump formed in my throat, and I choked back tears. It was upsetting and frustrating, but that was how it was.

In that moment, I decided that whatever I discovered about Miki during this investigation would be forgotten as soon as it was over, as payment for his help, and then I would walk away and never see the man again.

I'd tell him that the next time I saw him. That way, we'd both know where we stood and neither of us would need to be concerned about betrayal from the other.

Sadness filled me at the thought of having no actual future with him. However, I pushed it aside. We'd work together, fuck, and then part. It would rip me to pieces when that time came, but I'd eventually get over him.

For now, I would bloody well enjoy every second I could with him, make a lifetime of memories to warm my nights when he was no longer around, and indulge all of my fantasies while I could. Because I had a feeling that I would never again meet anyone else like my sexy Russian.

Another wave of sadness threatened to bring me to my knees, and I grabbed onto the car door for support. Oh lord, I was so screwed.

Tears pricked at my eyes, but I wouldn't let them fall. There was no way I would let future worries interfere with my current enjoyment. I was a grown woman who'd had temporary relationships before. I could handle this.

Mind made up, I took a deep breath, mentally pulled my big

girl panties up so high I almost gave myself a wedgie, climbed into my car, blasted some tunes by Pink, and sung along all the way home.

By the time I got there, I was convinced that I was not only a sexy siren who could *love them and leave them* with ease, but I was a badass one, too.

However, when I stepped out of my car, I had that feeling of being watched again. It was likely just paranoia, but after overhearing that conversation between Martin and the mystery man, I wasn't taking any chances.

Grabbing the large metal torch I'd hidden under my front seat; I furtively scanned around me.

The air was still, as if holding its breath the way I was.

"Is someone there?" I whispered into the darkness, wondering what the hell I would do if someone appeared.

Brain him and run! The annoying voice in my head said, obviously thinking it was being helpful. It so wasn't!

What the hell was I doing? This was like the opening of a horror movie, and everyone knew how that worked out for the stupid lone female who challenged her creeper to come get her.

Realising the utter stupidity of my actions, I turned and ran to the front door. Hurrying inside, I closed it behind me and threw the switches on the lights before resetting the alarm.

My security system was state-of-the-art, but since Miki had got in, I didn't feel as sure of it anymore. In fact, here alone, I was bloody scared.

So, with torch gripped high in both hands ready to swing if necessary and heart thundering in my chest with nerves, I crept around the house, flicking on all the lights as I went and checking every possible hiding place.

When I was sure nobody was inside, I slumped against the kitchen counter and breathed a sigh of relief.

My hands shook and my stomach churned as I poured

myself a shot of tequila. The burning liquid ran down my throat, its warmth soothing me and calming my nerves.

After another shot, I did as I'd said and made copies of my files and all the photographs I had taken. Then I emailed them to Miki.

We'd agreed to meet tomorrow night to discuss it all and anything else Marko found out in the meantime and make a plan about how best to move forward with things then.

After everything Miki had told me about Mathieson and his vendetta against Miki's family, I empathised with him. Especially over the death of his sister, Krissa. That was bloody awful.

No wonder he was determined to bring Mathieson to justice. Miki had as much reason as I did, perhaps even more. I wasn't sure we had the same thing in mind when we talked about justice though, but that was a problem to worry about another day.

Trudging upstairs, I changed into my pyjamas, and smiled at the memory of Miki thinking they were "cute."

Weariness tugged at my eyes, making them droop. It was time to get some rest. Tomorrow I had to endure another excruciating day at work and yet again I needed to have my game face on and my wits about me.

Huffing, I pulled the covers over me and prayed this would all be over soon because I really wasn't sure how much more of it I could take.

CHAPTER 18
MIKI
THE FOLLOWING DAY – SEXTING

Eilidh was true to her word and sent over her files as soon as she got home last night. And Marko and I had spent a few hours going through them.

The video surveillance from Mathieson's office hadn't yet provided us with anything useful. However, Marko had finally cracked the password to the hard drive we had copied, and we had unearthed some good stuff before we eventually fell asleep.

Despite the lack of hours in bed, I felt remarkably alert and cheery when I woke up. Partly because of the information we now had and partly at the prospect of seeing my Little Miss Red again tonight.

After a run, trip to the gym, shower, and breakfast, I reviewed everything again while Marko did some further digging into Mathieson's financials.

It turned out that Mathieson didn't just work for the Thomas gang as a defence lawyer; he helped run it! He and Gerry Thomas were partners. So, he wasn't just a very successful but shady criminal defence lawyer; he was implicit in a prominent drugs and people trafficking empire.

What a fucker!

Of course, I couldn't condemn him for dealing in drugs. After all, we dealt with drugs too; but at least we only dealt in Molly and coke now, and ours was quality stuff. The Thomas gang dealt in anything, and they didn't care about quality.

Worse than that, they brought girls in from eastern Europe, and forced them to work in their massage parlours and whore houses or sold them on to others. They were a nasty bunch, and he was the head.

That certainly solved the mystery of how a criminal defence lawyer, albeit a corrupt one, could afford the money it took to finance the attacks against my family and the Polish Mafia over the last few years.

My eyes narrowed and my mouth pulled into an evil grin as I mulled over the start of an idea.

I placed a call to my Cousin Viktor in the US and then after a quick chat; I rang Jim MacArthur and told him what I needed.

While I waited for them to get back to me, I drank a cup of coffee and let myself daydream for a few minutes.

Eilidh's face immediately came into my mind, and I smiled. I was so looking forward to seeing her again this evening.

Last night, we had made significant progress in our relationship, and I thought she'd started to trust me. I thoroughly enjoyed her company, and everything about her captivated me.

I'd been surprised she'd found Marko's tracker, intrigued that she had discovered who I was, and bloody impressed that she got a tracker on me without me even suspecting it. Throw in her safe breaking skills and my Little Miss Red was one hell of a woman.

Eilidh's commitment to her investigation, the thoroughness of her planning, and her ingenuity reminded me of, well, of me. She was the perfect match for me. Of course, I needed to convince her of that.

Checking my watch, I saw it was nearly time for her shift to be over.

She should have received the flowers I sent to her work by now. I hoped she liked them. They were part of my plan to woo her, but I'd also sent them to the station deliberately because I wanted her colleagues to know that Eilidh was no longer alone.

My sexy detective needed backup, and I was going to provide it, however I could.

Grabbing my phone, I typed out a quick text to her.

"Did you get the roses?"

A few minutes later, my phone vibrated in response.

"Yes. They are beautiful. Thank you."

Smiling, I text another message.

"What time are you coming over tonight?"
"When do you want me?"
"Immediately and preferably naked in my bed!"

The little dots moved, and I waited with bated breath for her reply. Excitement coursed through me. This was fun.

"Are you planning on using your belt again? And will you be wearing your balaclava this time?"

I read the reply and burst out laughing as I imagined her amused expression as she'd typed that out.

"Not unless you're naughty. And only if you want me to."

The dots moved again, then stopped, then moved again.

God, I hoped I hadn't scared her off... Nah, don't be stupid. Had I?

Finally, her reply came, and I breathed a sigh of relief.

"Into spanking, are you?"

She'd added the wink emoji.

Oh, did she like that idea? Was she into it?

I liked that idea. My cock thickened at the thought. Oh yes. I could definitely be in to that.

Shit, what should I say? *Think, man!*

"I could be. LOL."

"Ooh, now I'm wondering what else you might be into."

This really was fun.

"We'll have to explore the possibilities."

There was no reply.

Was that too much? Should I call her?

God, I was out of practise with flirting.

Not that I'd ever flirted via text before. This was all new to me.

Eilidh had a way of bringing out the lighter side to my character that I'd thought I'd buried with my parents when I'd taken over as pakhan. There had been no time for light-hearted fun since then, and certainly no time for flirting.

The few relationships I'd had over the last five years had been more like business arrangements for mutual convenience and based entirely on sex.

I had a few ladies I contacted when I had an itch to scratch, and a bit of do-it-yourself wouldn't suffice and in return, they enjoyed some no strings attached fun. However, we didn't date; we didn't flirt and we sure as heck didn't sext.

A short while later, my phone vibrated again. *Finally!* Disappointment flooded me as I read the message.

"Sorry, something's come up. I've got to go. I'll get back to you."

Damn it! I'd really been enjoying myself. Oh well, it couldn't be helped.

"Okay. Be careful!"

Little Miss Red sent a thumbs up, and the conversation was over.

Vlad entered the suite at that point.

"Who's on Eilidh?" I asked.

"Boris," he replied.

Good, Boris was an excellent tracker, almost as good as Trigger and Vlad. He'd ensure Eilidh stayed safe while she was at work.

Or he had better. If anything happened to my sexy detective while he or any of my men were supposed to be taking care of her, I'd kill them.

The phone rang, disturbing my thoughts. It was Viktor. He provided me with the information I'd been looking for.

A few minutes after I'd hung up on him, Jim rang.

"Did you get me someone?" I asked him.

"Yeah, one of my guys is in the lobby with him now, if you want to go talk to him," he said.

"Do you trust him?"

"Normally I wouldn't trust any of the Thomas gang, but

they killed his brother a couple of weeks ago and he's out for revenge. I'd say this plan of yours will be exactly what he's looking for. Add some cash into the mix and I'm pretty sure he'd be more than happy to agree."

"Great. I'll be in touch," I told him before hanging up and heading for the lift.

The guy was indeed happy to sell his gang out for revenge, and I was more than happy to exploit the fact. As I watched him leave the hotel with Jim's man, I grinned.

Finally, things were coming together.

CHAPTER 19
EILIDH

Biting my bottom lip to contain my grin, I read Miki's text.

Who knew my Mr Sexy Lips would be the type to sext?

We were having fun, and things were getting interesting when the Sarge shouted.

"Eilidh, you're with me. There's been a fatal stabbing over in the East End."

My mood plummeted.

Damn it! Seriously?

The shift was nearly over, and I'd already completed my paperwork. I was supposed to be heading to Miki's later tonight to discuss all of our information. But after he'd started the texts that quickly turned into sexts, my lady parts were all hot and bothered, and I was ready to head over there the minute I was free and explore some of those possibilities he'd just hinted at.

"Hurry up!" the Sarge shouted again.

Shit!

Why me? I pouted in annoyance. He usually partnered with Steve.

This was so unfair.

After sending a quick message to let Miki know the situation, I grabbed my stuff and ran to catch up with the Sarge.

"Where's Steve?" I asked as we headed to the location.

"He had to pick up his kid from school. His wife's sick," he replied.

Great! That explained why I got the privilege of staying late. Oh joy! As if the day hadn't been long enough.

I creaked my neck and rubbed it. My shoulders ached with tension, and I badly needed to relax. Preferably with a sexy Russian man with a body to die for and lips that could almost make me come just by thinking about them. A rush of liquid in my knickers was a testament to that.

Oops! This was hardly the time or the place to get horny.

Get a grip, Eilidh! I chided myself. I had to stay alert and not let thoughts of Miki distract me. Not when I was with one of the bastards I was investigating. Things were hard enough as it was.

My thoughts drifted back to the day I'd just had.

Spending almost all the shift in a car with Martin had been awful, so when we'd returned to the station to finish our paperwork; I was so bloody relieved.

I'd been hyperaware of everything he'd said and did all day, looking for clues in his behaviour which would let me know if he really was aware of my investigation.

Martin had looked at me a lot and flirted outrageously. None of which was unusual.

Although nothing in his demeanour hinted at him knowing what I was up to, the tension I felt in his presence made me ill.

Every second with the guy was torture. My nerves were frayed from trying to appear normal and not show how much I longed to hit the fuck over the head with my baton.

When I approached my desk and saw the enormous bouquet

of red roses that awaited me, it was just the distraction I'd needed.

As I read the card that was with it, I couldn't contain my grin.

Roy, the slimy toad, slithered up to my side.

"Someone's got an admirer!" he said, and attempted to read the card, but I slipped it into my pocket before he could.

Ignoring him, I bent and sniffed the flowers. Their fragrance calmed me.

"So, who's my rival?" Martin asked, in a tone that made my eyes shoot to his face.

There was a glint in his eye that hinted at jealousy, but the smile on his face was pleasant. I thought I must have been mistaken when he waggled his eyebrows.

Martin had enough women falling at his feet. He was a player. He wouldn't care that I wasn't interested in him, and he certainly wouldn't give two hoots if someone was interested in me. Or at least that was what I told myself.

"Well, are you going to tell us who they're from?" Roy asked, standing close enough to make me feel uncomfortable.

Roy often invaded my personal space. He had done it since I was a child, and I was used to it. It had never bothered me before.

After all, we'd been close, and he'd always acted like the doting uncle as I grew up. Swinging me around, lifting me onto his shoulders, giving me piggyback rides and stuff like that when I was really young.

Then, as I got older, he would put his arm around me or give me a peck on the forehead whenever I visited. It had all felt natural enough then. Now, after seeing the picture of the young woman in that passport, it gave me the bloody creeps.

"No," I said, moving away from him.

After that, I'd taken my notebook out and got started on my paperwork, ignoring everyone until Miki messaged.

The sexting had been another great distraction from the presence of the men I'd grown to despise.

However, here I was again, stuck with one of them.

At least he didn't flirt with me like Martin did or get in my personal space like Roy. He was also quiet. The Sarge wasn't one for small talk and I was glad about that.

As we reached the scene of the stabbing and he strutted around giving orders to the uniformed officers and our forensic team, I was struck by how good at his job he actually was, and I fucking hated him for it.

A cop who was as good as him shouldn't be corrupt.

To be honest, all of my colleagues were good at their jobs, which was probably how they could hide their corruption so well for all of these years.

However, the Serge had a certain flair about him that always reminded me of one of those detectives off the telly from years ago. Columbo, he was called. My dad had liked him.

It galled me that men who should have remained on the right side of the law had not only gone bad but had likely been involved in the murder of their friend and colleague who hadn't.

Every day, it got harder not to confront these bastards. I was desperate to let them know I knew what slimy toads they were. But I couldn't. Not yet.

Not just because of the danger I'd put myself in. But if I disclosed what I knew, they could destroy the evidence before an official investigation could take place.

Then it would be my word against theirs. Me, the newbie detective with unresolved issues over my dad's murder, against four seasoned and respected officers. Nobody would believe me, and I'd lose everything, but most of all, I'd lose the chance of justice for my dad. Possibly even my life.

So, I kept my anger wrapped tightly in a ball in the pit of my stomach and got on with my job.

When we finally finished, it was one o'clock in the morning and I was completely shattered. I'd sent a text to Miki earlier to say I'd no idea what time I'd be done, and I'd see him tomorrow night instead.

My eyelids were heavy, my neck ached, and my movements were sluggish as I climbed into my car and headed home with only one thought in my head: sleep.

Despite it being the end of August, it was pitch black and raining heavily by the time I got home, and I hurried inside. As I took off my jacket and went to hang it up, something hit me on the back of the head. The force of the blow made me dizzy, and I cried out in pain as I staggered and fell, hitting the ground with a thud that jarred my whole body, and suddenly everything went black.

CHAPTER 20
MIKI

After Eilidh text again to say she was still stuck at work and wouldn't be over tonight, I dragged myself to bed filled with disappointment.

Unable to settle, I tossed and turned for a while before giving up on sleep.

Although I knew Eilidh wouldn't be finished working until very late and had to get up early again tomorrow, I needed to see her. She might not have come to me tonight, but I intended to go to her. I wanted her in my arms again, even if it was only to sleep.

It was crazy how quickly the sexy detective had got under my skin, but nothing felt right without her.

When I'd seen the way Romi and Glowacki had looked at their brides with love in their eyes, I'd been admittedly jealous. I'd thought I would never be lucky enough to feel that way.

Yet in just a few short days, here I was smitten with a woman who should be my enemy but was instead my obsession. A woman I believed was my future.

There were still obstacles in our way, secrets that could

make or break us, but I held on to the hope that we'd work it all out.

Loving Eilidh was a risk, but it was one I couldn't stop myself from taking. Trusting her with the secrets of my life, however, was a different matter. I couldn't risk the repercussions to my family, and my Brotherhood, if she betrayed me.

I'd need to tread carefully, continue to build her trust and gain her loyalty. Then, when I was sure she had developed genuine feelings for me, I would tell her who I was.

Being pakhan was my birthright, and I tried to be a good one, but it wasn't who I wanted to be. Once she knew me better, and understood me more, I hoped my criminal side would be easier for her to accept. Especially when she saw the effort I was putting in to change things for the better.

Considering her colleagues were corrupt and her world was no longer as black and white as it had been, I believed she wouldn't be as averse to being with me as she would have been if we'd met under any other circumstances.

Of course, if we had, a relationship with us would never have had the chance to begin, so I guessed I should almost be grateful to the corrupt bastards.

"She's on the move!" Marko shouted from his own room.

I opened the tracking app to watch the little dot.

"See you tomorrow," I shouted back as I grabbed my jacket and car keys.

I'd already dismissed Boris earlier, and he was now back at the hotel and asleep. There had seemed no reason to have him wait to tail her home when I planned to meet her there, anyway.

The other guys were off duty too, so it would just be me and my Little Miss Red, and that was how I wanted it.

Smiling, I wondered how Little Miss Red would react when I turned up unexpectedly again.

I checked the little dot. She was closer to her house than I was, but I expected I'd get there just moments after she did. Then we'd have the rest of the night together.

My cock perked up at that thought, but it would need to bloody well behave itself. If Eilidh was exhausted, I would be content just holding her as she slept, but if she was up for more, I'd be happy with that too. I'd take whatever I could get. So long as I was with her.

Wind buffeted the car and rain battered against the windscreen as I sped towards Eilidh's house. It was exhilarating. Excitement coursed through me the nearer I got to her home. I couldn't wait to see my sexy detective.

However, as soon as I left the motorway, I ended up stuck on the slip road behind a line of traffic.

There had been an accident and the only thing I could do was wait for it to be cleared.

Damn it!

As I sat there impatiently tapping my fingers on the wheel, Marko called.

"I just got an alert. Someone's inside Eilidh's house!" he said.

"I'm pulling up the feed now."

"It's just one guy. He's tearing the place apart, obviously searching for something."

"Shit! I'll call and warn her. I'm near her house but stuck in traffic. I don't know when I'll get there. Keep watching and keep me informed," I said before switching lines and ringing Eilidh's mobile.

It rang, then went to voicemail.

Shit, shit, shit!

I tried again.

Pick up Eilidh! Please, baby!

"Fuck!" I cried in frustration when it went to voicemail once more.

I doubted she would hear it before she got out of her car, but I left a frantic message, anyway.

"Eilidh, don't go into your house; someone is there. Stay away! I'm on my way to your place now. Wait for me!"

My stomach churned with worry as I watched the little dot on my screen get closer to its destination.

My heart pounded and sweat coated my body as I waited for the last of the cars to be loaded onto a breakdown truck.

It was taking too bloody long.

Come on! I shouted and banged the palm of my hand into the steering wheel in anger.

As the little dot moved closer to Eilidh's street, bile rose in my throat as I realised I might not get there until too late.

My agitation grew as the seconds ticked by. All the while, Marko gave me a running commentary on her intruder.

"He's pouring petrol all over," he cried.

Fuck, he was going to torch her house!

And Eilidh was almost home. If she ran into the intruder, anything could happen.

God, I felt bloody helpless being unable to warn her. I was going insane sitting there when finally, the line of traffic started moving again.

As soon as I was passed the accident, I overtook the few cars in front and put my foot down.

"She's just parked outside the house now," Marko informed me.

Don't go in, baby! Check your messages first! Please, please check them! I pleaded, as if she might just be able to hear my subliminal messages. Or maybe somehow the universe would step in and help.

Neither happened.

"Shit! The bastard just hit her with something. She's been knocked out!" Marko shouted.

My heart stuttered, then pounded hard against my ribs and I roared in fury.

"I'll be there in a few minutes," I screamed down the phone.

Rage filled my veins. This guy was a dead man. I was going to fucking kill him.

"He's gone. The fire brigade and an ambulance are on the way," Marko said as I screeched to a halt outside my woman's home.

Darting towards the house, I saw that the fire had already taken hold. There were flames in the living room. I pushed open the front door and was immediately hit by the heat.

My eyes stung, and the smoke made me cough as I hurried over to Eilidh's crumpled form. Luckily, she was lying in the hallway near to the door. A coughing fit took me to my knees, but I managed to lift her up and stagger with her outside.

The first fire engine arrived just as I collapsed with her in my arms. The wind and rain hit us in the face, and she woke up coughing and wheezing.

Relief filled me as I hugged her to my chest. She was alive, but I couldn't believe how close that had been.

I brushed my lips against the top of her head and murmured.

"You're safe, baby. I've got you!"

Eilidh's body shivered, but she didn't seem to notice as she stared at the flames consuming her home.

After a few minutes, she started to cry. As my Little Miss Red sobbed her heart out, I held her close and vowed to find the bastard who'd done this and end his life.

Fury bubbled inside me, and I had to fight hard to keep a lid on it. I needed to be calm right now, for Eilidh's sake. She needed to know she could rely on me to protect her from now on. And protect her, I would.

CHAPTER 21
EILIDH
THE SAME MORNING – UP IN SMOKE

"You're safe, baby. I've got you," Miki murmured into the top of my head, brushing his lips against my hair.

His words broke through my daze, and the blood drained from my face.

They knew!

The bastards had found out I was on to them and tried to kill me. Just like they had killed my dad.

Suddenly, I was filled with a rage more powerful than anything I'd ever felt before, and I practically vibrated with anger.

These men needed to be stopped. They had to pay for their crimes.

Staring at my home being consumed by smoke as fire fighters tried to control the blaze, I vowed I would do whatever it took to make that happen. I wasn't even sure that I cared how they paid now; just that they did.

With a shaky hand, I touched the back of my head and winced as I felt the lump forming. I was going to have one heck of a headache later. But at least I was alive.

As I watched the firefighters from the second engine join the others, a feeling of utter despair hit me. My vision blurred as tears slowly ran down my cheeks.

My home was gone!

The place I'd grown up with my dad was in flames. All our stuff, all our memories, were going up in smoke.

A sob broke free as the floodgates opened.

Miki tightened his arms about me, hugging me close.

"You're safe now, baby. Let it all out," he murmured, stroking my hair in a soothing gesture.

So, I did.

Great sobs wracked my body and tears streamed down my face uncontrollably. There was no stopping them.

With every tear, my mind assaulted me with images of all my treasured memories being slowly destroyed by the flames. All I had left were the clothes on my back and they stunk of smoke and would likely not recover.

My world had been turned upside down when my dad had been murdered, but I'd clung to my life as an officer, my colleagues, especially Uncle Roy, and my treasured memories to get me through it all.

They'd been my lifeline when I'd felt like I was drowning. But over the last few weeks, bit by bit, that lifeline had been systematically destroyed, until there was nothing left.

As my sexy Russian's arms tightened around me, I realised that wasn't true. There was him. Held firmly in Miki's arms, I felt safe and no longer alone.

That thought helped, and my sobs quietened down to mere sniffles.

While I lay there in his arms, I was struck by the fact that if I hadn't decided to work with him and sent him copies of all the evidence I had collected, tonight all of my hard work would have been for nothing.

As it was, the only thing that had been lost was Martin's notebook. I hadn't had time to copy that properly and had planned on handing it over to Marko for him to decipher. I guessed we'd likely never know what all the information inside meant. But at least that was all the evidence we'd lost.

The paramedics arrived, and I didn't protest when Miki carried me to the ambulance. Inside, he kept me firmly on his lap as the medic examined me and again I didn't protest. After what had happened, I needed him close, and I could tell, by his reluctance to allow any distance between us, that he felt the same.

As the doors to the ambulance closed, I got one last look at what was left of my house and a fresh wave of sorrow washed over me as I mourned the loss of all I had ever known.

Miki was making soothing circle motions on my back that comforted me. Relaxing against his chest, the thought that my past had gone up in smoke, but my future held me firmly in his arms, entered my mind.

Wait, what? My future?

No, that was just my vulnerability talking. I still wasn't sure if we could be anything more than temporary.

However, one thing I was sure of was that he was here with me in the present, and I was comforted by that. In fact, as his warmth seeped into me, my body became aware of our closeness, and suddenly, and very inappropriately, perked up.

My nipples hardened through my soaked top and my core clenched.

Not the time, Eilidh!

My eyes felt puffy and sore, my head throbbed, my hair was a sodden mess and my clothes stunk of smoke.

Geez, I must look awful!

Not to mention the fact that I badly needed to blow my nose. Sniffing loudly really wasn't sexy at all.

And I hadn't even thanked Miki for saving me. He must think I'm an ungrateful bitch!

"Thank you," I whispered, looking up at him.

"No need to thank me, baby. I won't let anyone hurt you," he replied, and I believed him.

My sexy Russian leaned down and kissed me gently. This wasn't the usual devouring of my mouth. This was slow and sensual, and it made my toes curl and my core wet.

Oh, my!

If I thought I was in danger of falling for this guy before, now I knew it was too late. I'd been a fool to think this thing between us could ever be just sex. This went way beyond anything I'd ever felt before. That thought should worry me. But it didn't.

We were worlds apart, and I really didn't know how we could bridge that gap, or if it was even possible, but I refused to let that bother me right now.

I'd nearly died in that fire tonight, and so I planned on living for the moment. The future could take care of itself. What would be, would be! For now, I was going to take my earlier advice and enjoy every moment I could with this man.

Reaching up, I stroked his cheek. Miki closed his eyes, leaned into my hand, and sighed. My heart clenched at the look of peace that settled on his face at my touch.

God, he was beautiful!

What Miki had been doing at my home tonight, I didn't know. I'd have to ask him about that later, but regardless of the reason, I was grateful he'd been there.

My Mr Sexy Lips had saved my life, and I would never forget that.

———

A short while later, I was dry and modelling one of the very stylish bottom, revealing hospital gowns that patients just loved to wear.

Luckily, apart from some smoke inhalation and the lump on my head, I was otherwise unscathed.

The doctor insisted I be admitted for observation in case of a concussion and, having nowhere else to go, I reluctantly agreed.

I'd need to sort out somewhere to stay and so many other things, but I'd deal with it when my head wasn't bloody splitting.

Miki had been checked over too, but was fine. Sitting on top of the hospital bed, I watched him pacing the floor as he spoke rapidly into his phone. His Russian voice, harsh but sexy, made me shiver in delight.

Mr Sexy Lips was used to being the boss. Anyone observing him like this couldn't fail to see that. He was powerful, handsome, strong, and sensual, and I longed to jump his bones.

Unfortunately, I didn't have the strength.

After I hung up on Marko, I turned to see Eilidh sitting staring at me.

"How are you doing, Little Miss Red?" I asked as I leaned over and kissed her forehead.

She smiled and chuckled.

"Like I've been hit over the back of the head and dragged from a burning building."

My heart clenched at her words, but at least she was attempting to joke about things now and wasn't sobbing her heart out like she had done earlier.

Luckily, she only had minor smoke inhalation and although she coughed quite a bit after I'd pulled her out of the fire and she'd woken up, it didn't seem to be an issue for her now.

However, I was concerned about her head injury.

The doctor was keeping her in the hospital for observation in case of a concussion and although he had wanted me to leave after an offer to provide a very substantial donation to the hospital; he agreed I could remain with her.

My stomach was still in knots over the whole situation, and I could only imagine what my poor Little Miss Red was feeling after losing her home. I was furious that those bastards she worked with had attempted to kill her.

When I'd called Marko, I told him to make sure they were being followed, and we'd got some of Jim MacArthur's men involved to help our guys. I was more determined than ever now to bring these fuckers down.

As soon as I knew Eilidh was okay and I'd got her out of here, I'd step up my plans to do just that.

There was a knock on the door and a couple of young, uniformed police officers came in.

After introducing themselves, they separated us to take our statements. I didn't like it, but since we remained in the same room and I didn't need to let my Little Miss Red out of my sight, I didn't protest.

Because of the nature of the attack, they had wanted to post a uniformed officer outside her room to stand guard just in case the person came back to finish the job. I refused. The thought of any police officer keeping watch over her while she slept filled me with dread. She wasn't safe with any of them because we didn't know who could be trusted.

Glancing at Eilidh, I saw her gulp. She was likely thinking the same thing.

"No need, I'll remain with her, and I will post one of my own men outside," I stated. I'd planned to do that all along anyhow.

Naturally, they weren't happy with that at first, but when Eilidh agreed, they capitulated and left.

"I will keep you safe, Eilidh," I said.

"I know you will," she replied and stood up to embrace me.

My heart swelled with pride knowing that she trusted me, and I hugged her tightly.

Not long after, Marko and Vlad arrived.

"This is Vlad, my bodyguard," I said, introducing him.

"Nice to meet you," Eilidh said with a small smile.

Vlad kept his usual stoic expression firmly in place, but he gave her a slight nod of acknowledgement.

Marko, on the other hand, smiled widely when he saw her.

"You gave us all quite a scare, Little Miss Red," he said.

"Tell me about it," I mumbled, sitting down next to Eilidh on the bed.

She smirked at me, and my heart clenched.

"Why were you at my house tonight?" she finally asked.

"I needed to see you. I couldn't wait any longer," I replied truthfully.

A slow grin spread across her face, and she blushed.

It was cute, and I couldn't resist leaning down to capture her lips.

"Oh, here we go again!"

The sound of Marko's snigger and a grunt, which I was sure came from Vlad, was accompanied by the loud clearing of a throat.

A middle-aged nurse stood at the bottom of the bed with a tray in hand and an expression that could freeze hell.

"This is a hospital, not a hotel. Perhaps you can leave the kissing until a more appropriate time and place," the prudish old bird said in a haughty tone.

Biting back a smirk, I got up and moved to stand beside Marko.

Eilidh's cheeks flamed with embarrassment, but her eyes were filled with mirth as she took the pain medication the nurse gave her.

The second the old prude left, we all burst into laughter. Even Vlad sniggered before his face settled back into the poker face he usually wore.

Laughing made Eilidh wince in pain and I rushed back to her side.

"You need to rest, baby," I told her as I adjusted her pillows behind her back to make her more comfortable.

The guys said goodbye to Eilidh and left the room. Marko was returning to the hotel to get back to work, but Vlad would remain here with us.

Eilidh had removed her wet clothing earlier and was now in one of those flattering hospital gowns, but I hadn't bothered with that. There was no way I was flashing my arse off in one of those things, but I'd enjoyed the few glimpses I'd got of Eilidh's. However, my clothes still stunk of smoke, so after the guys left, I popped into the little ensuite to change.

When I was done, Little Miss Red was just dropping off to sleep, and I had just settled into the chair beside her bed when the door burst open, and her corrupt partner, Martin Johnson, barged in.

We'd never met, of course, but I recognised him right away as I'd studied the photographs of all her colleagues to make sure I knew exactly who they were.

Eilidh roused as the fucker ignored me and sat in the chair on the opposite side of her bed. I barely held back my anger as I watched him to see what the fuck he was up to.

If he tried to hurt her, I would gladly murder the bastard. The only thing that stopped me from doing just that right now was that it was a hospital, so I gripped the sides of my chair and imagined it was his neck instead.

"Eilidh, sweetheart, I just heard from the uniforms that someone attacked you and torched your home. Are you alright?" he said, oozing false charm. He hugged her quickly, then moved away but kept hold of her hand.

My eyes narrowed, and I glared at him, daring to touch my woman. If he didn't remove his hand from hers this instant, I was going to rip the fucking thing off.

"I'm fine, thanks," she said, tugging her hand away.

"When they release you, come to stay with me until you get things sorted out," he told her, sitting on the bed beside her and continuing to ignore my presence.

Who the hell did this arsehole think he was?

"I'll take good care of you and keep you safe," he murmured before reaching his hand towards her face.

That was it!

I'd had enough. I shot to my feet. The movement finally drawing his attention.

"She will stay with me," I stated, keeping my tone controlled even though I wanted to strangle him. How dare the slimy creature put his hands on my woman?

This is a hospital, and he is still a police officer, I kept telling myself, trying to remain calm.

"Oh, and who are you?" the cocky bastard asked.

Eilidh was about to say something, but I jumped in before she could reply.

"Her boyfriend."

Eilidh's eyes flicked my way, and a look of shock crossed her face before she quickly hid it. Johnson didn't notice as he was too busy looking me up and down, a look of contempt on his face.

"Her boyfriend?" he asked, sneering at me in disbelief.

"Yes, that's right, he is," Eilidh smiled up at me long enough to ensure that Johnson noticed before turning her head towards him.

"So, you see, I am perfectly well looked after and quite safe. Thank you for coming to see me, Martin, but you can go home now. I'm fine," she told him before yawning widely.

"Yes, she is fine but tired and needs to rest, so as Eilidh said, you can leave now. Thanks for coming," I said through clenched teeth as I stepped over to the door and opened it for him, making it clear it was time for him to go.

"Are you the one who sent the roses?" he asked.

"Yes," I replied, lifting my chin in a silent challenge.

Huffing out a breath, he sneered again.

I moved towards him, ready to punch him in the mouth, but Vlad took that moment to step into view. He shook his head at me, and I forced myself to rein in my temper.

I'd deal with this prick another time.

Dismissing me, he turned his head back towards Eilidh.

"You know where I am if you need me," he told her, then thankfully left, glaring at me as he went.

Standing in the doorway, my hands tightly fisted, I watched him leave, and made myself a silent promise to myself that the next time we met, he wouldn't survive to walk away.

"It's a good job I got back in time, or we'd be having to explain why you'd killed a cop," Vlad said. "You're not normally so easily riled," he observed quietly.

Pushing a hand through my hair, I huffed out an annoyed breath. Vlad was right. I rarely ever lost my cool. Or at least not with anyone other than my siblings and Romi, but the events of the evening had taken its toll. I was exhausted, stressed and downright pissed, not to mention still suffering from the aftereffects of the terror I'd felt at almost losing Eilidh.

"The hospital shop only had pyjamas, but the ones I got should fit," Vlad said, handing me a bag.

"Go in to your woman and get some rest. I've got your back."

Nodding in gratitude, I left him sitting on a chair directly outside the room and closed the door.

"Boyfriend, huh?"

Eilidh asked with a smirk.

"Oh, I intend to be your boyfriend, Little Miss Red. In fact, I intend to be a lot more," I said, stalking towards her with a wicked grin.

"I intend to be your everything," I told her as I gently took her head in my hands.

Careful to avoid her sore spot, I kissed her. She moaned, and I climbed onto the bed with her. Stretching out beside her, we hugged and kissed until my cock threatened to burst out of my pants.

I was desperate to take her right there and then, but she was injured and exhausted and so finally I reluctantly pulled away. Eilidh tried to cling to me, but I gently remove her hands from me and stood.

"You need to sleep, baby."

"What about you?" she asked.

"I'll sleep in the chair," I told her, sitting back in the chair I'd settled in before.

"Why don't you come and lie here beside me?" she said.

Scooting over, she made room for me and patted the space.

"Come on. I'll rest better if your with me. Please?" she said with a mischievous pout.

How could I refuse?

It was a narrow single hospital bed, but I didn't mind getting up close and personal with my Little Miss Red, so I agreed.

Eilidh lay down and moved onto her side, and I pressed myself behind her, holding her close. She let out a satisfied sigh, and I smiled. This was the way I wanted things to be from now on.

"I can't believe that asshole came to see me!" she said.

"It had to be him, one of my other colleagues, or perhaps that man he was talking to the other night, who attacked me at the house."

I tensed.

"What man?"

She mumbled, "Shit," under her breath.

"Eilidh, what haven't you told me?" I asked through gritted teeth.

With a sigh, she relayed the story about following Martin and the conversation she'd heard with the mystery man.

Now I knew what had prompted her change of heart about working with me and exchanging information.

"You should have told me," I told her firmly.

"I know, but I wasn't sure if I could truly trust you at that time, or if my being in danger would really matter to you," she said.

Fuck!

"Eilidh, you being in danger very much matters to me. *You* matter to me! And you can trust me, I swear."

I turned her face toward me.

"Is there anything else you need to tell me?" I asked gently.

She shook her head.

"Good. You are special, Eilidh," I said, watching as her eyes widened, then she gulped and licked her bottom lip.

"I know we have only known each other for a short time, and we still have a lot to learn about one another, but I already have feelings for you. I've never felt as connected to anyone as I do to you, and I want very much to see where this relationship between us can go."

Little Miss Red blinked a few times. I hadn't wanted to lay all my cards on the table just yet, but I couldn't seem to stop myself as I stared into her eyes.

"Eilidh, I want a chance to really be with you. Is that something you would like?" I asked, holding my breath as I waited for her to respond.

"Yes," she said, smiling shyly.

Yes! I felt like leaping up and shouting for joy but refrained and settled for grinning at her instead.

"Good, and tomorrow, when you are feeling better, I'm

going to show you exactly how I feel about you. But for now, you need to rest. We both do," I said, leaning over to brush a light kiss on her forehead.

Turning her back around, I settled in behind her again.

"Sleep, sweetheart."

Nodding, she snuggled close and after a few minutes, her breathing changed, and she drifted off as I held her tight.

CHAPTER 23
EILIDH
STILL THAT MORNING – IN HOSPITAL

My eyes flickered and slowly opened. Light filtered in from the window, illuminating the room in a soft glow.

The back of my skull ached and something heavy was wrapped around my waist. No, not something; someone. Miki.

His big body was spooning me from behind.

Lying there in the warmth of his embrace, I listened to his soft snores as he slept. It was comforting. I wouldn't mind waking up this way every morning.

After everything he said last night, it seemed that we were both feeling exactly the same about each other, and that gave me a warm glow inside.

We had a lot to talk about and a lot to find out about each other, and I wasn't sure how easy things were going to be for us, but knowing we both felt so strongly about each other had me believing that whatever was ahead for us, we would deal with it, together.

Just lying here made me feel protected and cared for, and I loved that feeling.

The uncomfortable sensation of a full bladder made me

grimace. I really needed to pee. Unwilling to move because I didn't want to wake Miki and break the spell I was under in his arms, I clamped my thighs together tighter. I didn't want to face the day ahead. Not yet.

My home had been destroyed, I had no place to live, my colleagues likely wanted to kill me and all I had to my name was a phone, which had thankfully been in my suit pocket and not my jacket.

At least I had insurance. Although that couldn't replace the loss of my personal items and memories, it meant I wasn't totally destitute.

Sighing, I felt the weight of it all pressing on me as badly as my bladder was.

Trying my best not to disturb Miki, I reached a hand up and gingerly touched the back of my head. It was still swollen, but it wasn't pounding this morning, so the few hours of sleep I'd had, and the pain medication, had done the trick. For now. I expected it would bother me again soon enough. However, I'd take a headache and a bit of smoke inhalation over the alternative.

If Miki hadn't got me out, I'd be dead. My insides felt queasy just thinking about it. With everything I'd lost, it might not seem it, but I was lucky to be alive. So, as soon as I could rally my spirits enough, I'd need to sort things out. Some clothes and somewhere to stay would be the first things, but it was obvious from my near escape that I needed protection, too.

Miki would help with that for now, I supposed, and while that thought made me grateful, it also concerned me. Dad had encouraged me to be independent, and I wasn't used to relinquishing control to someone else. If this whole thing had taught me anything, it was that I had to be careful who I trusted.

My sexy Russian wanted us to build a relationship together and, as vulnerable and exhausted as I was last night, I'd happily agreed. But now, in the cold light of day, I questioned the hastiness of my decision.

Oh, I still wanted to give us a shot. I mean, the guy was rich, sexy as hell, and had just saved my life. Of course, I wanted to give us a shot. However, I reminded myself that he was still hiding things from me and even if I thought I could trust him, my judgement had been impaired before.

After all, I had trusted Roy all my life, and then my colleagues, without ever thinking I couldn't, and I had been so wrong. What if I was wrong now? I could be mistaken about my feelings and letting my lust for Miki cloud my judgement because I felt scared and alone. What if whatever he was hiding made him as bad as Roy and the others? Or, god forbid, worse?

No, despite everything, I didn't believe that.

My only actual concern was if I could handle Miki's truth.

Miki exuded power and danger and while that should have put me off him, instead, I found it drew me more to him. I thought about how well he'd handled the police, the doctor, and then Martin.

The man was an obvious leader and with the criminal vibe and the Russian accent; I was still definitely leaning towards him, being a member of the Bratva. Maybe even a high-up member. The star on the wolf's collar of his tattoo certainly suggested a link to the Bratva at least.

Lying there in his embrace, I mulled that idea over in my head.

Could I really be with him if that was true?

The thought certainly wasn't as off-putting as it would have been just a few short weeks ago. My belief in the police and law enforcement had been lost, and my view of the world had transformed.

After taking a walk on the wild side myself, him being a criminal didn't bother me so much. It was more the nature and extent of his activities that could be the problem. We'd need to talk about everything, and soon.

Something pressed into my back, and I realised Miki was sporting some serious morning wood. All thoughts of talking flew straight out of my mind for more pleasurable thoughts.

Thinking of our first time together and the amazing orgasms he'd given me made my nipples tighten and my pussy clench. God, I wanted him badly.

Remembering how he'd tied me to the bed and taken control of my body, I bit back a giggle. I'd loved being at his mercy. It was a complete, and yet unexpected, turn on for me. I hadn't thought I'd enjoy being submissive in bed, but his dominance did it for me and I needed more of it. A lot more.

Maybe we could try that during the sexy exploring he'd promised me. I giggled and my bladder threatened to burst.

Oh oh!

Unable to hold off peeing any longer, I wriggled out of Miki's arms, and ran towards the toilet with a hand clamped tightly between my legs.

"Sweetheart, where are you going?" he asked in a sleepy voice that sent shivers of desire down my spine.

"For a pee!" I cried, giggling as I made it to the ensuite just in time.

CHAPTER 24
MIKI

Movement woke me as Eilidh slipped out of my arms.

"Sweetheart, where are you going?" I asked, trying to shake the last remnants of sleep as I sat up.

"For a pee!" she cried, giggling as she ran to the toilet.

My cock was already hard from having been pressed against her all night, and the sexy sound of her giggle went straight to my loins. Fuck!

Down, boy! Not here! I told it as I climbed out of bed and stretched.

When Eilidh returned, I grabbed her and gave her a long, lingering kiss. My cock might not be about to get any action, but my tongue hadn't got the memo.

A feminine chuckle alerted me to the fact we were no longer alone, and I reluctantly broke off the kiss. Vlad stood in the doorway with a young woman carrying a tray of food. He smirked at me as I helped Eilidh back onto the bed so she could eat her breakfast.

"I'll nip downstairs and get us something," Vlad told me.

"Can I get you anything, Eilidh?" he asked.

"No, thank you," she said, looking shocked that he bothered to ask her.

He nodded and turned to leave.

"Actually, a latte would be nice. If that's okay?" she called after him.

"No problem. I'll get you a strong one. You're going to need to develop a strong coffee habit if you are going to put up with Miki," he said, winking at her.

I huffed in annoyance as he left, but the grin she sent him secretly warmed me. In his own way, Vlad just let us know he expected her to stick around, and that he approved.

As his pakhan I didn't need his approval, he was loyal, and I knew he would follow me no matter what, even if he disagreed with me, but as a friend and someone I considered family, I enjoyed having his approval, nevertheless.

A few minutes later, the two uniformed officers who'd taken our statements stopped by again to check on Eilidh before they finished their shift and brought disturbing news. Martin Johnson's police warrant card was found partially burnt in the hallway of Eilidh's house. Other uniformed officers had gone to his home to question him, but he wasn't there, and he had failed to turn up at work this morning.

That cocky bastard had been the one who tried to kill my woman. And now he was on the run. Fuck, I should have given in to the urge to strangle him while I could.

Damn it to hell! Well, he'd get what was coming to him. I'd bloody well make sure of it!

***

It was early afternoon when the doctor discharged Eilidh from the hospital, and I took her back to my hotel.

We'd discussed it and she'd agreed staying with me was the

best thing for her right now, especially with Johnson being missing.

That solved one of her issues. Next, we needed to tackle her lack of clothing.

She was wearing the pyjamas and slippers Vlad had bought at the hospital shop, but we needed to get her some proper clothes. Not that having my Little Miss Red naked and in my suite would be a problem for me, but I suspected it might be for her. So, I asked the receptionist to call a local department store and arrange for one of their personal shoppers to contact us.

As soon as we were in the suite, Eilidh turned on her phone and she saw all the missed calls and my voicemail. Her eyebrows raised in question as she listened to my frantic message.

"I'll explain after we eat," I told her.

As we ate the sandwiches I'd ordered from room service, the personal shopper called. I told her what was needed then sent her Eilidh's measurements and a picture.

"How am I going to pay for this?" my Little Miss Red asked, sounding worried when I finished explaining to the shopper what was required.

"You're not. I am," I told her as I took another bite.

"Erm, no. You can't buy me an entire wardrobe," Eilidh stated incredulously.

"Hmm hmm," I said around a mouth full of sandwich. Of course, I was buying them.

"Erm, no you can't," she said, sounding frustrated.

"Can and I will," I mumbled between bites, and tried to keep from smirking. God, she was sexy when she was all riled up.

Of course, she was sexy all the time, I thought as I took in how she sat glaring at me with her hands on her hips.

When I said nothing and just continued to finish my sandwich, she huffed out a breath.

"You're infuriating!"

With a wink, I grinned at her. I'd been told that a lot. Especially by my siblings. I was used to getting my way, so she'd need to get used to that.

"Okay, I tell you what. You can loan me the money until I get a payment through from the insurance company. Then I'm paying you back." She stated like it was a done deal.

Smiling in amusement, I let her think she'd won the argument.

There was no way I would accept the money back, but she didn't need to know that right now. My woman was independent, so getting used to being looked after would take her some time. However, I intended to ensure that she was thoroughly looked after in every way so she would indeed get used to it.

"Whatever you say, sweetheart," I said before pulling her off her seat and on to my lap.

After a long and extremely enjoyable kiss, I stood up and set her on her feet.

As much as I wanted to continue kissing her, and a lot more, we had stuff to do before I could indulge myself.

My unruly cock jerked in protest, but I ignored him. There'd be time for him to have his fun later.

"Go call your insurance company and then we will talk about everything else," I said, patting her bum as she took her phone and headed to the sofa.

Looking over her shoulder, she threw me a saucy wink and emphasised her wiggle.

I laughed at her antics. It was good to hear the sound. I didn't laugh as much as I would like to these days because the pressures of my responsibilities weighed me down. Eilidh's mere presence lightened my world, and I loved her for it.

As Eilidh talked with her insurance company, I went to speak with Marko, who'd moved into the suite next door with Vlad and our other guys so I could be alone with Eilidh in ours.

———

A short while later, I returned to our rooms filled with anticipation. My plan was coming together, and it was time to involve my Little Miss Red.

She was just hanging up on a call when I entered.

"Did you get everything sorted out?" I asked.

"Yes, it will take a while for the claim to go through, but they didn't foresee any problems. I also called the bank. They will issue me with a new card and arrange for me to get some emergency cash," she said, smiling when I wrapped my arms around her.

"Good. Well, let me know if you need my help with anything," I said, leading her over to the sofa.

"It's time to talk, sweetheart."

Settling into the seat with my arm around her shoulders, I told Eilidh everything Marko had learned about Mathieson's involvement in human trafficking, and how he was the actual leader behind the Thomas gang.

That knowledge was as much of a shock to her as it had been for us.

We also discussed what she'd found and my belief that each of the corrupt bastards were keeping files on the others, as none of them really trusted each other. There was no loyalty between their kind, and that made them unpredictable, but it also meant they could be used against one another if needed. However, it looked like we'd be able to take all the bastards down together, and that was the plan.

The informant from the Thomas gang had told me their next batch of trafficked girls would be due in four days at an old factory in the Govan area of Glasgow. Some girls would be selected to remain in Scotland, and the others would be split up and sent elsewhere.

Apparently, during the handover, Mathieson himself would be there to inspect the cargo along with the four corrupt officers from the CID.

"Bloody pigs!" Eilidh exclaimed.

"I can't believe anyone could treat another human being like property to be bought and sold," she said, shaking her head in disgust.

"I agree."

"Do you think Martin will be there, even though he's in hiding now?" she asked.

"Yes, human trafficking was a lucrative business, and I doubt he will want to miss out on his share of the proceeds. Especially now that he's on the run and will probably need all the money he can get," I replied.

Even if Johnson was planning to leave the country, which I expected him to do, I imagined the cocky bastard would likely stick around to exploit one last opportunity to make some money.

My Cousin Viktor in New York had a friend who gave him the details of an Interpol officer who wasn't corrupt, and I intended to use him to create a sting operation. With Eilidh's colleagues taking part in the trafficking and hopefully Mathieson there too, they could all be caught in the one trap.

"And you trust this Interpol officer?" Eilidh asked, chewing on her lip.

"My cousin vouched for him, so yes, I do."

She nodded.

"So, the plan is to involve Interpol, get them to arrange a sting to intercept a human trafficking handover, and in the process, catch the Thomas gang, Mathieson, and Roy and the others red-handed?" Eilidh asked as she summarised things.

"Yes."

My sexy detective grinned.

"And on top of that, we get to stop a major human trafficking ring?" Eilidh asked, sounding impressed.

"We do," I confirmed, grinning back.

"Brilliant plan," she said, beaming at me, and I couldn't stop my chest from puffing up a bit at her approval.

Stopping a human trafficking gang was definitely a tremendous bonus. However, the icing on the cake was that by taking out one of Jim MacArthur's biggest rivals and thus removing a thorn from his side, he would owe me, and that would be a benefit during our future negotiations.

After Interpol had caught the traffickers, they would investigate everyone involved further. Homes and offices would be searched, and all the other evidence of their crimes would be uncovered. Including the murder of Eilidh's dad and Timmy Neilson. Everyone involved would then go to jail for a very long time after that.

Or that's what I told Eilidh, anyway. What I didn't tell her was that they could all go to jail for all I cared except for Mathieson. He was mine.

Oh, and that bastard Johnson! I reminded myself. I wanted him too.

The exact details of how I would grab them were still being worked out, but basically I would do it during the chaos caused when Interpol arrived.

When summarised, the plan sounded simple. However,

these things rarely were. Nevertheless, I'd do everything I could to ensure it was.

The two guys with us, Boris and Akim, who were tailing Mathieson, would continue to do so to ensure that he did indeed go to the handover. If he changed his mind, we would need to be ready to grab him elsewhere.

My best friend Luca was driving up from London to join us, so he could help.

At the time of the operation, Eilidh would stay here with Marko and me where we could ensure her safety. Vlad and Luca would go to the handover site and grab Mathieson and Johnson, and they would then take them directly back to London to be kept at the C until I got home.

Marko had already contacted the Interpol officer anonymously and started the ball rolling.

As Bratva, the least involvement we had, the better. However, like my father before me, I was aware of how much easier it was to let others do my dirty work and get rid of my enemies when possible. Especially when those enemies were people whose disappearance or murder would draw too much unwanted attention.

That was why getting Interpol to deal with this for us was an ideal solution.

My brother had also hacked the phones of Eilidh's colleagues, and Vlad had placed trackers on their cars so we could monitor them until the operation took place.

So, the plan had been set in motion and all that was left was to finalise the intricacies.

Once we'd finished discussing what was in place so far, Eilidh's questioning of the night before began. Just as I'd suspected it would.

My Little Miss Red had stood up part of the way through her interrogation and now paced the floor. The pinched expression and annoyance in her eyes told me she was not amused by my actions.

"So, you're telling me you have been tracking my car, watching my home and had men trailing my every move, since you came to my home the other night?" she asked when I'd answered all her questions.

Holding my hands up in a placating gesture, I shrugged.

"Well, yes. But in my defence, I needed to ensure your safety," I said with a sheepish grin.

"Harrumph!" was the only response as she continued her pacing again.

Eilidh's fists opened and closed at her sides, and she mumbled under her breath.

I opened my mouth to placate her further, but then thought better of it. Instead, I kept my lips clamped firmly shut and let her work through her feelings over my intrusion into her life in her own time.

After a while, Eilidh turned to me, narrowed her eyes, and glared, then resumed her pacing once more.

Oh dear.

She really was pissed.

Mentally crossing my fingers, I hoped my Little Miss Red would get over it soon and realise that if I hadn't taken such liberties, she'd be dead right now.

Just as I thought that, she stopped, took a deep breath, and turned to face me again.

"Miki, I'm not happy that you did that. I don't like you spying on me, but I guess I should be grateful that you did," she sighed heavily.

"Just promise me you won't do it again," she stated more firmly this time.

Standing, I walked towards her and took her into my arms.

"I can't promise you that and I will not apologise for it.

Eilidh, you are important to me, and I will always do whatever it takes to keep you safe. You might not like that, but you need to accept it because that is how it is. My life is filled with danger and if you remain with me, then so will yours be, but trust me when I say I will die before I ever let anything happen to you," I told her truthfully.

Eilidh was in danger now, but she had to understand that being with me held an element of danger too, and so she would need to get used to being protected.

As she stared into my eyes, I held my breath and prayed she would accept my words.

I hadn't told her I was Bratva yet. That conversation was for another time, but she knew I was a criminal, and that life came with danger.

Eventually, she nodded her head, and I let out a relieved breath.

Thank god! We were one step closer to her, accepting me altogether.

Leaning down, I tilted her head up to me and captured her mouth. My 6 step plan to seduce my sexy detective was well under way and I would do everything I could to make sure step 6 came sooner rather than later.

Things were getting heated when Vlad came in and spoiled things as usual. That was becoming a habit, and I glared at him. He simply smirked and reminded me we had a meeting to get to.

Damn! Being a pakhan was a pain in the arse at times.

CHAPTER 25

EILIDH
THAT AFTERNOON – THINGS TO GET USED TO

Miki smiled and gave me a wink before closing the door behind him as he and Vlad headed out to a business meeting.

My lips still buzzed with the remnants of our kisses, and my core throbbed. God, I wished he hadn't had to go out.

However, I knew he had important business to attend to and so I consoled myself with the fact that we'd be sharing a bed again tonight and the thoughts I'd had of jumping his bones could be given full reign then.

Miki had explained how he'd known about the fire at my house and, to be honest, I hadn't taken it well at first. I hated the idea of being spied on in my own home and tracked everywhere I went.

No wonder I always felt as if I was being watched. It hadn't been paranoia after all.

What he had done felt like such an invasion of my privacy, and of course it was, but in the end I realised how lucky I'd been that he'd done all of that to keep me safe.

After all, in a way, it had helped save my life.

And of course, the sexy Russian was right. If I was to be in a relationship with him, then I'd better get used to the fact I'd need to take security precautions.

Even Miki had a bodyguard and I'd bet that Marko had a tracker on him too. So, if Miki could endure these sorts of security measures, then so would I. It was certainly better than the alternative. I'd just have to get used to it.

Right now, though, it seemed I was safe enough without all of that.

Miki had taken over the whole of the top floor of the hotel. There were only a couple of suites; we were in this one, and Marko, Vlad, and a couple of their guys I'd still to meet were in the other.

Marko moved out of this suite so Miki and I could be alone, which was sweet of him.

However, although I was on my own in this set of rooms, Miki had said Marko was next door if I needed him, so I wasn't completely alone.

Knowing someone was nearby made me feel less terrified, and I felt quite relaxed in the hotel.

Just before Miki and Vlad had left, the clothes from the personal shopper had arrived. Watching them being wheeled into the room had filled me with excitement, and I couldn't wait to try them on.

Hurrying into the bedroom, I grinned.

Wow! I shook my head in awe.

There were so many things.

Joy filled me and I bounced on my toes, practically vibrating with excitement as I looked at all the bags. I'd never had a personal shopper pick out anything for me, and certainly not a whole bloody wardrobe full of stuff.

That was another thing I'd need to get used to.

Miki really lived in a different world from me. I was a normal working-class girl, and he was born rich and privileged. He was from a world where personal shoppers and designer clothes were the norm. I was more of a Primark or Next kind of girl.

However, as I pulled one beautiful item after another out of their bags, I couldn't help but think that I wouldn't mind getting used to this at all.

Trying on the first outfit that took my fancy—a gorgeous little black dress and some matching heels—I preened in front of the mirror.

It looked great, and it fit me perfectly.

A beautiful blue silk shirt and navy pants were my next choice, and they were just as fine. Posing ridiculously in each outfit, I took some selfies just for fun.

Dresses, trousers, tops, shirts, boots, shoes, bags, underwear and even swimsuits littered the room a short while later, as I entertained myself with my very own fashion show.

It had been a long time since I'd bought myself clothes and I was thoroughly enjoying having my wardrobe replaced.

The reason for it, however, was not enjoyable.

That thought soured my mood. I wanted to kill that fucker Martin, and if I ever saw him again, I just might.

Of course, I hoped that I never would. Or at least not until his trial, when the bastard had been caught and I could look him in the eye and take satisfaction knowing that he was going to jail for what he had done.

The uniformed officers had asked if I had any idea why he would do such a thing, but I played dumb, saying I hadn't a clue. All going well, they'd find out soon enough.

As I put away the outfits, I thought back over Miki's plan. It really was a good one.

I'd been shocked to find out the extent of my colleagues' corruption and that Mathieson was the head of the Thomas gang. Human trafficking sickened me and the thought of being able to end a gang involved in that was thrilling.

All going well, and Miki's contact got a sting operation arranged in time, when Mathieson, Roy and the others were apprehended while taking part in trafficking girls illegally for the sex trade, everything else would come to light and finally I'd get justice for my dad.

It was just such a pity it all had to be done anonymously. I would have loved to have been part of the Interpol operation and been there to see the faces of Roy and the others when they were caught.

However, I understood Miki's reasons for not getting involved, even if I didn't know everything about him yet.

So, I consoled myself that I'd be able to watch the whole thing via the cameras the guys were setting up.

Besides, it was my information as much as Miki's that was making this plan possible, so in the end, being directly involved on the take down didn't matter. Only the outcome did.

As I put all of my new purchases away, my eyes caught on the sexiest little black nightdress and a set of gold silk underwear.

Oooh, I was definitely going to put these little beauties to use!

Imagining how Miki would react when he saw me in them made me as horny as hell.

Excitement bubbled inside me as I thought about how I would use the sexy items to tease my man. God, I hoped he'd get back soon. It was time for me to thank him properly for saving my life.

CHAPTER 26
MIKI

LATER THAT DAY – ALL TIED UP

When I returned from meeting Jim MacArthur, Eilidh was sitting on my bed watching TV. A big smile lit up her face when she saw me, and my heart clenched.

"Did you have fun trying on your clothes?" I asked.

"The clothes are great, thank you!" she squealed and jumped into my arms.

"My pleasure, sweetheart," I said, laughing and kissing her.

Grabbing my arm, she tugged me over to the wardrobe.

"Wait until I show you all the beautiful things," she said, grinning.

Eilidh's excitement was adorable. I made all the right noises as she systematically showed off each outfit with matching accessories, but I barely registered any of them as I couldn't take my eyes off her face. She was so happy, and her enthusiasm was catching. I wanted to see her like this always.

As my sexy detective put the last of the outfits back into the wardrobe, she turned and held up some tiny pieces of gold silk.

"I got these too, along with some others," she smiled.

"What do you think?" she asked coyly, holding up the tiny thong I was sure would barely cover her modesty.

My mouth went dry. I gulped hard and cleared my throat as my legs nearly buckled when I imagined her wearing the bra and thong before I stripped them off her. Fuck!

"Don't you like them?" she asked, pouting, and fluttering her eyes to look innocent, which made me chuckle.

"They're beautiful!"

"What about this?" she asked with a teasing grin, showing me a short and very sheer looking black lace nightdress.

"Another beautiful item. I'll look forward to seeing you both in and out of them later," I told her with a wink and grin as she laughed and stuck them back on the shelf in the wardrobe.

As she did so, she bent over and wiggled her bottom at me.

Little tease! My Little Miss Red would pay for that later. I grinned in expectation of exactly how I would have her do that.

As I took my jacket off, I caught her flirtatious look as she licked her lips and grinned naughtily.

"Oh, my, you look great in a suit, Miki!" she said.

"You like my suit?"

"Hell yeah, I especially love the silver-grey tie; it really brings out your eyes!" she said, biting her bottom lip as she stared at me.

I laughed at the saucy look, my semi hard cock thickening in response.

"You like ties, huh?" I asked, a naughty thought entering my head as I stalked towards her, licking my lips and stripping off.

She backed up and sat on the bed again, watching me with a mischievous grin.

"Like what you see?" I asked.

"Not sure yet; I might need to see some more!" she said with a saucy wink.

Naughty little minx.

I stood in front of her in only my boxers, still holding my tie. My hard-on obvious.

Eilidh was wearing her pyjamas from earlier, and I grabbed her and yanked her top off.

Gasping, she bit her bottom lip again, giggling as I pushed her back on the bed and straddled her. Bending down, I kissed her and lifted her hands over her head, using my tie to bind them together.

"Leave them there," I told her, and she did.

Little Miss Red's mischievous eyes followed my every move as I yanked off her pyjama bottoms and then walked to the wardrobe and returned with several more ties.

With one of them, I tied an end to her bound hands and the other end to the leg of the headboard and repeated that on the other side so she couldn't move her hands. Then I wrapped another around her eyes, blindfolding her.

Eilidh protested, but I kissed her and murmured in her ear.

"Relax, baby, you'll enjoy this."

Next, I grabbed her ankles and tied them to the bed until she was laid out naked and spreadeagled in front of me.

I'd never been one for tying up my women before, but it was something I felt right for this moment, and I really liked it. Tying up Eilidh was my thing. My kink. Who knew?

My eyes took in every inch of her. She was like an offering to be devoured. And I had every intention of doing just that and savouring every second.

Starting at one foot, I feathered kisses all the way up her right leg until I got to the V between them and blew lightly across her mound, noticing she was wet already. She gasped.

Grinning, I licked her slit in one long motion. Rewarded by her shuddering breath, I did it again.

Loving having my sexy detective at my mercy, I repeated the motion, enjoying the way she bucked and moaned.

Chuckling, I moved my mouth away. I knew what she wanted, but I was not ready to give her that yet.

Instead, I moved down and feathered kisses all the way up her left leg. Again, when I got to the V, I stopped. This time I kissed her mound and licked her just once.

Little Miss Red was even wetter than before, and I smirked, thrilled at how well my woman reacted to me. I'd barely started on her, and she was soaking.

"Such a good girl!" I murmured, my mouth close to her pussy, my breath making her shiver.

"Please Miki," she begged, but I was nowhere near ready to give her what she wanted.

"Not yet, baby, first I'm going to make you come on my fingers, then if you are a good girl, I'll reward you with my cock."

My Little Miss Red would have to wait for me to fill her up. That was my payback for her earlier teasing!

Leaning over her, I kissed her deeply. But it was not just any kiss, this was me staking my claim. This woman was mine and when I finished with her and let her come, she'd be in no doubt of that.

Palming her breasts, I squeezed them together and sucked first on one nipple then the other, lavishing both with the same amount of attention. Like everything else about my sexy detective, her boobs were fantastic, fitting my hands perfectly, and I thoroughly enjoyed playing with them.

As I kissed and nibbled at her neck, an overwhelming need to bite came over me and I gave in to it. Nibbling and sucking, marking my woman. I'd never done that before. I looked at the reddened patch of skin, the first ever hickey I'd given, and a primal sense of possession swelled inside me. Now everyone would know my Little Miss Red was mine.

My cock leaked more at the sight, and I closed my eyes as I

fought back the urge to bite her all over and mark her everywhere. Not this time. Maybe one day I'd give in to that urge if my sexy detective was receptive to it, but for now, this one mark was enough.

Returning my mouth to her nipples, my fingers drew small circles on her body, moving my hand lower and lower and then across until slowly, very slowly, I was finally back where she wanted me to be, and I rested my hand on her mound.

Eilidh whimpered and pushed against it.

"Please," she begged, making me smile. I gave her a little reward and stroked her clit lightly.

"Yes, more, please more," he cried, wriggling her hips in desperation.

Grinning, I kissed her on the lips, sliding my tongue inside her mouth as I slid two fingers inside her pussy.

She was slick with juice, and I plunged my fingers in and out of her, quickly matching the rhythm of my digits with my tongue, fucking her with both.

God, she felt so good. My cock was bloody throbbing, feeling like it would explode if I didn't get inside her soon, but I needed to wait; I needed her to come for me first.

So, I picked up speed with my fingers and kissed my way down her fantastic body, then drew her clit into my mouth and sucked hard.

"Oh fuck, Miki!" she gasped as sweat broke out all over her.

My sexy detective continued bucking her hips into me, matching my rhythm. I growled into her pussy. The vibration and the pounding of my fingers were all it took. Her channel clenched and my cock leaked with need, as she came with a shuddering cry.

With one last lick, I kissed my way slowly back up Eilidh's body as she lay under me, panting hard.

Reaching her breasts again, I nipped on her nipple. She

moaned with the slight and unexpected pain and shivered as I brushed my fingertips lightly over it. Dipping my head, I alternated between licking one nipple and tugging and twisting at the other.

My cock throbbed painfully. To ease it, I shifted my hips to let it rest against her drenched pussy.

The material of my boxers was the only barrier between us, and as she rubbed her wet core along my length, the friction of her movements was such exquisite torture for both of us.

"Please, Miki. I need you!" she begged in frustration.

It was time. My Little Miss Red needed my cock, and I was more than ready to oblige.

As I crawled back over her, all I could think was *Mine!*

Lining up, I thrust inside her to the hilt in one quick movement.

"Fuck!" she cried in a cross between pleasure and pain.

Slowly, I pulled back until just the head of my cock was inside her, then thrust hard into her tight, wet core again.

I repeated this several times slowly until I couldn't take it anymore and had to speed up, thrusting into her like a rutting animal. It was fucking amazing. *She* was fucking amazing!

Eilidh's cries of pleasure set me on fire. I kept pounding into her, grunting and groaning as her tight little channel took all of my hard cock.

Little Miss Red's need was building again with each thrust, and I reached between us and played with her clit while trying to maintain my frantic pace. She cried out one last time and came gushing all over my cock, and that was all I could take. My movements became jerky and out of control as I thrust a few more times before I exploded into her.

Exhausted but unwilling to leave her hot little pussy, I remained poised above her until my forearm spasmed and threatened to give way, giving me no choice but to pull out and move aside to avoid crushing her.

As we lay there gasping for breath, I couldn't help the big grin on my face. I looked over at my sexy detective, still tied up and blindfolded. She had a matching grin. I chuckled, and she did too.

We were a brilliant match and such a good fit in every way. I couldn't imagine how I got along all these years without her.

"Can you untie me now, please? I need to pee," she said, laughing.

Chuckling at her admission, I quickly undid her restraints and removed the blindfold.

"That was flipping amazing!" she told me before leaning in, giving me a quick peck on the lips, and then jumping up and running into the bathroom.

As I watched her flee, my cock was already hardening, ready for round two.

CHAPTER 27
EILIDH
THAT NIGHT – PLAYTIME

While I washed my hands, I checked myself in the mirror. My hair was mussed, lips were swollen, and the patch where Miki sucked and nibbled on my neck stood out bright and red.

The bugger marked me as his! I should be annoyed, but, instead, I grinned at the sight like a lovesick idiot.

Taking in the rest of my appearance, I looked, well frankly, I looked well fucked.

You certainly were! A little voice said, and I giggled, then frowned. I was not usually a giggler, except where Miki was concerned, it seemed. He made me feel and act like a horny teenager.

Everything he did to me set me on fire. The sex between us was amazing, but the connection I felt to my Mr Sexy Lips was even more. I would never have believed I could trust any guy enough to let them tie me up. Yet with Miki, not trusting him didn't even cross my mind.

It was odd that the sexy Russian made me feel so safe; he was definitely a dangerous criminal, so I shouldn't feel safe with him, yet I knew without a doubt that I was.

Things were moving so fast between us and with every second I spent with Miki, I fell further and further under his spell. And I loved it. All thoughts of caution flew out of my mind with each look, hug, kiss, and smile from that man.

Miki had looked great in his suit, and the silver-grey tie really brought out the colour of his eyes. I smiled. I'd never really taken much notice of what tie a man wore before. However, I didn't think I'd ever be able to look at one again without thinking about what we just did.

It had been so much fun, and I felt so sated now. Who knew tie play was my thing? Or, more likely, it was Miki that was my thing, and the tie play was just an added bonus. Anything Miki did to me made me hot, needy, and wet. Every time with him was fantastic, and it just kept getting better and better.

After finger combing my hair, I gave myself a quick wash under my arms and between my legs, ensuring I smelt nice and fresh again, ready for another round.

I hope Miki is too, I thought, giggling again.

Seriously, Eilidh, at least try for a bit of sophistication! I chided myself, shaking my head at my silly schoolgirl-like reaction. Lord, I needed to get a grip! I was acting like Miki was my first crush or something.

More like first love! That annoying little voice chimed in.

Love? I gulped. Yes, in such a short time, I had to admit, if this wasn't love; it was damn well close and it wouldn't take much for Miki to solidify the deal.

The idea filled me with mixed emotions.

For anything permanent to be between us, I knew I would need to leave the police force and perhaps compromise my morals.

While, after everything that had happened meant the former wouldn't be that difficult, the latter might. Although I guessed I'd already did just that when I broke into Mathieson's office.

So, perhaps it wouldn't be as much of a problem for me after all.

The thought disturbed me, but didn't horrify me. It was strange how just a few days could not only turn your world upside down, but completely change your perspective of it.

A couple of weeks ago, I would have laughed at the absurdity of the idea that my colleagues were corrupt and I was falling for a criminal. Yet here it was happening.

A mix of disappointment, anger, and confusion at my situation threatened to overwhelm me. Closing my eyes, I sighed heavily and tampered down on the feeling. I didn't want to think about my life right now. There were more important things to deal with, like jumping my man again.

After that, I would help him plan our revenge and then I would resign from the police and decide what I was going to do about us. Because love or not, committing to a man like Miki was a huge thing and would likely mean a forever commitment. It wasn't something I could do lightly.

It was also not something I could do without a shift in our power dynamics. So far, Miki had been the one to control everything and if we were to be together, it needed to be an equal partnership.

That meant he needed to understand that while I didn't mind letting him dominate and control me in the bedroom sometimes, it wasn't something I would put up with in other areas of my life. It was time to turn the tables on my sexy Russian, and I knew just how to do it.

Grinning wickedly, I opened the door.

As soon as I stepped out of the bathroom, Miki picked me up.

"Not finished with you yet, sweetheart!" he said, throwing me on the bed and looming over me.

And I'm not finished with you either, sweetheart!

Smirking mischievously, I pushed at him, licking my lips.

"My turn!"

Miki raised his eyebrows and smirked, allowing me to push him onto his back. He was still naked, and his cock hardened as I stared at it. Yum!

This was going to be so much fun. It was time to see how he enjoyed being at my mercy. I bit my lip to stop from cackling like an evil witch at the thought.

"Close your eyes, babe, and keep them closed," I said, and was pleased when he did so without protest.

Slipping off the bed, I walked over to his trousers, grabbed the belt, and then some of his ties, and hurried back to his side.

Grabbing his wrists, I secured them with his belt, and he chuckled.

"Relax, baby, you'll enjoy this," I whispered in his ear, repeating his comment to me earlier and making him chuckle again.

God, I loved that sound. It went straight to my core and my pussy gushed.

"No peeking!" I said as I pulled his arms above his head before tying them to the bed with his ties, just as he'd done to me.

When I'd finished tying the last knot, I saw that he'd opened his eyes to watch me and lay there grinning.

"Naughty! I didn't say you could look!" I tutted and pouted.

Chuckling, he closed his eyes again, but it was too late. He'd disobeyed me and he would need to pay for that later.

I took a step back to admire his gorgeous body spread out before me. What a view!

The man was a living god. Total perfection in every dip and curve of him. From the top of his head to the bottom of his feet. Geez, I thought no man could have such sexy looking feet.

Taking another tie, I covered his eyes like he had done

mine, but didn't bother tying up his legs. I knew Miki could easily break out of the bonds if he wished, so there was little point. He would either remain tied up for me or not. His choice.

It all depended on how much he was willing to give up some of his control to me. It was a little test, and we both knew it.

"Looking sexy all tied up," I whispered, and he chuckled as I kissed him lightly on the lips.

Straddling his hips, I studied him. I truly loved his body. It was big with hard muscles and made me feel delicate and so small in comparison. Placing my hands on his pecs, I slowly and lightly dragged them down and over his abs, watching with excitement as his body shuddered under my touch. I loved I could make him react like this.

Feeling powerful at turning the tables on my sexy Russian, I slowly tortured him with kisses as he had done me. Kissing and licking, I nibbled my way around his body, avoiding his rigid length, which was now standing proudly erect again.

Miki groaned and grunted with pleasure as I rubbed my boobs against him. My nipples were so hard and sensitive that every movement caused sweet sensations to shoot directly to my core, making my pussy wetter and wetter.

Oh my, even with him at my mercy, the man made me almost lose control. And he hadn't even touched me.

Like I did when he had his boxers on, I rubbed my soaking wet pussy against his cock, moving slowly up and down his length, drenching him in my juices. Fuck, he felt so good! I longed to have that length buried deep inside me, but I was determined to hold off for now, needing him to beg me the way I had him.

Miki had to know he needed me as much as I needed him. If we were going to have a future together, I had to show him I was strong enough to stand by his side and match him in everything. That included sex!

So, I continued with my slow rhythm, rubbing my pussy over the length of his cock, teasing and kissing him. Our tongues danced and fought for dominance. Every time he thought he was taking back control through our kiss, I pulled away. He moaned in frustration, and I smirked. *Uh, uh, lover, my turn to be in control*!

Miki was a man who was used to being in command. So, for him to give up control, even this little, couldn't be easy for him. I knew that, but I wanted more. For us to have an equal partnership, Miki had to give me everything, just like I knew he would demand of me. The only way to know if he could do that was to push his boundaries and see how far he would let me in.

Nipping the side of his neck, I sucked his skin, marking him just like he had done to me. He laughed when he realised what I was doing. It pleased me he didn't stop me. I was pretty sure him sporting a hickey around the guys would get him the ribbing of a lifetime and the fact that he would endure that for me made my heart swell.

When I was sure that he would have a mark to rival my own, I gave it a last lick and pulled back.

Time to make him beg!

Still rubbing against his length, my need building, I braced my hands on his chest and positioned myself, so my pussy sat against the head of his cock, but I didn't sink down onto it. Instead, I circled my hips, letting his cockhead slip teasingly in and out of my folds.

"Eilidh," he growled in a warning tone.

Playing innocent, I whispered in his ear, "Do you want me, Miki?"

"Yes!" he said through gritted teeth, obviously trying to hold back from losing control and ripping away his restraints.

"Are you sure?" I asked innocently.

"Fuck! Hell, yes!" he cried.

"You need to beg me! If you want me to ride you, you need to beg me to!" I murmured, letting him hear in my voice how much I was enjoying the sensation of his cock playing through my folds.

"Okay baby, ride me!" he said in a commanding voice, obviously thinking that qualified as begging.

It certainly didn't. Nope! Not at all!

"That's not begging, Miki," I chided, leaning down and nipped his nipple, making him grunt in protest at the slight pain.

Upping my game, I allowed my pussy to sink down a little further onto his cock.

"Yes!" he gasped out before I pulled off him completely.

"Beg me, babe," I whispered in his ear again.

"Eilidh! Please, I need you!" he cried.

This time, I heard the pleading in his voice. It made me feel sexy and powerful and it was all I could do not to come right then. I lifted over his cock and impaled myself in one quick movement.

He grunted.

"God, that feels so good!"

It did. It felt bloody amazing!

Slowly I rode his cock, rocking up and down his hard length, then picking up the pace. Our gasps rang out as our release built into a frenzy. My breasts bounced, and my heart pounded as I slammed down on him repeatedly.

"Ride me, babe, ride me! I need you!" he pleaded, over and over until the words became incoherent.

Miki had relinquished full control to me, and that was my undoing.

Slamming down hard one last time, I came with a cry before slumping over him, exhausted.

But he wasn't done yet. Growling loudly, he yanked his arms free from his restraints, ripped off the blindfold, grabbed my hips, and took back control.

Thrusting me up and down his length until he, too, cried out, coming hard and shooting his cum deep inside me.

"Oh, fuck!" he shouted, and I couldn't stop myself from coming again.

Dear god, the things this man did to me!

Falling on top of him again, we stayed like that, with me lying over him, unable to move my limbs, his cock still inside me as we gasped for breath until he softened completely.

Eventually, he shifted me off him, chuckling as he tucked me into his side and kissed my forehead. Still unable to move and completely drained of energy, I fell into an exhausted sleep.

CHAPTER 28
MIKI
THE NEXT MORNING – TELLING EILIDH

Glancing at Eilidh's sleeping form in my arms, I smiled. After she'd rode my cock last night, we'd slept for a short while before I woke her up for another round. I'd done that a couple more times throughout the night. It was as if I just couldn't get enough of her. Completely sated, lying with her in my arms, listening to her gentle breathing, I'd never felt so relaxed.

Brushing her hair back from her face, I gazed at her beauty. This had to be how I woke up every day. There was no alternative. I had to win her over, or I'd never be able to function properly again.

Later today, I would need to tell her exactly who I was and pray it wouldn't put her off. Worry prodded at the edge of my thoughts, but I pushed it aside. The chemistry between us was undeniable, and the last few weeks had changed her view of the world. I knew she didn't see things as black and white as she once did.

Eilidh took a step into my world when she broke into Mathieson's office, then a further step when she continued to do illegal stuff in her unofficial investigation. She was no longer the lily white newly promoted detective she'd been a couple of weeks ago.

Besides, she already knew I was some sort of criminal and accepted it readily enough, so finding out I was a Bratva boss surely wouldn't be a deal breaker. At least I prayed she could see past that and accept me for who I was.

Watching her sleep, I pretended she already had, hugging her tighter to my chest. She snuggled into me, and I let the worry drift away.

The next few days would be fraught with enough tension as I put my plan into action, so I wanted to enjoy this moment of peace with her wrapped in my arms. The calm before the storm!

A little while later, Eilidh woke up, and I slipped out of bed, returning with the gift I bought her yesterday.

Marko had already added a tracker to it and re-wrapped it, so she would never know. It was one of his creations, and it was so tiny it was almost undetectable to the naked eye. I marvelled at the genius that was my brother for a second before handing the wrapped box to her.

"This is for you, sweetheart; I hope you like it," I told her, feeling nervous.

She gave me a questioning look before opening it. When she saw the contents, she gasped, and a smile lit up her face.

"It's gorgeous!" she squealed in delight and hugged me.

Yes! I mentally high-fived myself, pleased by her reaction.

"It's rose gold too. How did you know that is my favourite?" she asked.

"I thought it would go best with your colouring, Little Miss Red," I said, grinning at her.

"Also, the stone matches your amber eyes."

"Wow, I love it. I have never had anything so beautiful, thank you," she said, reaching forward to give me a kiss.

"Turn around, and I'll help you put it on," I said.

She lifted her hair and twisted to give me access and I clasped the necklace around her throat before kissing the side of her neck where my mark was darkening nicely. Seeing it there felt so right. My cock jerked in agreement.

"I want you to promise to wear it from now on," I told her, neglecting to mention the tracker inside. After her annoyance with me over the other tracker and the cameras in her home, I wasn't taking any chances that she would refuse to wear it.

"Okay," she agreed.

Darting to the mirror, she twisted from side to side, admiring it.

The huge smile on her face pleased me. I hadn't seen her wearing any other jewellery except the small rose gold studs in her ears, and I vowed to ensure she had many more items to add to her collection in the future.

Eilidh's naked body with only my necklace and hickey as its adornments was a sight to behold, and I longed to grab her, throw her back onto the bed, and make her scream my name.

Unfortunately, I had another meeting to attend later and before that we needed to talk to the guys, as we still had to figure out a significant part of our plan.

So, instead of indulging my fantasy, I gave her a quick kiss, explained the situation, and headed to the bathroom to get showered and dressed.

A short while later, I returned to the bedroom to find Eilidh looking through her outfits, choosing something to wear. Wrapping my arms around her from behind, I picked up a cute little white lacy lingerie set.

"Wear this, so I can imagine you in it until I can strip it off you with my teeth later," I whispered in her ear, handing her the set.

That earned me a delightful giggle as her body shivered in response.

She grabbed the items, kissed me, and walked to the ensuite, with an exaggerated wiggle throwing a saucy look over her shoulder.

God, I wished I could join her in that shower instead of spending the day dealing with business. Being a pakhan really, really sucked.

While my sexy little detective was getting ready, I headed into the living room. Marko and Vlad were already there with Luca, who had just arrived from London.

We talked over the main part of the plan, and Marko updated us on the whereabouts of the key players.

"Have you figured out how we will get Mathieson out yet?" he asked.

"Still working on it," I told him.

"Luca, you and Vlad will take him directly down to the C once we have him, but it is getting him away from the police operation that will be the hard part," I said, running my hands through my hair in frustration.

My mind had rejected many ideas as I'd tried to come up with a way to get my guys in and out of the old factory where the handover was to take place safely, without them being caught up in a fight with the Thomas gang, arrested by Interpol, or worse, killed.

"There must be some way to get Mathieson out of there. You'll figure it out, Miki. You always do," Luca said.

"What do you mean, get Mathieson out?" Eilidh asked in a voice that could have made hell freeze.

Shit! My mind had been too busy with this bloody problem that I hadn't even heard the shower turn off.

Little Miss Red would not like my plans for Mathieson, and I'd hoped to avoid telling her, at least until I absolutely had to.

Sighing in resignation, I turned to look at her.

Eilidh stood staring at me with her hands on her hips, looking livid.

Oh, oh!

"I guess we have more to talk about," I said, sighing again. I'd planned on discussing things with her today, just not this.

"It sounds like it!" she said through gritted teeth, her eyes glinting at me in fury.

"We'll talk in the bedroom," I said, and she turned and stormed back inside with a huff.

"Bring Luca up to speed with everything else," I told Marko.

He smirked at me, obviously amused at my predicament, and I sent him one of my signature death stares before following Eilidh into the bedroom.

Closing the door behind me, I took in the tension of her posture as she stood next to the bed, arms folded and mouth in a tight line.

God, I wanted to kiss that mouth.

So, I did.

Eilidh held herself rigid at first, but within a few seconds, she was putty in my hands.

Thank god!

"I'll explain everything," I told her when we finally broke apart. Relieved to see kissing her had been the right call, and she was much calmer now.

We sat on the bed, and I told her everything about being born into the Bratva, my parents' death leading to me becoming pakhan for the UK, and the issues my family had faced since. She already knew about Krissa's murder and how Mathieson had been not only involved with that but also about the recent attacks against our business. So, I just went into a little more detail.

"However, although we do illegal stuff, one thing we don't and never will do is human trafficking," I told her.

"And I can assure you that I've been working hard to reduce the amount of criminal involvement we have. My family wants out. Unfortunately, it isn't a life you can just walk away from. But know that I'm trying hard to make that happen. In the meantime, if you remain with me, you'll need to accept me for who I am and know that I will never harm you."

One thing I didn't do was go into the exact nature of my illegal activities. She would find out more about that later if she stayed with me. In the meantime, I couldn't forget she was still a police officer, and it was better that she didn't know for now.

While I believed I had the first three steps of my plan to woo her in the bag, and I was sure I was well on the way to step 4 - winning her love - her loyalty was still in question. For even if she loved me, her moral code might lead her to betray me and above all else, I had to protect my family from that.

Everything I'd told her to date could be denied. She had no witnesses to my words; it would just be her word against mine and without evidence, it would be hard for her to prove anything.

I didn't believe she would betray me, but without winning her loyalty with her love, there was always the slight possibility, and I needed to ensure she was completely mine before I divulged anything more.

Eilidh was quiet the whole time I spoke, simply looking off into space as she listened intently to my words. My stomach churned with nerves. It wasn't a feeling I was used to, and I hated it.

Finally, I finished speaking. There was silence between us for a moment before she released a long breath and smirked.

"I thought you were Bratva, and was pretty sure you had to be high up if you were," she stated, surprising me.

Of course, I shouldn't be surprised; she was an intelligent woman and a detective. I should have known she would figure it out, and in all truth, it wasn't that big of a leap to imagine that a Russian oligarch who she knew to be a criminal of some sort, would at least have some link to the Bratva.

However, that despite suspecting I was Bratva, she still got intimate with me and was developing feelings for me. That gave me hope.

"So why do you want to get Mathieson away from the police op?" she asked.

"I need him for questioning," I explained.

"And then?" she asked, frowning and biting her bottom lip.

"Then I need to ensure he can never threaten my family again," I replied, watching her intently.

"So, are you planning on killing him?" she questioned.

"Yes," I said without hesitation.

She was silent again, and I could see her mulling things over in her mind.

Waiting for her response was killing me, but I said nothing, leaving her to figure her feelings on the matter out for herself. All the while, I prayed she could deal with it.

If she couldn't, I would have her moved to a safe house, kept under my protection until I'd dealt with her colleagues and Mathieson, and then I'd let her go. It would break me, but I would do it.

Please let her accept this! I begged the universe.

Eventually, Eilidh took a deep, steadying breath and nodded.

"But you don't know how to get him?!" she said, more of a statement than a question.

Little Miss Red stood and paced the floor, biting at the skin on the side of her thumb as her mind worked overtime.

Watching her, I remained silent and waited for her to work through whatever was going on in that brain of hers.

My little detective was thinking hard, and then suddenly, I saw her lightbulb moment. Her eyes widened and a triumphant grin spread across her face.

She's got something!

"Glasgow has a secret network of underground tunnels which were created during the Second World War, including one that leads to Govan where the factory is," she told me.

A slow grin spread over my face as I listened to the rest.

"The tunnels were made to ensure the telephone lines for the war cabinet were far enough underground so that if the enemy bombs destroyed the buildings, the phone network would remain operational. They also connected various important buildings together and bomb shelters so people could use them to escape from the bombing, too," she told me.

"After the war, the tunnels were sealed off and forgotten about, but they still exist. That old factory building has been around since then, and there was a shelter nearby, so it might have an underground tunnel. If it does, that might be the answer," Eilidh finished, grinning.

The woman was a genius!

"Let's get Marko to check," I said, feeling excited at the thought she might have solved our problem.

Pulling her to me, I rewarded her with a kiss before we headed through to the living room.

It took a while, but finally, Marko found the plans for the underground tunnels.

Eilidh was correct, and the guys look suitably impressed. I was so proud of her and couldn't stop holding her close and kissing her, and to my joy, she didn't seem to mind. In fact, she seemed very responsive to my affections, and I hoped that meant that when everything was over, she'd agree to be mine.

Marko pulled up the old blueprints of the factory building, and we were happy that there was indeed a tunnel with an entrance directly inside the building itself. We just needed to make sure that we could actually use the tunnel, but from the information Marko discovered, it looked possible.

We ate breakfast together, and then I sent Vlad off with one of our other guys to explore the tunnel and make sure it was indeed a viable option.

Before leaving, I promised Eilidh I'd take her to dinner in the hotel restaurant that evening so she could wear one of her new outfits, then I reluctantly kissed her goodbye and headed off with Luca to set up the cameras we'd use to monitor things.

CHAPTER 29
EILIDH

THAT AFTERNOON – COMING TO TERMS
WITH EVERYTHING

After Miki and Luca left to place cameras near the handover site, Marko headed to his room to work, and I was left alone with nothing to do but think.

Vlad had gone to check that my idea of using the old tunnel network to access the factory was possible. I was pleased with myself for remembering about the tunnels and I really hoped it was indeed the solution to their problem.

When I'd thought of the idea, they had all been impressed, and it had made me proud. We'd discussed the possibility of it being a viable option and it had been thrilling to be a part of things. I'd listened to Miki's input and was blown away by his ingenuity. The man was bloody brilliant in the way he thought of every eventuality.

Warmth spread all over my body as I thought of everything else that man was brilliant at.

Just as he'd asked, I was wearing the pretty white lace underwear, and I couldn't wait for him to make good on his promise later. Shivers of excitement ran down my spine at the thought and I was back to being horny as hell.

Lord, it seemed like that was becoming a permanent state of being for me.

Not that I was complaining. Hell no!

My man turned me on, and I was more than happy with that thought.

I was quickly learning that there wasn't anything he could do that would make me unhappy with him for long.

Even after overhearing the guys discussing getting Mathieson out, and not knowing what to think, all it took was a kiss from him to calm me down.

I'd been livid, wondering why they would want to help Mathieson escape. It had crossed my mind that Miki had lied to me, and he was actually working with the guy. Although I hadn't wanted to believe it, I hadn't understood why else they would get him out. Yet one touch of those sexy lips of his and I'd been putty in his hands.

Even now, just thinking about his kisses made my lips tingle, and I wasn't just talking about my mouth!

Thankfully, after Miki explained things, I understood his need to make Mathieson pay for his crimes. God, how I'd changed!

It was almost a relief to know exactly who my sexy Russian was because now I could reconcile with the fact that he was indeed Bratva, as I'd suspected. I'd known he would be high up too, but I hadn't considered that he was the pakhan. That blew my mind.

When he told me he had unwillingly inherited the position from his dad but had done his best to fulfil the role of Bratva boss and family protector since, I could hear how much his responsibilities weighed heavily on his mind and my heart went out to him.

Miki's life was a difficult and dangerous one, yet he seemed to navigate it with his own moral code.

Even so, it was a scary thought for me to have become such a different person that I would be happy to get into bed, literally as well as figuratively, with a man who was part of a Mafia organisation. Yet I knew that no other man but Miki could have made me want to.

The way Miki looked at me and the way he treated me made me feel like I was special. No man had ever made me feel the way he did and despite his background, my Mr Sexy Lips was probably the best man I'd ever met.

My whole body warmed as I thought about how much he laughed and smiled at me. I got the impression he didn't do that often, and I loved I was the one who could bring a little lightness into his dark world.

I'd thought that accepting Miki for who he was would be difficult, and yet it was turning out to be a lot easier than I'd expected.

I still didn't know the exact extent of the criminal activities his Brotherhood was involved in; all he had told me was that they didn't hurt women and weren't involved in human trafficking.

That, at least, was an immense relief to me.

An even bigger relief was the fact that Miki had said that his family was trying to get out of their criminal lifestyle. While I doubted the possibility of that, I was happy that he was at least trying. It said a lot about his character, and it endeared him to me all the more.

While Miki talked, I had quietly listened and allowed myself to process it all. After he finished telling me everything he was comfortable sharing, I had been stunned because it didn't matter to me.

Even when he admitted he planned on killing Mathieson, it hadn't made a difference. In fact, after everything Miki had told me about the guy, I actually agreed that he deserved it. Jail was too good for people like him.

It was a shock to agree with what Miki planned to do to Mathieson.

I had always done everything by the book, lived my life playing by the rules, and kept the laws of the land. I'd believed in our law enforcement and our justice system, and never agreed with people acting as vigilantes. But when the upholders of the law were bigger perpetrators of crime than most criminals, that changed a person's perspective.

A sense of grief washed over me as the last vestiges of the person I was, died.

Even knowing Miki was a killer, if I was truthful, I could see more morality in my Bratva pakhan than in either Mathieson or my colleagues, who were morally obliged to uphold the law but had failed dramatically.

Shaking my head at my revelations, I had to admit; I was completely, totally, and utterly, one hundred percent in love with my Bratva man and while the old me would have been horrified, the new me simply accepted it. There was no point in even trying to deny it. I had it bad, and that was all there was to it.

The sexy Russian was never far from my thoughts and had become an obsession. I wanted to be with him every minute and thought about him constantly when I wasn't.

Fingering the necklace Miki had given me, I smiled.

The rose gold tear-shaped pendant was set with an amber stone surrounded by tiny little diamonds. It matched the rose gold studs in my ears and complimented my colouring, just as Miki said.

I was touched, not only by the gift, but by the amount of thought Miki had put into buying it for me. It really was stunning, and I would enjoy wearing it.

As I examined it more closely, I realised it would also compliment my gold underwear, which had little rose gold bows in between the cups of the bra and the sides of the thong.

Today Miki wanted to remove my black lace set with his teeth and I intended to make sure he did. But another day soon, I decided I'd bring the little gold set out to play.

Ooh la la! I couldn't bloody wait. The thought sent a gush of wetness straight into my white lacy knickers, and I bit my lip as I anticipated the evening ahead.

I was looking forward to going to dinner with Mr Sexy Lips later and would wear my little black dress and strappy heels. Then afterwards we'd come back to the room, and I'd give him dessert.

Smiling mischievously, I made a call and ordered a couple of little items to be delivered to the room later. Miki had given me a present and tonight I planned on giving him one in return.

In the meantime, I had an entire afternoon ahead of me and nothing to do, so I settled in the suite's living room and put on the TV, turning to the local news. The story of my attack and the fire was running, with an image of Martin, as the suspect wanted for questioning.

My heart sped up as I looked at his smug face staring back at me from the screen, and I couldn't suppress a shiver of fear.

A detective constable being attacked in her home and left for dead as it burnt around her would be news on any day. However, with the suspect being another detective and her partner, who'd gone missing, it was a major story.

I'd left a message on Aunt Maisie's phone to tell her I was okay, just in case she was worried. The Chief Superintendent had left a message on mine telling me how sorry the department was for what had happened, but I hadn't called him back. I still didn't know how far up the chain of command this whole corruption thing went, so I didn't want to talk to him.

Thankfully, the reporters didn't know where I was, or I expected the hotel would be inundated. Miki had paid the manager for the staff to be discreet, so I just hoped it stayed that way. It would be difficult for us to carry out our plan if we had to navigate the so-called great British press. And I really wouldn't want to bring Miki and his family any unwanted scrutiny.

Tears stung my eyes at the images of my house in flames. I couldn't believe how close I'd come to being killed only two days ago, and by a colleague, too. The sooner Martin was caught, the better. I just prayed he would be at the handover, as I didn't like the thought of him out there somewhere, possibly waiting to attack me again.

The very idea had me feeling sick with nerves.

I'd joined the force to follow in my dad's footsteps and I had been so proud to be a police officer, but with officers like Martin, Roy, and the others, I wasn't any more, and I bloody hated each one of them for stripping me of that pride.

Of course, if they hadn't, Miki and I would never have met or got together.

My breath hitched as that thought hit me like a bucket of water being thrown over me.

However, as much as I adored Mr Sexy Lips, it wasn't like I was going to be grateful to a bunch of murdering scum for his presence in my life.

No, fate had put us in each other's path. Chemistry and common goals had brought us together, and now love would bind us and bridge the gap between two worlds and two people that otherwise would have remained apart.

When the next couple of days were over, I'd resign and follow Miki to London. I wasn't sure what I would do there, but it would be a fresh start, so I supposed I could do anything I wanted.

With TV not an option and nothing else to do, by mid-afternoon, I was bored and about ready to climb the walls, but thankfully Marko and Vlad came in to check on me.

We ordered room service, ate little cakes and sandwiches, and sipped tea together while chatting about the plan for the next day. It was odd to think these Russian men enjoyed such a British tradition.

Watching them sip from China cups balanced on little saucers was pretty funny, and I had to bite my lip to avoid laughing each time Vlad took a sip. He was a big guy, so when he held the cup, it looked like a child's tea set in his hands.

Regardless, both men looked sophisticated, and it was hard to remember they were more than the Russian Oligarchs they appeared.

As we discussed the plan, I asked Marko lots of questions.

"Don't arrest me," he said, laughing as I marvelled at his skills in hacking and tracking.

"I promise not to," I replied, laughing in turn.

I liked Marko; he was nice and had a nerdy sort of charm about him, but he was hot too. He was not your typical nerd, that was for sure, and he carried that hint of danger, just like the others, that added to his attraction.

Vlad was a quieter person. He was as tall as Miki, but even more muscular. Yet, like Miki, they appeared more down to genetics and training rather than steroids. He had a calming air and seemed to be one of those people who was rarely fazed by anything, and I could see why he was Miki's friend and bodyguard. I liked him too.

We laughed and chatted, and I thoroughly enjoyed their company.

After about an hour, I noticed Vlad yawning. He had slept little in the last few days between tailing me, Bratva business, staying up, guarding my hospital room, and helping put our plans into motion. The poor man was shattered, and no wonder.

All those times I thought I was being watched; it had been Vlad.

"You scared me by creeping around, following me in the dark," I told him.

"I'm sorry," he said quietly, and I believed him.

"Of course, you scared me too," he went on.

"Me? I doubt that." I laughed incredulously.

"That day when you challenged me to come out with that torch in your hand and that glint in your eye, I was pretty sure that if I did, you'd brain me with the thing and that would be the end of me," he smirked.

"Oh ha, ha!" I said, laughing.

Bonding with the guys gave me the warm fuzzies and made my decision to be with Miki feel better. I had a feeling that was the intention of our little get together and it worked.

We were having fun, but after I caught Vlad covering another yawn with his hand; I insisted he go take a nap.

Marko followed a few minutes later to do more of his hacking stuff and I was left to my own devices, once again, which wasn't a good idea.

Within ten minutes of them leaving, I was going stir crazy. I really needed to get out of the room, so decided to go for a swim in the hotel pool.

After quickly getting changed, I headed down to the Spa.

I thought about telling Marko where I was going, but quickly talked myself out of it. Marko was busy, and I didn't want to disturb him or wake up Vlad.

One of them would have probably insisted on coming with me if I had told them, and that wasn't fair because Vlad needed his sleep, and Marko needed to be doing whatever he was doing to make sure everything ran smoothly tomorrow. Besides, it wasn't as if I was leaving the hotel.

A staff member directed me to the woman's changing room, where I took off my clothes and put them in a locker. I debated keeping my promise to Miki and leaving my necklace on, but was scared to lose it in the pool, so I took it off and tucked it into the locker as well. Just as I closed the door, I felt a presence behind me.

Before I could turn to look, I was pushed up against the locker door. A hand closed over my mouth, and I felt a prick in my neck. I was suddenly very weak. My knees buckled, but I was held in an iron-tight grip so instead of falling, I simply slumped over the arm around my waist, powerless to fight the waves of tiredness that made my head lull and my eyes heavy.

Unable to move my limbs, I couldn't stop my hands from being cuffed behind me. My mind was sluggish, and I couldn't seem to think coherently as I was slung unceremoniously over someone's shoulder.

I wanted to struggle, but I couldn't sum up the energy and I didn't seem to care as the world wavered in and out of focus. Instead, I just hung there, limp, while I was carried away, fighting to stay conscious.

A few minutes later, my assailant bundled me into somewhere small, and I heard a noise above me like a boot closing. A car! I was in a car. My mind registered the fact, and I vaguely thought that I should try to escape, but it was impossible. I couldn't even muster a scream.

Lying curled up in a ball, I felt the vibration of the engine as I was driven away from the hotel. I must have passed out because I woke again as the car turned a corner and I was thrown against the side. That should have hurt, but it didn't. My mind felt like it was floating, and my body was warm and relaxed.

I'm high!

Did I get injected with heroin? I wasn't sure, but I didn't seem to care. My eyes grew heavier again, and I drifted off.

The jolt of the car as it went over a bump woke me the next time.

A short while later, the vehicle stopped. Nothing happened for quite some time, and I lay there practically paralysed, but finally my thoughts cleared a little. I was still too weak to do anything about my predicament, but aware enough to know I was totally screwed.

Thankfully, I was still too high to panic.

CHAPTER 30
MIKI

After reluctantly leaving Eilidh at the hotel, Luca and I headed off to the old factory building in the Govan area of Glasgow to look around before putting up the cameras for our surveillance.

We'd easily located the entrance to the tunnel, which was a hatch within the floor of a small cupboard at the back of the factory. Just where Marko said it should be. There was some musty old carpeting over it, and we pulled it up.

Dust flew around and we both sneezed.

There was a bolt keeping it closed, but it was in surprisingly good condition, considering the time that passed since the tunnel had been in use.

However, even though it didn't take too much effort to open the bolt, it immediately became clear that the tunnel was sealed from the inside.

Damn! I knew it was too easy.

"We'll need to get the other end opened and then access this one," I told Luca.

On the way over to the factory, I'd called Jim MacArthur to inform him about the plan, and he sent one of his guys out to meet with Vlad. Apparently, the guy had worked at the old docks on the banks of the River Clyde and knew about the tunnels, and so, with his help, Vlad had already located the other entrance we'd use to access the factory.

After relaying the carpet loosely back over the top of the hatch, we headed off to meet them and inspect the other end.

Just like with the factory end of the tunnel, it was in an old building that was empty but still accessible. We were lucky because there was a lot of development going on in the Govan area, especially along the Clyde side where the building was located, and that could have caused us a significant problem. Thankfully, it hadn't reached that area yet.

However, the tunnel had been sealed well and needed special equipment to re-open it. Jim MacArthur kindly provided a crew, and the equipment. He and his crew arrived within the hour and his men got to work right away.

Of course, for his help, Jim had requested I return the favour and bring another guy out for him. Since Mathieson was mine to deal with, he wanted Gerry Thomas, the other leader of the Thomas gang.

Naturally, I agreed. Gerry Thomas had been a problem for Jim for a long time and had caused him a lot of trouble. Jim wanted his revenge just like I wanted mine.

Unfortunately, that meant things were even more complicated as now we had three guys to get out: Mathieson, Martin Johnson, and Gerry Thomas.

Since Vlad had slept little in days, I made him return to the hotel to get some rest and help Marko look after Eilidh. Luca and I remained at the site with Jim for the tunnel to be opened up.

It took a few hours, but when it was finally opened, we were pleasantly surprised that it was still intact and, all things considered, in perfect condition.

The air was stale, but in general the quality wasn't bad and even though we needed to take shallower breaths than usual, we didn't need the oxygen that Jim's men brought with us as we explored. That was an enormous relief, because getting the three men out was going to be hard enough without having to worry about having enough oxygen.

Once inside the entrance, the ground sloped downwards for some distance until we got to the deepest part. The semi-circular shape and dark grey concrete walls reminded me of an unused subway tunnel. Electric lights were spaced out at regular intervals but wouldn't be of any use to us. However, the camping lanterns we carried lit the small space well enough for our purposes.

This tunnel wasn't part of the telephone network Eilidh mentioned, but one of the old escape routes which connected air-raid shelters.

The hairs on the back of my neck pricked up as I thought of people rushing through the passage while bombs rained down on the city above.

It was actually strange walking through it and realising this tunnel had saved thousands of lives during the war. It was also strange to think that my family would have been on the opposite side of said war, and the people that had hid in these tunnels, were our enemies. Having been in the UK for so long, the country and its people held a large place in my heart, and so that was a sobering thought.

The tunnel was about a mile long and sloped up again as we neared the factory entrance, where it met with a metal stairway that took us directly to the other side of the hatch.

That side had simply been bolted, then closed with a large padlock. One of Jim's crew that accompanied the three of us through the tunnel made quick work of opening it and, just like that, we had the most important part of our plan complete.

My mind ran through what we'd need to do to get the guys out easily, and I told Jim's men what else we needed. As we wanted the men out alive, we would drug them and use wheelchairs to wheel them through the tunnel. It was a good plan but would take around thirty minutes, less if we were very lucky, to complete, and that was my only concern.

Not only did we need to get three human traffickers away from their gangs without issue, but we also needed to do it during a time when Interpol officer would try to arrest them. Not a simple task and one made harder with every moment it took us.

However, the chaos the Interpol operation would create would help with actually snatching the guys. We just needed to ensure we weren't seen or followed back through the tunnel once we'd got them.

Frowning, I pinched the bridge of my nose. This whole thing was giving me a headache and the lack of fresh air wasn't helping.

However, after a brief discussion with Jimi's crew, we rigged some small explosive charges part of the way down the tunnel. Not big enough to cause damage to the surrounding area, but just big enough to collapse that part of the tunnel.

Marko would remotely discharge them. He'd wait for our guys to pass, then detonate them. That way, no gang members or Interpol officers could follow us through.

Hopefully, with the Thomas gang to deal with and women to rescue, our guys would be gone, and the charges detonated, before any officers even noticed a tunnel existed. I didn't want to kill innocent parties if it could be avoided.

Jim was providing several guys to help us implement my plan, and they would get Gerry Thomas out. We'd concentrate on the other two. Once our guys had exited the tunnel, cars would wait for them. Luca and my two other guys would take

Mathieson and Johnson straight to the C and Jim would take Gerry Thomas wherever he wanted.

Vlad would remain here with me and Marko. We'd conclude our business with Jim and then follow them later.

Finally, we had all the arrangements in place. There was nothing else to do but wait until it was time to put the plan into action. By this time tomorrow, hopefully, it would all be over.

After leaving some of Jim's men to guard the tunnel, we said goodbye to him and headed for the car.

"Let's get back to the hotel," I said to Luca, feeling exhausted.

I needed something to eat and a bloody strong coffee, or maybe a vodka or two. And I needed Eilidh. Just the thought of her lightened my mind. I'd promised to take her to dinner this evening and was glad to see that I would be back in plenty of time to do so.

I'd missed my Little Miss Red and wondered what she had been up to all day. On the drive back from the factory, all I could think of was that little white lacy bra and thong she was wearing. All thoughts of exhaustion fled as I imagined fulfilling my promise to remove them with my teeth. The sooner I fulfilled my promise of dinner, the sooner I could fulfil my other promise.

My cock thickened, happy with that idea, and as soon as we were in the hotel, I practically ran inside. Luca sniggered at my enthusiasm.

"You've got it bad, man," he said, chuckling as I pressed the button to the lift repeatedly in my impatience.

"Wait until it's your turn," I told him with a grin.

"Not likely," he replied.

Luca was a charmer and a bit of a ladies' man. As far as I knew, he'd never been ensnared by the charms of the women he'd dated, but there was always a first time and those that protested the most often fell the hardest. I imagined Luca panting after a woman the way I was after my sexy detective and laughed. I really couldn't wait to see that.

And I couldn't wait to see my Little Miss Red, either. Tapping my foot in annoyance, I pressed the bloody button again and finally; the door opened.

"Hey baby!" I shouted as soon as I got to our suite. But there was no answer. She wasn't there.

Trying not to panic, I headed to the suite next door.

Maybe she was there with Marko and Vlad, or maybe Vlad took her somewhere? I pounded on the door, and Vlad opened it yawning widely, looking like he had just got up from a nap.

"Where's Eilidh?" I shouted.

"Eilidh should be in your room. She was there earlier, before I took a nap," he stated in confusion.

"Eilidh's gone!" I cried.

"Aw shit!" he said as I pushed past him and headed into Marko's room.

Marko had his headphones on, listening to some conversation members of the Thomas gang were having, but he removed them the minute he saw me enter.

"What's up?"

"I need you to bring up Eilidh's tracker now!" I said, my voice sounding frantic.

Worry flickered across his face, but he said nothing, just did what I asked.

"What's going on?" Luca asked, emerging from the bathroom.

"Eilidh is missing," Vlad said.

God, I felt sick at his words.

Where the hell is she?

Eilidh shouldn't have gone anywhere without Vlad. I was

annoyed at her, but tried to stay calm. She wasn't used to having a bodyguard after all and probably didn't think.

Also, I realised I only told her to get him if she was going out. She probably assumed that meant if she was going out of the hotel, not just the room. Next time, I would be far more explicit about the rules for her safety.

"Looks like she is in the hotel, the Spa, women's changing area," he told me.

"Both her phone and necklace trackers say she's there," he added, and I breathed a sigh of relief. I'd assumed that was the most likely option.

She probably thought the hotel spa was safe enough. I knew, however; it wasn't. If someone wanted to grab her, that was the best place to do it, when she was in the changing room, without her protectors. It was certainly where I would do it.

That thought had my heart pounding hard again and my stomach churning with nerves.

Even though her tracker was there, she might not be safe.

Please let her be safe!

I repeated the plea in my head as I ran to the lift and frantically pressed the button, with Luca and Vlad at my heels.

As the lift took us to down to the spa, I tried to calm myself by taking slow deep, breaths, but my lungs were having none of it as they continued their shallow panicked breathing despite my best efforts.

Calm down, she's probably only gone for a swim, I told myself, but I couldn't stop the panic rising inside me or the sense that something was terribly wrong.

Luca and Vlad went to check the pool and gym while I knocked on the women's changing room door. After a few seconds, when nobody answered, I entered.

It was empty. Only a few lockers were being used, and I

noted their numbers and hurried outside just as Luca and Vlad returned, confirming she was nowhere else in the Spa either.

Fuck!

According to Luca, there were only two women using the gym and none in the pool. However, there were three lockers being used, leading us to believe the third might belong to Eilidh.

Luca approached the women and worked his charm, briefly chatting with them while glancing at the numbers on their locker keys.

Once we had the number that might be hers, we headed to the reception. It was the same receptionist who'd checked us in yesterday and arranged for the personal shopper.

Unwilling to divulge the truth yet, I told her Eilidh had intended to use the pool but was unwell and returned to our room. I also said she had lost her locker key and the woman kindly agreed to open the locker and retrieve Eilidh's belongings.

We waited outside as she returned with Eilidh's clothes, shoes, and necklace. My stomach clenched at the sight.

She must have planned on swimming after all, and took the necklace off. She probably didn't want to lose it.

Bile rose in my throat as I stared at it in my hand.

Fuck, she really was gone, obviously taken by someone as she wouldn't leave without her clothes, phone, or new necklace, and now I have no way of tracking her!

Shit, I should have told her there was a tracker inside and that she was to keep it on, no matter what.

Even if she hadn't liked the idea, I'm sure I could have persuaded her to keep it on, regardless. Why the hell hadn't I tried?

I was a bloody fool.

Next time I was getting Marko to put one in both of her

earrings, she never took them off and if there had been one in them instead of just the necklace and phone, she wouldn't be lost.

In fact, I'd make sure every piece of jewellery I got her from now on contained a tracker.

I just needed to get her back first.

After checking the spa, we found an employee-only entrance right next to the women's changing area, which led around the side of the building and straight to the carpark. That was obviously how the person had got her out.

Who, though, and where had they taken her? Was it that fucker, Johnson? Or someone else? My mind bombarded me with questions I couldn't answer.

"Get the locations of Mathieson, Roy Allen, and Eilidh's other colleagues. Check all their communications and look for Johnson again; one of them must have her!" I barked down my mobile to Marko.

"Already on it!" he told me.

After a quick discussion with the manager and a promise that there would be a significant bonus for him and his staff for their help and discretion, I talked him into pulling up the security footage.

Sitting there waiting for it to re-wind, my hands clenching and unclenching, I tried not to punch anything.

I should have taken better care of her. I failed! Just like I failed Krissa and almost failed Sonia. Shit!

Guilt threatened to overwhelm me, but I forced it aside. I needed to focus so I could get Eilidh back.

Finally, an image appeared on the screen. A man wearing a dark jacket, jeans, and a baseball cap exited with a woman wrapped in a towel over his shoulder, hands cuffed behind her back and some sort of bag over her head. She was limp. She could be knocked out or drugged.

Narrowing my eyes, I zoned in on the image of the guy. It was hard to see who he was at first, but at the last minute, the camera captured the lower half of his face, and it was enough to recognise the cocky bastard. Martin Johnson had Eilidh!

But why? He had tried to kill her before, unless that had actually been an accident. He'd ransacked the place and was pouring petrol on it before she arrived. Maybe he had just been trying to get rid of evidence and not her. So, why kidnap her now?

Was I the reason? Did he know who I was and had kidnapped her because we were obviously not only working together, but an item?

Mathieson knew who I was, and Johnson worked for Mathieson, so it was a possibility that he recognised me yesterday. What did that mean? Would he be in touch? If so, what would he want? Did he plan on ransoming her, or was there another reason for taking her?

These questions assaulted me as we returned to our suite to find out what Marko had discovered.

Apparently, Mathieson was in court today. Roy Allen had just returned home from his golf trip and was in his house. The other two officers were working and were at the scene of a robbery, so they were all accounted for and none of them had communicated with Johnson.

"Fuck!" I roared in frustration.

"That bastard has my woman, and I do not know where he has taken her or what the fuck he is doing to her or if she is even still alive!"

God, my whole body shook with rage. I wanted to punch something, or better yet, someone. That fucker Johnson!

"We'll get her back!" Marko stated, gripping my shoulder reassuringly.

We had to. I needed to save her. What the hell would I do if I couldn't?

Sighing, I sunk onto the sofa, holding my head and feeling utterly defeated.

I rubbed at the hollow ache in my chest.

Eilidh hadn't been in my life long, but she was already my world. My heart belonged to her.

"He kidnapped her. That's a good sign that she is still alive. He could have killed her in the changing room if he had wanted her dead. He wants her alive, and she is smart. She's a trained detective; she will do what she can to remain alive, giving us time to find her and bring her back. You need to stay positive and focused," Marko told me firmly.

"Miki, you are the best planner and strategist I know; you solve problems daily. This is another problem. Focus on solving it like you do any other!"

I blew out a breath and nodded. He was right.

"Keep monitoring everyone and let me know the second anything happens about Eilidh or the handover! While you're at it, hack into the investigation on Johnson and the fire again and see if anything gives us a clue where the bastard might have taken my woman. Luca, you help Marko with that."

"Vlad and I will head to Johnson's place and see if we can get any information. There might be something they missed."

To be honest, I doubted it. However, there could be something, a photograph, anything that might hint at where the bastard taken Eilidh, so I had to try it. Besides, it gave me something to do to stop my anger from getting out of control.

The place was clean, almost void of personal items, and nothing in Johnson's house gave us any bloody clue where he had taken my heart.

———

Several hours later, we were still no nearer finding Eilidh. My stomach was clenched in a tight knot and my heart pounded in my chest, and I was amazed that it could still beat under the pressure of the mix of anger and utter despair I felt.

Unable to sit still, I paced the suite, my fists clenching and unclenching in agitation. My nostrils flared with my short shallow breaths and my jaw ached from grinding my teeth. I was ready to explode, barely holding on to my anger and my sanity. My mind bombarded me with questions I couldn't answer.

Where was she? What the hell was he doing to her? Would he contact me? Try to ransom her somehow?

What if he took her somewhere, and I never saw her again?

Fuck! I hated feeling this powerless. Fury boiled my blood.

Unable to contain it any longer, I let my rage engulf me.

With a loud roar, I hurled a lamp, smashing it into the wall. I was vaguely aware of Luca jumping out of the way as I launched a vase next. The sound of breaking glass, serving only to heighten my anger.

Yelling in fury, I smashed the television on the floor, the screen cracking and splintering. I upended chairs, tore down the curtains, threw anything I could get my hands on, and ripped apart cushions, imagining I was ripping apart Johnson, limb by limb.

By the time I stopped, the room was in shambles, a chaotic mess that mirrored the storm inside me, and I slumped into the sofa, completely drained.

Marko, Vlad and Luca stood off to the side, all wearing matching looks of shock. Nobody moved as they held their breath while I panted and fought to get mine under control.

As my breathing calmed, my gaze tracked across the room and landed on the broken pieces of a vase. Images of my sister's broken, battered body flew through my mind and I roared again, this time in despair.

God, please don't let that be Eilidh's fate, too! I pleaded, praying for the second time in as many days to a deity I wasn't sure even existed, desperate for any help I could get.

As I sat slumped on the trashed sofa, with my head in my hands, I was unaware of time passing or the guys quietly rearranging the furniture and tidying up the mess I'd made.

After a while, Marko placed a hand on my shoulder rousing me from my stupor.

"Eat!" he said, holding out a sandwich for me.

I grimaced and shook my head.

"Eat! You need your strength. You look like you are about to pass out," he said firmly, and shoved the sandwich into my hand.

"Bossy bugger," I mumbled.

"What? You don't like the tables being turned for once?" he laughed, and I growled at him in response.

The thought of food made me nauseous. With every passing second my worry for Eilidh grew and I knew, just like the others did, that the longer she was gone, the less chance there was that she would be found safe and well.

Marko must've known what I was thinking by my expression.

"You really need to eat, Miki. Or you'll be no good to Eilidh when we locate her...and we will!" he raised his hand, cutting off my words as I was about to argue.

"We will find her, and we will get her back. We won't stop looking until we do."

"Now eat!" he barked in a tone that brooked no further argument.

Like all of my siblings, Marko was an annoying little bugger at times, but he was right. My body needed fuel, whether or not I felt like it. So, despite my stomach's protests, I forced down the sandwich.

A while later, I was regretting it. My head was pounding, and my guts churning so much that the threat to lose every bit of what I'd eaten was very real.

My agitation grew as the hours clicked slowly by.

I was not a religious man, probably just as well given my line of business, but for the first time in forever, I sent up a silent prayer to the big guy begging him to help me find my Little Miss Red.

CHAPTER 31
EILIDH
THROUGHOUT THAT NIGHT – KIDNAPPED

After being left in the boot for a while, I was unceremoniously hauled out and slung over the guy's back again, in a move that knocked the wind out of me. The bastard wasn't in the least gentle, and I was jostled about like a sack of potatoes.

Not long after, I was thrown onto a thin mattress so hard I bounced. My head banged off a metal frame, almost knocking me out.

"Ow!" I cried as I struggled to remain conscious.

While someone moved about the room, I desperately clutched the headboard and tried to sit up in a valiant attempt to escape. My limbs were stiff, and I was still groggy and weak from the aftereffects of whatever drug I'd been given, and I barely lifted my head before the man grabbed me again.

My cuffs were removed, and I was pinned back onto the mattress by a hand on my throat as a heavy body straddled me. Chains rattled, and my hands were roughly hauled above my head. A second later, my right wrist was secured in a metal cuff, and then my left, and I realised I was being chained to a bed. *Fuck!*

"Get the hell off me!" I cried.

The only response was a low chuckle and a tightening of the hand on my neck, making breathing hard. I desperately tried to breathe through my nose, but the air inside the hood was stale and only made me panic more.

Bucking my hips, I attempted to throw my captor off. It was useless.

Weak and nauseous from the after-effects of whatever drug he used on me, and with his weight on top and my lack of breath, all I could do was wiggle ineffectually under him. Not a brilliant idea, I realised too late. Something dug into my stomach, making me freeze. Oh fuck, no!

"Keep it up. I like it!" a voice whispered. It was Martin.

"Fuck you!" I cried.

"Be careful or you'll get your wish," the fucker stated with a chuckle, but thankfully, he moved.

As his weight lifted, I kicked out, unable to see but hoping to connect with whatever part of him I could. Thankfully, I did, and the asshole grunted in pain. I felt a second of satisfaction, but that was all, before I was punched hard in the stomach, knocking the breath from my body once more.

"Want to play rough, do you, babe? Don't worry, I like it that way myself. Plenty of time for that later!" he chuckled again.

Oh, dear god no! Please no!

I was still trying hard to catch my breath while my legs were restrained, and I found myself once again unable to see and spreadeagled on a bed.

However, while being restrained similarly by Miki was exciting and sexy; it was bloody terrifying now! Especially as the towel I had wrapped around me when I was kidnapped had come off in the boot, and I only had my swimsuit on now. Thank God it was a one-piece, at least! Though I doubted it would be much protection if he planned on doing anything.

The bag over my head was finally ripped off, and I blinked hard. It took a minute for my eyes to regain focus after so long in the dark, and I cringed at the sight before me.

"Hi Eilidh, fancy meeting you here," that fucker Martin said with a smarmy grin, but it wasn't that which made me cringe. It was his appearance.

The usually handsome ladies' man was gone. The man before me was dishevelled and unshaven, his clothes were rumpled and dirty, and his eyes were frightening. They were glazed with a hint of madness in their depths, and he looked high.

Oh, fuck!

He reached over and grabbed my hair, pulling hard.

"Do you know how much trouble you've caused me with your investigation, you little bitch?" he spat out, spittle hitting me on the face with each word.

"You just had to stick your nose in where it wasn't wanted, didn't you?" he cried.

Pain burst through me, and my head jerked to the side as he slapped me hard across the face. The room spun.

"Well, you'll get yours soon enough!" he told me ominously before he stalked out of the room and closed the door. I didn't like the sound of that. Not at all!

Now that I could see, I glanced around, trying to get my bearings.

I was in an old building which looked like a warehouse. The room was quite large and there were some old filing cabinets in one corner beside an old wooden desk that looked well used. The walls were probably white at one time, but had yellowed with age, and the carpet tiles on the floor looked worn and stained.

It might have been used as an office once, but that definitely wasn't the purpose of this room now. I gulped as fear gripped me.

The bed I was chained to was an old double bed with a metal frame, and the chains restraining me look well-used, but unfortunately still solid. The mattress was thin and lumpy and had definitely seen better days.

There were several tripods with cameras attached set up in the room, all facing the bed. I didn't want to think about what this room was likely used for, but considering my colleagues were working with a gang involved in human trafficking, it was hard not to.

Now that my faculties were returning to normal, I tested my restraints again.

It was useless.

No matter how hard I tugged, they didn't loosen and, with every pull at them, I felt my strength ebbing further. I wouldn't be getting out of these chains easily, that was for sure. Or at least not by my own volition.

With nothing else to do and trying desperately to keep a hold of my growing panic, I kept tugging on them, anyway.

I knew I should conserve my energy, but every time I stopped my futile attempts at getting loose, my mind started racing, flooding me with every worst-case scenario it could come up with.

It seemed stupid for Martin to have kidnapped me. I mean, why would he bother? He could have got revenge simply by killing me.

Martin had always flirted with me, but I never truly believed he was that interested in me, and certainly not obsessed with having me enough to bother kidnapping me so he could rape me.

There seemed more to be more to this than I knew.

Perhaps he was planning to hand me over to the Thomas gang? They couldn't be happy that a cop on their payroll was now being investigated for attempted murder. Did Martin somehow think that handing me over to them would in some way compensate for that?

Of course, that scenario was no better for me. They would not bother trying to traffic a trained police officer. They wouldn't want that sort of trouble. So, whether I remained with Martin or was passed on to someone else, there seemed to be only one outcome for me.

Unless I could escape.

Tears threatened, but I refused to let them fall. I would not give in to the despair I could feel rising deep within.

Blinking hard, I sniffed loudly and pulled air in through my mouth until I was a little calmer. Then I gave myself a pep talk.

I would get out of here. So, what if I couldn't get out of my restraints by force? I was smart; I would find another way.

Martin was interested in me. Or at least his body was. That was obvious, so I would use that to my advantage.

I'll get out of this, somehow, whatever it takes! I vowed.

It was time to stop wasting energy I would need later and take back some control over the situation, however small. I stilled and concentrated on my breathing, counting slowly with each inhale and exhale, willing my body to relax and rest.

———

After a while, I must have dozed off because I woke as Martin entered the room, just in time to see him putting a phone away in his back pocket. I watched quietly as he walked over to the desk and put a bag on it, before removing a bottle of water and walking towards me.

"Lucky for you, the boss wants you alive and well, for now," he told me before unscrewing the bottle.

Fisting my hair, he lifted my head and poured water too quickly down my throat.

Coughing and spluttering, I wrenched my head away.

Martin pulled me back, annoyed, but let me sip the water this time, and I managed to get a few mouthfuls before he pulled the bottle out of reach. I didn't realise how parched I had been.

"Thanks," I murmured, letting my lips twitch into a slight smile.

It galled me to thank him, but I was determined to put my plan into action.

The bastard nodded approvingly and allowed me another few sips before making a show of pouring the rest of the bottle over my boobs.

"Oops!" he laughed.

"Always liked those. I bet you'd win any wet t-shirt competition," he said, chuckling and staring at them.

Keep it together, Eilidh! You need to use his attraction and get yourself out of this mess! I reminded myself, although the very thought made me want to puke.

Martin reached out and squeezed my breasts.

"You really have great tits, Eilidh," he told me, licking his lips.

"I'm going to bite them hard later. Mark them, good. You're going to love it!" He laughed as he leaned down and roughly nipped one of my nipples through my swimsuit.

"Ow!" I cried out.

"We are going to have so much fun, baby!" he whispered in my ear.

"I'm going to make you scream for me!" he said, smirking.

Dipping his head again, he nipped the other nipple. I bit back my groan of pain, and he kissed the abused bud.

"Don't hold back, baby. I want your pain. Give it to me!" he said, biting the other nipple again.

Squeezing my eyes shut, I grimaced and cried out. Tears coursed down my cheeks at the pain. Oh, god! I couldn't do this.

"By the time I'm finished with you, you'll love this as much as I do!" he said.

His smug look was all I could take, and before I could stop myself, I spit in his face.

"Fucking pervert!" I screamed.

Martin's hand flew out and slapped me hard across the face. *Fuck!*

"That's it! Keep fighting me, Eilidh!" he said, panting hard.

That fucker! I spat at him again. This time it was a good one and hit him square in the eyes, earning me another slap, which made my ears ring.

Martin wiped his eyes with the back of his hand, and the look he gave me told me what a huge mistake I'd made. He was enjoying my reaction. He really got off on this.

Slowly, he reached out again, his smirk widening as he pulled my swimsuit down below my breasts. Straddling me again, he used both hands to tweak my nipples, twisting them cruelly until I cried out in pain.

I tugged hard on my restraints again, but there was nothing I could do but lie there and take the abuse.

"If you thought that was painful, baby, just wait. We've only got started. I have so many ways to make you scream," he sneered.

Fucking bastard! When I got out of here, he was going to pay for this.

If you get out of here! A treacherous voice in my head said, but I ignored it.

Fighting back the tears that sprang to my eyes at the pain he'd inflicted, I vowed again that I would get out; I just had to figure out how.

I wouldn't even consider the idea of not getting out of here. That meant never seeing Miki again, and that was so not happening. I'd known the guy for a short time, but I couldn't imagine not being with him. It was kind of crazy, but it was the truth.

The very thought of Miki fortified my intent, and I knew I would do whatever it took to stay alive and get back to my man.

Thankfully, before Martin could do anything else to me, his phone rang.

"Fuck!" he stated, removing it from his pocket and leaving the room.

Thank god!

I sighed in relief, glad of the respite to get my thoughts together.

My whole body ached and my nipples stung like hell, but I was alive and that was all that mattered.

My reprieve didn't last long. Martin returned a short time later, looking angry, but thankfully didn't approach me.

He paced around the room, mumbling to himself, sniffing loudly and shooting glances my way every few seconds. The man was agitated as fuck. That didn't bode well for me.

While he'd been away, I'd thought about my predicament and figured that Martin must have the key to my restraints somewhere on him. I needed to get it.

As I observed him, my eyes were continually drawn to the phone in his back pocket. That was another thing I needed. If I could get that phone, I could contact Miki, and he could rescue me.

So, I needed the phone and the key to my chains. I just didn't have any idea how I was going to get them.

My eyes closed as despair washed over me, but I took a long, shuddering breath and pushed it aside. There would be an opportunity at some point; I just needed to be ready for it.

Meanwhile, I tried to remain calm, and not draw attention to myself again.

After a while, Martin went to the desk and sat before removing a little bag of what looked like heroin, a syringe, and some other paraphernalia.

Aw hell!

I hoped that wasn't for me.

Thankfully, after preparing it, he stuck the syringe in his arm.

Quietly, I lay and watched him close his eyes and smile as he injected himself.

Why did I never realise this guy was an addict? Seriously, how the hell did I miss that?

Thinking back, I realised the signs were there, but I was not paying attention because I was too wrapped up in investigating him for corruption.

The guy was a user, but obviously he'd been a high-functioning one. The recent events must have changed that. He had seemed desperate for his fix, and that made him unpredictable. But could I use that? And how?

Martin sat in his blissful state for a few minutes before opening his eyes again.

Gulping, I saw when his focus switched to me, and his eyes

slowly roamed over my body. A sense of dread built inside me. Eventually, he got up and strutted towards me, all smarmy confidence again.

Smirking, he stood above me, and I shuddered, my dread making my throat dry. He removed a knife from his pocket and made a show of flicking it open and closed, and open again.

"The boss said not to touch you, but I don't think I will listen to him. I have a few hours to spare before I need to do some business. I've always fancied you. After the trouble you've been, I don't think I should be denied fucking you!" he said, smiling at me, but unlike his usual smiles, this one was vicious.

"Seems to me that having a beautiful woman chained to my bed and not touching her would be a wasted opportunity."

"Stay the fuck away from me!" I cried, pulling frantically at my chains, but there was still no give in them, and my efforts only made me feel exhausted.

My breath hitched and my eyes widened in terror as he put the knife against my skin. I froze, holding my breath as he cut my suit off, leaving me naked and vulnerable.

Oh my god, no, this cannot be happening!

"You look hot, babe! I really should film this as a memento," he said, going over to the cameras and turning them on one at a time.

No, no, no!

Martin was going to rape me and film it. What a complete bastard!

Terror gripped me and my breathing became panicked. What the hell was I going to do?

"This is where we break in some of the new girls," he told me.

"It's always a lot of fun," he laughed at my look of shock, and I felt nauseous.

"Don't touch me!" I shouted, but he just laughed as he stripped off his T-shirt.

Seconds later, he lunged at me, sprawling on top of me, one hand holding my throat, squeezing slightly, the other roaming my body.

Then his lips were on my neck, and he was biting and nibbling me.

No, no, no! I closed my eyes and prayed for a way out of this nightmare.

"You are going to love this," he said.

"What the fuck are you doing?" Roy's voice shouted, and then Martin was pulled off me.

Oh, thank fuck!

Roy might be corrupt, but he'd been my "uncle" all these years. Surely he wouldn't let that fucker rape me?

They squared off against one another, each looking as if they wanted to kill the other.

"I'm going to fuck the bitch! Come on and join me. It's not like we haven't shared before, especially here, and it's not like them being willing ever mattered!" Martin said, laughing and turning back towards me.

They'd *both* raped women in here? Even Roy? I couldn't believe it. I knew he was complicit in human trafficking, but I hadn't suspected he was also a rapist.

"Leave her alone!" Roy shouted.

"The fuck I will! You just want her for yourself," Martin taunted, turning to me again.

"Did you know Roy's obsessed with you, Eilidh? He has a real thing for you."

Oh, my god! All the times he had got into my personal space over the years, and the way he would make any excuse to touch me, came to mind. Where it had seemed fatherly before, now it just seemed sick.

"Shut it!" Roy shouted and lunged at him.

He swung a punch, catching Martin on the chin.

"Oof!"

"You fucker!" Martin screamed, staggering back.

"You know it's true! You've wanted to get into her knickers for years. Ha, you even got yourself a girlfriend who looks like her and make her call you daddy! You sick fuck!" he laughed.

"Yeah, Eilidh, this sick fuck wants to be your daddy-dom so bad," he taunted.

"Enough!" Roy bellowed with rage and lunged again. This time, he grabbed Martin's arm that held the knife and disarmed him.

However, Martin didn't back off and ran right at Roy, shouldering him to the ground. They rolled, each one attempting to get control of the knife.

From my position, I couldn't see who had the upper hand until Martin grunted loudly.

"You crazy fuck! You stabbed me!" he said incredulously, holding his side.

Roy struggled to his feet and stepped back, panting hard.

Martin followed but instead of the situation calming down, as I thought it would, Martin ran at Roy again and punched him I the stomach.

Winded, Roy fell to his knees with a grunt. Martin was on him in seconds. A loud thud rent the air and Roy's head snapped back.

The pair wrestled, grunting and cursing as they fought to get the upper hand.

Martin let out a pained gurgling sound as Roy stabbed him in the neck.

But Roy didn't stop there. He continued to stab Martin repeatedly until he was nothing but a bloody mess on the floor.

I boaked and bit back the bile that made me want to puke at the sounds and sights before me.

As if in a daze, Roy stood looking down at Martin's body for a long minute, panting hard. When his breathing finally slowed down, he turned to look at me, and I cringed at the sight of him covered in blood.

Roy walked over to me, and I grimaced as one of his bloody hands cupped my face. The other was still holding the knife he'd just killed Martin with. His eyes were wild, and he looked crazy.

"Hey baby girl, daddy's here now. I'll look after you and keep you safe!" he told me, stroking my cheek.

Aw fuck!

Martin was right; he was a sick bastard. Pushing down the bile rising again in my throat as he stroked my cheek, I remained as still as possible.

Feeling sick to my stomach, I really wanted to pull away but didn't want to antagonise him, not when I was still chained to this bed and naked.

"I've got everything arranged. I have some business to attend to, and then we are leaving the country. We'll go abroad. I've got enough money for us to live in luxury and already own a large compound in Thailand. You'll love it there. We can be together at last." He smiled.

The man was nuts. A frigging psycho! I stared at him, completely speechless.

"Daddy loves you, baby, but I need to go take care of that business now, and then I'll be back for you, I promise!" he told me, kissing me on my cheek.

Shock still had hold of me when he stood up to leave, stopping to use Martin's discarded T-shirt to clean some of the blood off himself.

Shit, he couldn't go; I needed to get out of these chains, and I needed him to help me do that.

Martin's phone was on the floor and just under the bed, and I prayed Roy wouldn't notice it.

If I could at least get my feet unchained, I could get it. I needed to use the sick fuck's obsession with me and make that happen.

"Wait, please wait, Daddy," I said, feeling nauseous at my words, but playing his game was a necessity in order for me to survive.

Roy turned to me in shock before a smile spread over his face.

"Yes, baby?" he asked, approaching me again.

Taking a steadying breath, I pushed down my sense of disgust and pouted.

"I've wanted to call you that for a long time, but I didn't know you felt the same. It makes me so happy you do," I said, batting my eyelashes and trying to look as innocent as possible, a shy smile on my lips.

"I'm so pleased to hear that. We were always meant to be together," he proclaimed, smiling and leaning down to nuzzle my neck.

God, the guy had completely flipped if he believed me, and I could tell by the look on his face that he did. I tapped down on the feelings of disgust that made me want to shiver in revulsion and pressed on.

"I can't wait to go away with you. Can't you take me with you now?" I asked.

He chuckled.

"Sorry, baby girl, but daddy can't."

"Then can you at least unchain me? Please Daddy? I'm cold and sore!" I stated, adding a little whine to my voice.

His eyes tracked over my body, and then he glared at the bloody mess on the floor.

"I'm sorry he hurt you, baby girl."

Roy went to the body and rifled through Martin's pockets, then came back with the key.

Oh, my god! He was going to do it! He was going to free me!

Excitement filled me as he unchained my legs.

Being tied down so tightly had made my legs go numb, so I wiggled my toes to help them regain their feeling.

When he freed my left arm, I did the same with it, wiggling the fingers and shaking my arm until the heaviness abated.

But he didn't unchain my other hand.

Damn, damn, damn!

Instead, he placed the key on the desk, then retrieved a blanket which had been tossed in a corner beside it.

I held still as he covered me before kissing me on the forehead.

"I'll see you soon, baby," he said.

Well, at least I was almost free and able to move now, so I had to be thankful for that.

As soon as he'd gone, I avoided looking at the mess that was left of Martin as I got up and tried to stretch over to the desk, but the chain wasn't long enough, and the bed had been secured to the floor, so it wouldn't move.

Damn it to hell!

There was no way to reach the key, but I could get the phone.

It was locked, but luckily, it only required the pin to unlock it. Thankfully, I had been secretly watching Martin input it for so long now that I thought I knew what it was.

Yes! I was right. I felt like doing a jig when the home screen appeared.

After looking up the number for the Hilton, I called and asked to be put through to Miki's suite.

"Rominov," Miki answered immediately, in that sexy Russian accent that made me want to swoon and despite my current predicament, my lady parts tingled in response.

"It's me. Can you trace this phone?" I asked.

CHAPTER 32
MIKI

EARLY THE FOLLOWING MORNING – THE
RESCUE

My eyes stung and were blurry from lack of sleep. It was the early hours of the morning, and we still hadn't found my woman.

I was exhausted and frustrated and bloody angry with myself.

Why had I thought leaving her here alone was a good idea? Even with Marko in the other suite? I should have taken better care of my Little Miss Red.

Guilt washed over me.

Why hadn't I stayed here with Eilidh and let someone else go with Luca to fit the cameras and check the tunnel? If I'd been here, nobody would have got close to her, and I wouldn't be facing the possibility that I'd lost her forever.

We'd tried everything we could think of to find where Martin could have taken Eilidh and come up with nothing. Our other enemies had finished work, returned home, and remained there. There had been no communication between them since.

With nothing to go on, I was seriously contemplating rounding up her colleagues and beating them senseless until one of them told us where she was.

The only thing that stopped me was that I didn't want to jeopardise the upcoming Interpol operation. I couldn't risk it, not when it was just a short time away. It was unfair to do so when so many other women, ones currently being trafficked, could be freed and so many of our enemies caught all at once.

Frankly, if it was just up to me, I would do it in a heartbeat, but it wasn't. I had Jim and my Brotherhood to think about. And I also knew Eilidh would hate me for it if I did anything to disrupt our plans for revenge. So, I'd bided my time and waited, hoping Martin Johnson or one of the others would get in touch with me about her.

But they hadn't, and it was getting close to the time of the handover. I was at the end of my tether, thought, ready to find Roy Allen, at least and beat the shit out of him when the phone in my room started to ring.

Shock filled me and I grabbed it.

"Rominov."

"It's me."

My knees buckled in relief when I heard Eilidh's voice on the other end.

Thank fuck she was alive!

"Can you trace this phone?" Eilidh asked, and I told Marko to do just that.

"Sweetheart, are you okay?" I asked, unable to hide the worry in my voice.

"I will be when you ride to the rescue," she joked.

Chuckling in relief, I told myself she couldn't be too bad if she was joking.

I knew it would take Marko a few minutes to trace her location, so I asked her what had happened.

It was difficult to hear, and I knew she was holding a lot back from me.

The image of Johnson hurting her and touching her made

me livid, and I banged the desk angrily, knocking the lamp off and breaking it.

"I'll fucking kill him!" I vowed.

"No need; he's already dead. Roy killed him," she said before she told me the rest.

When I heard about Roy and his sick fantasy, I almost puked. No fucking way! I'd skin the bastard alive.

We hadn't even been aware that Roy had left his house yet. He must have left his phone and car behind. Fuck! What else didn't we know?

Marko gave me the thumbs up and then showed me Eilidh's location on his computer.

"Got you. You're in the building next door to the handover location. We're on our way!" I told her.

"Great, I'm in an old office," she said.

"See you soon, sweetheart," I told her before hanging up.

My Little Miss Red's call had arrived just as Vlad and Luca were about to leave to meet Jim MacArthur's men. They needed to get there in plenty of time to head through the tunnel and be ready for when the informant gave them the signal that Mathieson and the others had arrived. So, I grabbed a ride with them.

I'd already figured to that using the tunnel was my only chance at getting to my woman unseen.

On the way, I called Jim, explained the situation and told him to ensure that our men all had eyes on the other fuckers to ensure none of them slipped past us. We didn't need any surprises. For this plan to work, all the pieces had to line up just right.

We slipped through the tunnel. My anxiety level had been through the roof since Eilidh had been taken and even though I'd heard her voice, and she'd said she was okay; I wouldn't be able to calm down until I saw that for myself and held her in my arms.

My palms sweated, my stomach was in knots, and my heart was beating way too fast. It felt like I'd run a bloody marathon by the time I'd reached the end.

I hated not having everything under control. My plans were always meticulously thought out, and every scenario prepared for. But not this time. I hadn't prepared for this, and I felt like a fish out of water.

Marko said the building Eilidh was in adjoined the factory and that there should be an emergency exit on the upper floor of the factory building, which led directly into it.

That's how I planned on getting in and out with her, undetected by any police who were by now watching the building. It would be tricky though, as Roy and probably a good number of the Thomas gang would likely already be there. It was only about thirty minutes until the handover was due. Anything could go wrong!

Worry gnawed at me, and I had to admit, for the first time in my life, I felt truly scared.

Vlad went to climb the stair to the hatch, but I pulled him out of the way and headed up first. At the top of the ladder, I pushed my shoulder against the door leading into the small cupboard in the factory, moving the old carpet aside so I could peek out. It was empty, and I breathed a sigh of relief as I climbed into the cupboard.

"I'm coming with you!" Vlad said.

"No, stick to the plan," I told him.

"You need backup!" Luca stated.

"No, I don't. I can handle this. You two have a job to do. Do it!" I said.

Despite their continued protests, I made Vlad and Luca remain in the tunnel to wait for the informant signal as planned while I sneaked up the stairs and along the hall to the emergency exit door. It had been jammed open. I peered through, but there was nobody in sight. So far, so good!

All the doors were open except the one at the very end. I moved that way, double-checking the rooms were empty as I passed.

The last door was closed but not locked. I quietly turned the handle and pushed it open. Relief filled at the sight of Eilidh sitting on the bed, a bloody lump lying nearby, which I assumed was Jonson.

"Miki!" my Little Miss Red sobbed as I rushed over, pulling her into a gentle hug.

I was reluctant to let her go, but we needed to hurry. Pulling back, I opened up the blanked covering her and checked her over.

There were marks on her wrists, a large bruise on her abdomen, smaller ones on her head and cheek and what looked like finger marks on her neck, but otherwise, she appeared okay. My hands fisted at the sight of them. And she was fucking chained up like an animal too.

"Fuck!" I exclaimed in fury.

Closing my eyes, I fought the urge to go storming out to look for Roy. Since I couldn't kill the fucker Johnson, I'd be more than happy to kill him instead!

"I'm okay," Eilidh said, reaching up to cup my cheek, obviously seeing me upset at her appearance.

She wasn't, but I appreciated the attempt to make me feel better even while it shamed me. It should be the other way around.

"Let's get you out of here, sweetheart," I said, wrapping her in the blanket again.

Eilidh nodded and pointed to a key on the desk, and I grabbed it and freed her wrist.

I gave her a quick kiss, then passed her the clothes and shoes I had in my backpack. She smiled her thanks, and I was glad that even in my overly anxious state and haste to get to her, I remembered to bring her something to wear.

After she dressed, I took her hand in one of my mine, and with my gun in the other, we headed for the door. As soon as I opened it, a figure lunged at me, hitting me on the head. I collapsed to the floor, barely conscious.

Eilidh cried out, but someone grabbed her and pulled her away from me.

My eyes wouldn't focus properly, and I could barely make out the shapes of two bodies as I tried to force myself to stay awake.

"I hope you weren't planning on leaving daddy, baby girl!" a voice said.

Roy! I thought before darkness engulfed me.

Blinking my eyes open again, I saw the room was empty. They were gone. Fuck! So was my gun.

My head pounded as I staggered to my feet and lunged for the door.

Thankfully, I could only have been out for mere seconds as I heard a scuffle and saw Roy dragging Eilidh towards another exit while she struggled against his hold. He saw me heading toward them and shot, but Eilidh struggled so much in his arms that he missed.

The gun had a silencer, so the noise was muted. I hoped it wouldn't attract attention, but if I didn't get control of this situation soon, it definitely would, and then we'd be in even more trouble.

Eilidh continued to struggle frantically against Roy's arm, which was wrapped tightly around her neck as he tried to get her out the door. He fired towards me again but was too distracted to aim correctly, and once more, the shot went wide. Thank fuck!

It didn't stop me from heading towards him. Nothing would. Eilidh elbowed Roy in the ribs, and he loosened his grip on her. She grabbed his arm and smashed his hand against the doorframe, which made him drop his gun, but he backhanded her, sending her sprawling at his feet.

The fucker!

I lunged towards him, fists flying, punching him twice in the face.

Roy fell to his knees and threw himself towards the gun on the floor. Eilidh grabbed for it at the same time. She got it, and it went off.

Roy was dead!

Little Miss Red looked completely shocked. There were a few seconds of silence before I acted. Pulling her up off the floor, I took the gun from her limp wrist as she stared at Roy's dead body.

"Eilidh, baby, we've got to go," I said gently before tugging on her arm. That roused her, and we ran to the emergency exit, into the factory and down the stairs.

I checked the small corridor, and it was clear except for Vlad, who was heading our way. I should have known he would check on me if I took longer than expected.

With a relieved look, he led us back to the tunnel. Just in the nick of time, as chaos broke out in the factory above.

The sound of sirens, shouts and screams rang out as the Interpol officers arrived, and the traffickers realised they were surrounded.

Gripping tightly to Eilidh's hand, I hurried her through the tunnel, leaving the others behind for our plan to play out as expected.

I knew I should check on the progress of things, but looking after Eilidh right now was more important to me. Besides, if there were any issues, I trusted Luca, Vlad, and Marko to deal with them.

One of MacArthur's guys drove us back to the hotel, and I took Eilidh straight up to the suite. I needed to be close to her and desperately wanted to throw her down on the bed and show her how scared of losing her I was, but I didn't.

Instead, I ran a bath for her. I expected she would want to wash off the night's events, and I certainly wanted her to. The thought of either of those men touching her made me so angry I wanted to bring them back to life so I could have the pleasure of kill them, torturing them slowly, making them scream.

As the tub filled, I fought to control my emotions. They were gone and couldn't hurt Eilidh anymore. Killing them wasn't required; taking care of my Little Miss Red was, I reminded myself, finally calming down.

Eilidh sank into the bubbles and closed her eyes with a sigh. I stripped off, then grabbed some oil. Climbing in behind her, I sandwiched myself around her, needing to have her close. My cock was already hard, anticipating being inside her, but not yet, I told it. *Patience!* Eilidh had been hurt and been through a traumatic experience. My Little Miss Red needed to bathe and rest.

Pouring some oil on my hands, I gently massaged her shoulders. Eventually, I felt her muscles loosen as her tension slowly drained away and she became drowsy.

It was good to see her relax, but I didn't want her falling asleep on me yet.

So, I stopped what I was doing and moved my hands lower to cup her breasts, then squeezed them gently, nibbling lightly on her neck.

There were things I needed to say, and there was so much I hoped to hear.

"I was so scared I would lose you, sweetheart! The thought of never seeing you again made me crazy. I don't think I could survive it!" I whispered.

Turning her towards me so she straddled me, I looked into her eyes.

"Come home to London with me," I said, praying she'd agree.

CHAPTER 33
EILIDH

Miki looked so vulnerable when he said, "Come to London with me."

There really was only one answer.

"Yes," I said, smiling.

"You will?" he asked, trying to keep control of his eagerness, but I saw it in his hopeful look.

"Yes, Miki, I will," I replied.

He grinned, then his face fell, and he gulped and licked his lips.

"You would need to leave the Police," he said as if unsure if my agreement had been only a temporary thing.

"Uh, huh."

I nodded.

"Assuming this is to be a permanent arrangement, it would be very difficult to commute all the way from London every shift, wouldn't it?" I said, my lips twitching.

"Oh, this is to be a very permanent arrangement," my sexy Russian said, his accent becoming so sexily thick that I shivered.

"Then I guess I'd better resign," I said, smiling widely.

"You're sure?" Miki asked.

"Hell yeah!" I replied, and he pulled me in for a kiss, sealing the deal.

"I was scared I might never see you again, too, and I don't think I could survive that either," I told him, echoing his words from earlier.

"I'd already decided that I would resign from the Force and follow you to London, anyway. It's not like I want to remain in the Police after everything that's happened and even if I did, I would gladly give it up to be with you, Mr Sexy Lips," I confessed.

As he grinned, I couldn't resist letting my hand drift under the water to stroke his hardness.

Leaning into him, I stroked his length and kissed him, making it clear I meant every word. He palmed my boobs and gently stroked them in turn.

God, it was so good to be here with him. Miki's massage had made me so relaxed, but now I was feeling anything but, and I was suddenly overwhelmed with need. I didn't know if it was an accumulation of my nervous energy, my relief at getting away from a terrible situation, or simply Miki's amazing hands, but I was bloody horny.

Lifting my body higher, Miki took a nipple into his mouth and licked it. I gasped and tensed, anticipating pain. There was none. Just a slight ache, but Miki pulled away and looked at me.

"You okay, sweetheart?" he asked, his eyes searching mine.

"Yes," I said, brushing my lips against his.

"We don't have to do anything if you aren't comfortable, Eilidh," he told me, and my heart clenched.

My sexy Russian's eyes showed how desperately he wanted me. I could feel how hard he was, and I knew how worried he'd been. He needed to be close to me, yet he was ready to put aside his own needs and desires to ensure I was okay. If I didn't already know that I wanted to be with Miki, that would have confirmed it.

"I want this, Mr Sexy Lips."

"In fact, I need it," I told him, kissing him soundly, and bringing his hands back to my breasts.

I wanted to replace the memory of the terrible events of the last few hours with a new amazing one of our own. Lifting myself over his cock, I rubbed my aching pussy against it, and my boobs in his face.

My sexy Russian took the hint, sucking and licking gently at one tight bud and then the other as he squeezed my bum. I gasped in pleasure, and he moved one hand, sliding it between my legs and stroked.

God, I was soaking wet already, not only from the water, but from my own juices. Miki kept his strokes light and teasing, making me moan in frustration.

"I need more, Miki," I practically growled at him.

He chuckled and picked up speed.

"Yes, like that!" I cried as he kept up the pace, rubbing me so good I had to grasp his shoulders as my knees weakened, and he chuckled again.

"Mine!" he said, and I loved the possessive gleam in his eyes as he pulled me closer, his touch becoming firmer with each stroke of my clit.

I ground against his hand as he sucked a nipple, gently pulling it deep into his mouth, and my back arched against his lips.

My sexy Russian tugged lightly on one nipple with his teeth, then the other, sending shocks of desire straight to my core.

It wasn't long before I was gasping and murmuring his name repeatedly as his fingers stroked faster and faster. I felt his own excitement build with mine as his cock pressed against my pussy entrance.

"Miki, I need you inside me," I begged.

Bracing myself on his shoulders, I tried to sink into his erection, but he held me back.

"Come for me first, sweetheart," he said, keeping up his now almost frantic assault on my clit, with his mouth on my tits, alternating from one nipple to the next, paying them both the same amount of attention.

My orgasm built as he quickly thrust a finger into me, then another. My channel was tight, and I felt the walls of my wet pussy clamping down on the intrusion. As I gasped, I cried out.

"I'm so close!"

My gorgeous, sexy man kissed me deeply.

God, I was so near to ecstasy, riding Miki's fingers frantically. He reached around with his other hand and breached my back hole.

"Oh, my God!" I cried, panting.

"Come for me, sweetheart!" he commanded, his voice sounding as strained as his muscles as he thrust his fingers in and out of me, pressing his thumb against my clit until I couldn't take it anymore and exploded.

Hell yes!

Miki was sliding his tongue in my mouth, matching the rhythm of his fingers as he filled all my holes. I continued to ride him as he did so, ringing out every drop of pleasure I could, water splashing everywhere.

Finally, I collapsed limply against him, gasping for breath.

Before I could come down from my high, he removed his fingers, grabbed my hips, lined his cock up with my entrance, and in one quick thrust, he was inside me.

"Fuck!" he growled, and I felt him straining not to come.

I loved the control he had, but I wanted him to lose it, the way I lost mine. But with my body still weakened by my amazing orgasm, I couldn't do anything but let him move me up and down on his cock.

My sexy Russian's rhythm changed, his movements becoming jerky and less controlled. He mumbled incoherently as he thrust me down on his cock one last time before he finally released.

Panting hard, we clung to each other, unable to move.

That was so bloody amazing, I thought, when my mind could finally form a coherent thought again.

We stayed like that for a minute, and when our breathing was back to normal, we climbed out of the bath and dried each other off. Neither of us could stop smiling, touching, and kissing each other.

Miki's cock was hardening again, but when I reached for it, he moved my hand away.

"Later, sweetheart, you need to get some rest," he said before sweeping me into his arms.

"Who knew I would be swept off my feet by a Bratva pakhan?" I giggled.

"I did. The minute we met, and you sniffed me, then practically fell into my arms as we kissed," he told me cockily. I cringed at the memory and shook my head.

"I can't believe I sniffed you! Although I seem to remember you sniffed me right back, and *you* were the one who kissed *me*, Mr Sexy Lips," I said, pouting.

"Damn right I did," he laughed.

"How could I resist? I was lost the second your beautiful amber eyes met mine."

He smirked.

"Of course, feeling those luscious curves of yours pressed so closely against me might have had something to do with it, too."

"Oof!" he grunted as I elbowed him, then laughed.

"When I found out you were a sexy little detective with a penchant for ties, well, I have to admit that only excited me more," he chuckled, wagging his eyebrows.

I laughed and hugged him close.

"Everything about you excites me, Eilidh," he said, more seriously this time.

Smiling wickedly, I licked his neck, running my hands over his pecs.

"Ready for more excitement, big guy?"

Depositing me on the bed, he laid down beside me and snuggled close, spooning me.

"While I would love to do many more exciting things with you, Eilidh, it will have to wait."

I pouted over my shoulder at him, and he smirked.

"You've had more than enough excitement for now. You're exhausted, sweetheart. Time to rest," he whispered.

Mr Sexy Lips was right; I was exhausted. The events of the last few weeks were catching up on me.

There'll be plenty of time to explore how much we can excite one another; I smiled at the thought as my eyes closed.

Snuggled against him, I sighed, glad to be safe again.

The last thing I felt was my sexy Russian kissing the back of my head before I sunk into oblivion, safe in Miki's arms.

EPILOGUE
MIKI

LONDON - DECEMBER

Marko handed me the box and I smiled my thanks and pocketed it, the churning in my stomach making it difficult to speak.

As I walked headed to our room to collect Eilidh, my mind went over the events of the last few months.

We returned from Glasgow the evening after I'd rescued Eilidh. Marko, Luca, and Jim had ensured our plan was a success.

Mathieson was grabbed easily, and Luca brought him down to London. When the Interpol officers had arrived, Gerry Thomson was the first to open fire and was killed. Jim wasn't pleased, but at least the thorn in his side had been pulled out for good.

In the chaos, the other two cops from Eilidh's team were also shot. None of them survived. However, their presence at the handover, and the evidence of rape found in the cameras in the office next door, were enough for them to be investigated further.

The news had been going mad over the story but so far we'd avoided the reporters and I aimed to keep it that way.

My sexy detective wasn't one any longer. She had handed in her resignation, stating she was too jaded after everything that had happened, which was the truth.

I'd paid the hotel receptionist and hotel manager plenty of money to keep quiet so nobody else was aware of her kidnapping and we were keeping it that way.

Mathieson was taken to the C but was a pussy and didn't last long under torture. His heart gave out too quickly. We got all our questions answered except one. He never told us if he had been working alone.

Was he the last of our unknown enemies or not? We didn't know. I would have liked to believe he was, but something told me there was more trouble ahead.

Nigel Simpson was also still alive because of that. I had a feeling he might still be of use to me, so he had been given a stay of execution for now until I decided his continued existence was no longer necessary.

We'd made Interpol aware of some of the bank accounts Mathieson and the others had in their false names and the money had been seized under the Proceeds of Crime Act. Hopefully, it would fund more operations against human trafficking gangs. The rest of the money was sent to various charities that helped people who were affected by trafficking.

While we could have kept it all for ourselves, my family didn't want to profit directly from that type of crime. We had more than enough of our own illicit gains and the guilt that went with that.

However, we kept back information on one account of Mathieson's with a sizeable amount in it, which was in the name of Jessica Adams.

All the other accounts had been set up against his false

identities and all were male names, so this account seemed odd. We could not locate any females with that name which were associated with Mathieson, so it was a mystery.

From now on, Marko would keep a track of the account and if someone tried to access it, we would know. If Mathieson had been working with, or on behalf of someone else, it might lead us to them.

Letting Jim MacArthur expand his operation was proving to be a good choice. The first batch of drugs was delivered without a hitch yesterday and today we were celebrating. For now, at least things had settled down and everyone was safe and happy again.

As far as Eilidh and I were concerned, the past was now done. Our enemies were dead; Eilidh's father and my Krissa had been avenged.

My heart swelled with love when I entered our bedroom and saw Eilidh. All the steps in my plan to woo my Little Miss Red were now complete, and I'd claimed my woman in all but name, but I hoped that soon she would become a Rominov and mine forever.

She was stunning in a short gold dress which showed off her curves to perfection.

My mouth salivated and I checked my watch, wondering if there was time to grab her and take advantage of them before we had to leave. Unfortunately, there wasn't. Damn!

Later. Once we returned home, I'd take my time exploring every inch of her as I had done these past few months. There would never be a time when I would tire of that.

"Ready, sweetheart?" I asked her, forcing myself to only lightly kiss her on the lips. Otherwise, my resolve to leave would vanish the moment our tongues met. I was only human after all and resisting my Little Miss Red's charms, beyond me.

Eilidh nodded and we walked to the car.

Sitting in the backseat with my arm around her, my stomach twisted and turned with nerves. This was one of the biggest moments of my life and I didn't want anything to go wrong.

We pulled up to our best Italian restaurant, and as we entered, the manger greeted us.

As Eilidh turned to speak with one of the waiters she'd met before, I quietly asked, "Is everything in place?"

"Si, senor. It is all as you requested," the manager confirmed with a smile before leading us through to the private dining room.

Soft music played in the background and the room was lit only by candlelight. We ate a meal prepared beautifully by the chef, but I didn't taste a thing as I forced the bites down and waited for the right moment.

Time stretched on and I wished I'd not decided to wait until the end of the meal to do this. We chatted about the everyday running of my legitimate businesses which Eilidh had taken to helping me manage. However, I couldn't concentrate on anything much.

Finally, the time came, and the manager entered with a cake in hand. He passed it to me and with a wink left. Turning to Eilidh I walked to her trying desperately to not let my hands shake. Setting the cake down in front of her I watched as she read the words, *"Will you marry me?"* written in icing on top.

She gasped as she read, and I quickly got down on one knee. Withdrawing the little box from my pocket at the same time, I held it out to her.

"Eilidh, from the moment I looked into your eyes, you had me ensnared and I've been yours ever since. You are my heart, and you complete me in a way I never thought possible. I love you for now and forever. Be mine. Marry me?" I said, gulping as my mouth went dry and I swear my heart stopped as I waited for her response.

Her eyes lit up and she cried, "Yes!"

Jumping out of her chair, she threw herself into my arms as I stood.

"Yes, yes, yes," she said laughing as I swung her in the air and twirled her before setting her down. She held her hand out and I slipped the ring onto her finger.

She looked at it and beamed.

"It's stunning, Miki. I love you," she said hugging me. Kissing her soundly my cock jerked with longing and I thought about taking her right there and then, but she pulled back and stared into my eyes.

"I have something to tell you," she said, biting her lip.

"Yes, sweetheart?" I asked.

"We're pregnant!"

My eyes widened as I took in the words.

A grin spread across my face and I thought there would never be another day like this in my life, when I was so filled with joy I thought I could burst.

"Eilidh, you've made me the happier than I ever thought possible," I told her, picking her up and swinging her around again as we laughed in shared joy.

She leaned towards me and as her tongue slipped inside my mouth, my need for her grew. Sitting on a chair, I pulled her onto my lap and proceeded to show her just how happy she made me.

As my Little Miss Red whimpered in pleasure, my heart clenched with happiness. Life was good, and I was confident that with Eilidh and the family we were starting together, the future would be too, because no matter what life threw at us, we could deal with it as long as we had each other.

EILIDH

Smiling as I looked over at my fiancé chatting with Ash and Anton, I knew I'd never been so happy. The ring on my finger glittered and I still couldn't believe I was engaged to marry Mr Sexy Lips.

Miki had proposed yesterday and after a night of utter bliss in his arms, I had to keep pinching myself to make sure it wasn't all some sort of dream.

Happiness bubbled inside me as I watched my sexy Russian chatting with the groom who was starting to look nervous as we waited for the bride to arrive. We were at Ash and Gracie's wedding. The pair were lovely, and I'd become great friends with Gracie.

In fact, the whole of Miki's family and friends had welcomed me with open arms and I was amazed at how quickly I'd become part of their close-knit group. As I gazed around, I realised that I had never felt more like I belonged than I did here with a group of people and a man that just a few short months ago, I would have considered the enemy.

So much had changed for me in such a short time and while occasionally I felt a little overwhelmed by it, mainly I'd taken it in my stride. It helped that I had found a place for myself working with Miki on his legitimate businesses and supporting him in his endeavours to escape the life that was his birthright.

We'd left Glasgow the night after I'd killed Roy and the last few months with Miki had been great. Every day with him was an adventure. His family welcomed me easily, and I already felt like I belonged.

The Interpol operation had been a success, and many women were now free because of it. I'd resigned from the police and although I had felt a moment of grief when I signed the letter, I hadn't looked back since. As far as I was concerned, it was all over. My dad had been avenged and could rest in peace.

I never figured out who sent the photos of my dad's murder to John Aldridge, setting everything in motion, but I decided I no longer cared. As long as they were not a threat to me or my new family, it really wasn't important.

Miki laughed loudly drawing my eyes back to him. He looked pleased, exuding happiness. I remembered him telling me about the pangs of jealousy and loneliness he'd felt at the last family wedding and I smiled knowing that he'd never need to feel that way again, because now he had me.

As my sexy Russian came to sit beside me, I squeezed his hand and he smiled down at me before kissing the top of my head and brushing his other hand over my stomach in a gesture I thought would become familiar as the life inside me grew.

When we'd first had sex, I had told Miki I was on the pill, and I was, but somehow a little swimmer got through.

I had been nervous to tell him because despite being in love, everything between us had already happened so quickly that I worried it was too soon. My concerns had been foolish however, as he was overjoyed at the prospect of being a father.

As I watched Ash and Gracie exchange vows, excitement bubbled inside me at the thought of Miki and I exchanging ours. A few months ago, I had felt so alone. Now I had Miki, a new family, a baby on the way and a wedding to plan. God, I was one lucky woman!

I looked at Miki, and he grinned at me, making my heart flutter in my chest. I knew that my life with this man would not be perfect; he was a Bratva Pakhan after all, but I knew it would be filled with love and family, and I had never felt happier. There might be difficulties and more dangers ahead, but whatever we faced from now on, we'd face it together.

The future was ours to write!

ABOUT THE AUTHOR

Jax Knight is a fledgling author who finally gave in to the voices in her head, letting them come to life in her first dark contemporary romance series.

Jax lives in Scotland with her husband and son. She enjoys martial arts, reading and coffee and can often be found hiding away in a corner, glued to her Kindle or with her head buried in a book while sipping a Mocha.

A sucker for sexy, protective villains with morals and feisty, fun females, all her books have them aplenty and a guaranteed happy-ever-after!

Ash is her debut novel and the first of six books in her Bratva Blood Brothers Series.

If you'd like to keep up with all of her new releases and more, please come and join her newsletter or follow her on social media to stay up to date!

ALSO BY JAX KNIGHT

Bratva Blood Brothers

Ash

Romi

Miki

Marko

Luca

Anton